The new ship came into view quite suddenly. It was big, a squashed spheroid resting on four stilty legs like a giant half-limbed spider.

Michi could not stifle her gasp. "It's them."

Birk looked at her. "Who?"

She took her gaze off the receiver and looked straight into his eyes. "The aliens who invaded New Edo. They finally tracked me here. We're not alone any more, Birk. Whether you like it or not, the war has come to you."

A WORLD
CALLED SOLITUDE

Stephen Goldin

FAWCETT CREST • NEW YORK

A WORLD CALLED SOLITUDE

THIS BOOK CONTAINS THE COMPLETE TEXT OF THE
ORIGINAL HARDCOVER EDITION.

Published by Fawcett Crest Books, CBS Educational and
Professional Publishing, a division of CBS Inc., by arrangement with Doubleday and Company, Inc.

ISBN: 0-449-24486-5

Printed in the United States of America

First Fawcett Crest printing: February 1982

10 9 8 7 6 5 4 3 2 1

to Kathleen, for rescuing me from solitude
every day

ACT 1

ONE

"Arthur, how many times this month have I wished I were a poet?"

The robot barely hesitated. "Seventeen, sir."

Birk Aaland nodded absently. "Make that eighteen now. This world inspires poetry—or it would if I were any good at it. And I remember so damned little of the poetry I learned in school. It only goes to show that a good technical education can still have drawbacks."

The man and the robot were standing atop a rounded hillock overlooking a broad plain. The purple-shading-into-green flatlands stretched before them until the horizon stole it from view—a horizon that was clear and sharp, free of the haze and pollution of a human-occupied world. Low scrub dominated the scene, with some prickly pseudocactus and misshapen purple trees giving counterpoint.

The hot yellow sun rose behind Birk, warming the back of his neck. It cast long shadows of the two figures on the hill, the tall, robust man and the cylindrical robot beside him. Overhead, the gray of the dawn sky was bleached to the pastel shade of day.

It was not a still life Birk observed. The creatures he thought of as birds—even though they bore their young alive and had no feathers—filled the sky. Dawn and dusk were their prime hunting hours in this part of the world, though already most of the night-flying insects they preyed on had found their havens for the day—much to Birk's relief. Smaller creatures scampered about, little blurs at the edge of his peripheral vision. The air was clean, smelling refreshingly of herbs and damp leaves.

Two kilometers away was a herd of the animals Birk had named "lopers," already awake and grazing on the vegetation. The lopers were lumbering four-legged beasts nearly as tall as a man, two and a half meters long and weighing upward of two hundred kilos. They had tawny yellow fur clumped in odd patches over their skins, and long, flat tails dragging awkwardly in the dirt behind them. Their faces were piggish, their eyes dark and stupid. But despite their ungainly appearance, Birk knew they could move swiftly when alarmed.

"I tried writing poetry when I was in college," Birk continued, his gaze never wavering from the vista before him. "I suppose everyone does. I tried to fill it with passion and imagery, expressing the innermost secrets of my soul. Only my soul didn't have any secrets; not then, anyway. So my passion came out as pretension and the imagery came out as clichés. I had a problem, too, with lapsing into doggerel at the most inopportune places."

" 'Doggerel,' sir?" From Arthur's inflection, it was clear Birk had used a word beyond the robot's vocabulary.

Birk turned from the landscape to look at his partner. Arthur was a tall, silvery cylinder of metal and plastic with a variety of arms and sensors scattered over the upper half of his body. He was supported by four legs that could extend at will from a dozen centimeters to more than two meters. The legs could also be flexible or rigid, whichever was more useful at the moment.

"Yes," Birk said. "Doggerel is considered a bad sort of poetry, when your lines take on a singsong quality and content is sacrificed for meter; I can't define it any more precisely than that, I'm afraid. It's too bad I didn't save my old poems—you could have seen it in a minute."

He shook his head. "It's a shame I can't do more justice to this place. Sometimes the urge is overwhelming, it's all so beautiful. Look at the yellow and blue of those birds flying over that green patch of ground. Well, I can't do it any justice by just talking about it; let's move in closer and see if we can bag a loper for dinner." He gave a friendly pat to the spot where Arthur's shoulder would be if Arthur had shoulders.

They started down the hill at an easy pace. Birk couldn't have taken the delta any closer to the herd without spooking them, but a walk of two kilometers would be good exercise. Beside him, Arthur matched the pace, equally unhurried. Arthur had a patience no mere human could attain; after all, hadn't he waited here two thousand years with nothing to do until Birk's arrival?

They reached the bottom of the hill and had started toward

9

the herd when Birk suddenly began to laugh. "What's funny?" Arthur asked him.

"My own egotism," Birk said. "You write poetry to express your feelings to someone else . . . and there *is* no one else except you and the other robots. I already know what my feelings are, and you could never understand feelings or emotion. It would be a colossal conceit and a waste of time— an intellectual form of masturbation."

"You masturbate quite frequently," the machine commented.

"You have neither tact nor delicacy, do you know that?" Birk didn't even break stride, but smiled anyway. "I shall attribute it to jealousy, because you were created less than a eunuch and cannot enjoy the Supreme Pleasure. Yes, of course I masturbate; otherwise the pressure would build up until even *you* looked good to me. And I like you too much to rape you."

"There *is* another alternative . . . in the Black City."

Birk stopped and turned abruptly to face the robot. His teeth were suddenly clenched, his voice harsh, his hands balled into fists. "I know there is. And I've told you not to bring that subject up again."

Undaunted, Arthur stopped as well. "Yes, you're right. I apologize."

"And don't apologize so quickly. How can I get a good argument started if you apologize at the first little outburst?"

"I'm sor . . ."

"There you go again! Damn it, stop being so perfect."

"I am what I am. I can't help that." The robot extended one flexible arm and laid it gently on Birk's shoulder.

Birk shrugged away the touch with a sharp gesture and stalked forward angrily. "Forget it. We've got lopers to hunt. Let's go."

He strode across the plain at a pace nearly double his former easy gait, swerving every so often to avoid the larger rocks or bushes. Arthur would have had no trouble keeping up, but decided it would be more prudent to stay a few steps behind the human. He had seen Birk fly into these sudden rages before, and knew that the wisest course was to let the anger burn itself out and maintain a low profile in the meantime.

The trek across the open ground took twenty minutes, all of it in stony silence as Birk refused to acknowledge the robot's presence. The herd moved little from its initial spot; none of the lopers' natural enemies were in the area, and they did not recognize the two approaching figures as a threat. The strong, musky odor of the animals filled Birk's nostrils as the hunters closed to within thirty meters of the grazing herd. Birk stopped and unslung the gun from his shoulder.

The weapon was left over from the reign of the Makers—Birk's name for this planet's original inhabitants. It looked like a slightly squashed, yellow plastic volleyball with a vacuum-cleaner nozzle attached at the front. It weighed only a few grams, yet because of the awkward size and shape Birk had found it necessary to use both hands when firing. It had not been designed for a human's easy grip.

He stood there for a moment, eying the herd and choosing his victim carefully. His needs were modest, so he disdained the larger males, and he did not want to upset the breeding pattern by taking a nursing mother. He finally selected an immature female as his prey. Having made his selection, he aimed his weapon carefully and fired.

The gun emitted a series of high-pitched bleeps and a thin blue line of energy flew from the nozzle. The energy projection streaked through the air to its target. There was a crackling that reminded Birk of static electricity, and the loper cow collapsed onto the ground. The rest of the herd, on hearing the bleeping sounds, looked around in confusion and, at the instigation of one large male who seemed to be the leader, moved at a fast walk to a spot a few dozen meters away, leaving their fallen comrade behind.

Satisfied with his kill, Birk turned to Arthur and finally spoke. "All right, call the delta over and let's get our catch home."

Arthur obediently beamed out a radio signal and, from the other side of the hill on which they'd originally landed, their hovercraft lifted into sight and zoomed toward them. It had the triangular shape of an arrowhead without a shaft, ten meters from tip to base and nearly two meters high. It flew soundlessly, but its large bulk and quick motion startled the grazing herd. As a unit they bolted northward at a surprising speed.

Within seconds the delta was hovering overhead and, at another silent radioed command from Arthur, it floated gently to the ground three meters away. The cargo door in the back slid open, as did the plastic bubbles over the passenger seats on either side of the forward vertex. The ship turned off once more, awaiting further instructions.

11

Birk grunted as he bent down to drag, with Arthur's help, the heavy loper carcass over to the craft. They lifted the animal into the cargo section, and Arthur tucked it neatly away while Birk brushed the dirt he'd picked up from the body off his rough-skinned leather jacket. The two hunters climbed into their own seats and closed the plastic bubbles again. Though Birk had learned to pilot the delta, he preferred to let Arthur do the actual work today. He gave the robot a curt nod, and their craft lifted gracefully into the air to begin the long flight home.

The delta flew at the leisurely—for it—speed of 2,000 kilometers an hour. The character of the land beneath them changed as they passed over, progressing from purple scrub plains to brown wooded hills to tangled and overgrown green patches of level land. Birk stared stonily ahead, at first, but his anger faded gradually as the ground passed beneath him. *On Earth*, he mused, *all that would have been parceled out and divided into farm sections, all under cultivation to make maximum use of the resources. There would be squares and rectangles of different colors, all neatly plowed and carefully tended. Here—nothing but wild, uncontrolled growth.*

He grinned, taking a perverse satisfaction in the untamed quality of this planet. It was as though living on a savage world made him something of a savage himself.

Occasionally they passed over some of the smaller towns and villages the Makers had left. Years ago, Birk's curiosity might have compelled him to interrupt his journey and investigate these hamlets on the outskirts of the "civilized" world. But he'd seen enough of them in his eleven years here; with few exceptions, the smaller towns in this region followed a similar pattern. He would never have time to explore them all, but his early investigations told him that he didn't really want to.

After an hour's silent flight, the nature of the land below them softened, became more regular. Soon the outer fringes of the city he called Beta-Nu were passing beneath their craft. The delta began to slow its flight and drop lower. The sun was now well above the horizon, and Birk gazed out over the city where, in recent weeks, he had been residing.

The Makers had chosen to lay their city plans out in diamond patterns rather than rectangular grids as was customary on Earth. They loved to build tall and slender, so that many of their cities resembled pincushions: flat-topped buildings, needle slim, pierced the sky, thousands of them clustered together in impressive array. The Makers had loved colors, too, and each city was a rainbow of towers. Some of the buildings were even made of materials that changed their hue depending on the angle of the sun.

The delta homed in on the tallest building in Beta-Nu. Birk always chose to live in the tallest building of any city he was exploring; he could then look down from his tower and plot the course of his inspections. Plus, he would be able to find his way around in a strange city by using his home as a reference point.

This tower of stone, steel, and plastic was eighty-seven stories tall, small for a skyscraper on this world—but then, Beta-Nu was a small city. Arthur had said that Beta-Nu's population was only four hundred thousand at the peak period in its history.

The robot now settled the delta gently down atop the tower's flat roof and sent out another radio signal. Within seconds, a swarm of small gray helper robots appeared at the back end of the craft, unloading the dead loper and carrying it to the service lift. They would take it to the kitchen, Birk knew, where the carcass would then be skinned, cleaned, dressed, and prepared for half a dozen different meals. The kitchen robots were very efficient.

Birk emerged from his side of the delta, paying no attention to the mechanical dwarves. He walked to the edge of the low wall that enclosed the roof and leaned on it, staring down at the city below him. Beta-Nu, though small, was one of the more interesting sites he'd explored during his sojourn on this world. It was once known, Arthur had informed him, as an artists' haven; museums and galleries abounded, and even some of the individual homes and apartments showed artistic pretensions: entire walls of stained glass, unusual architectural designs, murals that covered whole rooms. So far, Birk had barely explored one quadrant's worth of richness; the rest of the city was his for the taking.

After some moments he was aware of Arthur standing slightly behind him, trying to attract his attention. He ignored the subliminal signals, forcing the robot to speak aloud.

"Sir, were you considering an exploration this afternoon?"

"Yes, I was."

"An excellent idea. Perhaps I could show you some of the . . ."

"I'll go alone if you don't mind, Arthur."

The robot hesitated just a fraction of a second. "If that's

13

what you want, sir." And, after another pause. "May I ask you a question?"

"Sure. But I won't guarantee to answer it."

"Are you feeling all right?"

Birk's first impulse was to snap back a quick "Of course," but then realized that Arthur wasn't inquiring about his physical health. An honest answer would be far more difficult. He tried to evade instead. "You're a robot. You don't even know what feelings are."

"Not from firsthand experience. But I can make inferences from the outward appearance and behavior you project, comparing them to your previous behavior. The difference is entirely too obvious, sir. If you want to hide your feelings from me, you'll have to be far more subtle than this."

Birk grinned in spite of himself. "Arthur, there are times when you've been the only thing keeping me sane in this place . . . and there are other times I'd gladly take you apart piece by piece. I don't know which feeling is uppermost at the moment, but I hope I never do reach the point where I dismantle you. That would be . . ."

"Sir?"

"What?"

"You haven't answered my question."

"Damn you!" Birk turned away, then turned back again almost immediately. The petulance was gone from his face. "There's a doomsday feeling that's been building up in me over the last week or so. Have you ever known that the world was going to end very shortly, and there was nothing you could do about it? Don't bother answering; that was just rhetorical. But that's how I feel right now."

"The world did end for me once, sir," Arthur said quietly.

Birk stared at him, nodding slowly. "Yes, you're right. I keep forgetting, even though the evidence is all around me. I think that's why I feel so close to you; we've each of us had our world end once. I'm sorry."

"No need to apologize, sir. I have no feelings, remember?"

"You're either being cynical or naïve. If I can ever figure out which, I probably *will* dismantle you." Birk shrugged. "Nevertheless, I'll be going out into the city today. Alone."

"As you wish, sir," Arthur said—the model of the perfect servant.

The streets were patterned mosaics in waves of colors. They echoed the soft clicks of his boots as he walked, while

14

the silence welled up inside him until it was a roar. The thoroughfares of Beta-Nu were narrow, made to accommodate only pedestrians; mechanized traffic was reserved to the underground tubeways. It was not that way in all the cities on this world, but Beta-Nu had been one of the newer, more progressive communities. Perhaps that was why Birk liked it so much.

Around him towered the city. Stone giants of blue and gold and red and green peered down at him, barely tolerant of this alien interloper and indignant that he should command the situation. The sturdy structures showed the wear of time and the wind, and the city was scented with the perfume of gentle decay.

The ubiquitous gray maintenance robots bustled all about him. Most were only waist-high, but they gave the city its only pretense at life. It was these mechanized legions who had kept the cities so well preserved centuries after their builders had perished. Birk had, by now, become accustomed to seeing them sweeping, dusting, removing foreign matter, or repairing cracks with their welding lasers; he paid them as little attention as they paid him.

And, as always, the streets were lined with ghosts. Birk had seen enough pictures of the Makers to visualize them quite vividly. Averaging more than two meters tall, with two arms and two legs apiece, they had heads that were squashed ovoids with narrow, pinpoint eyes, no noses, and a gash that only by generosity could be called a mouth. Skin colors varied from blue to green, but there was one minority race that seemed to have a pleasant golden cast.

The most blatant features of the Makers, though, were their enormous hands and feet. The hands each had seven digits, including two thumbs, and had twice the span of a human's. The feet were similarly oversized, and yet the arms and legs were proportioned normally for slender bodies.

Eleven years ago, these creatures had seemed bizarre; now, Birk was more used to seeing representations of them than he was to seeing humans. Even his own reflected image seemed strange to him. In some ways, too, he felt more of a kinship with the Makers. They existed in a place that was now out of time and reality—and so did he, cut off from all that was normal for his race.

A gentle breeze blew from his back, ruffling his unkempt dark hair still further. There were times when the wind could become strong enough to make the buildings vibrate. On

15

some of those occasions, Birk could feel as though the city were serenading him with a soulful siren song; yet at other times it was merely cacophonous vibrations, and he would stand in the middle of a room, holding his hands over his ears and screaming.

He ignored the taller buildings on this jaunt. He'd learned early on that they were usually either offices or apartment houses; and while there were always serendipitous discoveries to be made there, his soul today craved more momentous accomplishments.

He likewise walked right past the parks with their immense statues and monuments to war; they held no meaning for him today. Picking up a small pebble, he threw it at some birds to watch their hasty flight with grim amusement. He was looking for something special, and was angry with himself for not knowing what it was.

There were smaller buildings interspersed among the larger ones. Cubical and rectilinear architecture prevailed, though occasionally he would come across a whimsy that was a dome or pyramid or even some irregular conglomeration of straight lines and curves. These were the ones that attracted his attention now; only eccentricities would soothe his strange mood of the moment.

The first few he came to were shops of some sort, but whatever merchandise they'd sold had long ago turned to dust and been swept away by the efficient maintenance robots. Sometimes murals were painted on the walls, faded over the millennia; invariably they were scenes of great battles, dedicated to the glory of war. The best one he saw was of two opposing robot armies, clashing in a furious metallic assault. The din of that silent struggle was overwhelming, but Birk turned away, unmoved.

After three hours of random walking, he found what he'd been seeking: an art museum. In contrast to the war murals that graced public walls and the heroic statues that filled the parks, the art in the museums tended to be of a softer, more sensitive nature. The Makers put their spirit on display, but they held their soul in secret.

This building was an inverted truncated cone, held upright by three outside pillars. Inside, the gallery was arranged along a helical walkway that spiraled up the sides. The vast open space in the center—which grew larger the higher one climbed—was filled with mobile sculptures suspended from the translucent ceiling and with phantom images of animals and flowers that floated through the air courtesy of hidden holographic projectors. Standing at the foot of the walkway and looking upward, the effect was one of having the museum stretching out infinitely into space overhead, even though Birk knew the building was only ten to fifteen stories tall. He was suitably impressed, as the designer of this gallery had intended him to be.

He started casually up the ramp with the wall on his left, noting as he walked the artistic legacy that was now his alone. Some of the works had been done on a fabric-based material similar to canvas; these had been partially eaten away by this world's equivalent of mildew and bacteria, though not to the extent one might have supposed. They were, after all, indoors and protected from the elements and animals. The maintenance robots had done what they could to preserve these treasures, with more success in some cases than in others.

Later paintings were made on an artificial material that could be as thin as parchment while retaining color and lasting indefinitely. The paints themselves were mineral-based and faded almost not at all, despite the millennia that had passed since their original application.

There were other forms of art besides the paintings. Sculptures both of stone and of metal were set in niches along the wall as he ascended; the metals tended to be corroded, but the stone works were as fresh as the day they were cut.

In addition, there were some of the unique art forms that, for want of a better word, Birk had called "windows." A plate of what looked to be glass was framed flat against a wall, and yet looking through it gave the viewer a panoramic scene as though he were looking through the wall. The representation was perfectly three dimensional, yet the glass that held it was flat. Birk had once taken down one of these pieces to make sure there was nothing behind it but solid wall. He had never figured out the process that created these windows—it was certainly no holographic procedure he was familiar with—but he had to admire the technique and craftsmanship that went into them. Often they were the most striking works in any given display.

The works at the lowest level of this gallery had a martial flavor to them, but they were subtly different from the more public art forms. These paintings concentrated on the individual aspects of battle—bravery and loyalty, cowardice and betrayal. A few were even so bold as to depict the tragedy of warfare as well as its glory: widows mourning their loved ones, limbless veterans returning to shattered homes, terrified children dying for reasons they could not understand. Birk passed them by, observing but uncaring.

Next came a series of more surrealistic works: pieces where perspective shifted in and out of focus with startling abruptness; where there were several different references of gravity in one painting; where familiar objects were of unusual proportions or in bizarre juxtaposition; where colors clashed in outrageous combinations. There were times when Birk enjoyed standing before such works, wondering about the symbolism they carried to the audience they'd been intended to reach. But today he was in no mood for puzzles, and he pushed relentlessly on.

There were some strictly representational pieces, though not very many in this gallery—simple landscapes, or seascapes, or portraits, or scenes of ordinary events: merchants in a marketplace, craftsmen at their labors, children playing by a seashore. Birk spent a long time studying these last, hoping that they would speak to him, tell him something that could relate to life as he was living it. But they were just pictures, as lifeless now as their creators, and try as he would he could not bring animation to their subjects.

The higher he went, the harder it was to go on. His legs began to ache from the climb. His breaths were deep puffs. *One more time around the spiral,* he thought, *and then I'll quit.* He grew thirsty, and wished the Makers had believed in putting water fountains in public places. He climbed some more and rested, drawing deep breaths. *One more time around.*

He climbed.

He found what he didn't know he'd been seeking near the very top of the building. It was one of the windows, oval in shape, with the long axis nearly two meters tall and the short axis a meter across. The frame was glittery silver, sparkling with a life of its own. Birk took one look into the window and was transfixed by its awesome emotional impact.

The background of the scene was dark blue, verging to black as it faded into the distance; although there were no lines of perspective, the impression was of staring down a long, dark tunnel with no opening at the other end. Two figures inhabited the scene—both androgynous (if such a term could be used in reference to the Makers), both featureless.

One figure seemed smaller, though that might only indicate it was farther away from the viewer. It was pale blue

18

and lay on its right side, propped up on one elbow. Its neck was craned forward and its left arm stretched agonizingly toward the other figure in a gesture that could only be a call for help. Its cry of pain was implicit in the strain of its musculature, the angle of its head, the trembling fingers of its hand.

The larger—nearer?—figure was golden-skinned and had its back turned to the other. While it, too, had no facial features, it faced the viewer in a pose of disdain. Hands resting casually on hips, left foot forward and silently bent, the figure had its head cocked, listening. There could be no doubt that it heard the piteous pleas of its fellow on the ground behind it—and there could be even less doubt about its total lack of concern.

There in the window, the scene was staged in eternal simplicity: the blue victim, its silent screams echoing through the blue-black corridor, reaching out for help; and the golden ignorer, locked into its own world and refusing to emerge even to help a soul in agony.

Birk didn't know how long he'd been standing in front of the window before he realized he was sobbing. The devastating emotionalism of this single piece had lanced through him, touching scars he'd thought were long healed and making them bleed afresh. Birk sank slowly to his knees but did not—could not—take his eyes from the window.

Though the picture remained unchanged, he could see faces forming on those alien bodies. His face and—Reva's. He was on the ground, reaching up to her, reaching for his golden Reva. *Reva, I'm hurt. Reva, I need you. Reva, don't deny me! Reva! Reva. . . .*

There came a point at which he could no longer keep himself upright, even on his knees. He fell forward, then, to the walkway, and his eyes finally left the scene in the window. He lay there prone in an undignified heap with his arms outstretched and clawing at the floor, coughing as his tears flowed unchecked. The walls of the empty building echoed his cries of anguish.

After some time, the sobbing stopped. Birk rose unsteadily to his feet and staggered back down the ramp and out of the gallery. Not once did he look back at the window hanging silently on the wall.

The nightmares started up again that night.

They began with the peaceful fuzzy nothingness of his

19

normal sleeping pattern—but the fuzziness was suddenly shattered by sharp, painful images of bright lights shining in his eyes, of harsh stabbing at his limbs, of a relentless droning in his ears that grew louder and louder no matter how hard he tried to shut it out, until finally his eardrums threatened to burst. There was Reva, standing before him, naked in the golden glow of her beauty, smiling her warm, understanding, I-can-make-everything-better-with-a-touch smile. But as he stepped toward her she changed, snarling with fangs that would shame a guard dog, raking him with claws of burning iron.

He backed away and stepped into a pit. Cold, heavy chains bound him as he fell. As he hit the floor, he discovered that there were others around him, also in chains—faceless souls screaming against their bondage. The floor tilted and he was thrown together with them, jammed so tightly that the stench of their sweating bodies burned his nostrils. Then explosions, bright lights, shock . . .

He awoke to find himself crying in Arthur's arms. The robot was holding Birk tightly against his smooth body, swaying ever so slightly with a comforting rocking motion and stroking the man's hair tenderly. Birk could recall his mother holding him like that when, as a child, he'd awakened in the night with fear. As rational thought returned to him, he remembered teaching Arthur exactly the way it should be done.

"I . . . I think I'm all right now," he managed to say.

The robot loosened his grip, but did not entirely let go yet. "Are you sure, sir?"

"Yes, quite."

With the increasing confidence in Birk's voice, the robot took his hands away and backed off. He continued to watch Birk closely, however.

"Thanks for coming to me," Birk went on after a moment. "It's been a while since I've had an attack that bad, hasn't it?"

"Over three years, sir."

Birk shook his head. "It's all part of this feeling I was trying to describe to you earlier. I don't know what's come over me."

On impulse, he threw back the blankets and slid off the high bed to stand naked on the icy floor. The soles of his feet tingled and the air was bitingly cold all around him, but he forced himself not to notice. Instead, he crossed to the stairway and climbed up one flight to the roof.

A chill wind whipped him as he stood unprotected in the darkness, looking out over the black abyss that was the city below. Looking upward brought no relief from darkness, either; the night gripped him like a cold black fist and the sky was as barren as a witch's womb.

Behind him, Arthur emerged from the stairwell carrying a sleeping robe. Birk turned slowly and allowed his companion to dress him. "I do miss the stars, Arthur," he sighed. "They're the one thing I really do miss. These empty nights of yours give me a touch of claustrophobia."

"You said yourself, though, that being in the middle of a dust cloud kept other humans from finding you."

"True, true. But shooting my own arguments back at me won't cure me of nostalgia. The stars were always my friends, even when people turned against me. I may recognize the necessity for their absence, but I still miss them. Damn it, I do!"

As he spoke, a streak of light flashed across the otherwise black backdop of night. "A meteor," Birk said, his lips curling into a tight smile. "All right, then, I'll settle for that, if it's all this stingy sky will give me."

Alarm bells started ringing downstairs, and Arthur stiffened. After a moment, the robot relaxed again and addressed his master. "That was no meteor, sir. It was an artificial object, quite possibly a spaceship like the one you came in. It just crashed in the mountains five hundred kilometers north of here."

It was Birk's turn to stiffen. The night's chill had suddenly doubled its intensity. There could be only one reason why a ship would come here: they had found out about him. They were coming to take him back.

Perhaps it was, indeed, the end of the world.

TWO

"It's but a short flight, sir," Arthur continued, unaware of Birk's malaise. "We may still find survivors if we hurry." And he started back toward the stairwell.

Birk stood rigid, frozen in time and space. Arthur's words registered somewhere in his mind, like a mouse squeaking in a far corner of the next room. There was suddenly a hole in the bottom of his stomach, a queasy abyss through which all sensation was flowing, to be replaced by . . . what?

Arthur stopped when he realized Birk was not following him. "You are coming, aren't you, sir?" the robot asked politely. "I should think you'd want to supervise the rescue operations. There may be some decisions about whom to save and whom to leave, and you're much more capable of making such choices than I am."

Birk was suddenly aware that he was standing in the dark, with just a night robe draped loosely around his naked body. He was stricken with a fit of uncontrollable shivers and, even in his dazed state, that struck him as odd—the night wasn't *that* cold. He tried to answer Arthur's question, but his teeth were chattering so fiercely that he couldn't force the words out.

Seeing his master's difficulty, Arthur returned to his side and wrapped one tentacular arm around Birk's shoulders. "I've already summoned the medic team from the local area, and they're on their way to the scene. If we hurry, we can meet them there." He hesitated. "Unless, of course, you don't want . . ."

"No," Birk said. "I mean, yes, I do want . . . we must try. . . ." He was surprised how hoarse his own voice sounded.

"Good, sir, I thought that was what you'd say. But we must move quickly." With the arm around behind him, Arthur was pushing Birk back toward the stairwell. Birk found his feet leaden, but Arthur's gentle, inexorable pressure kept him moving forward. "Every second wasted could cost a life," the robot continued.

Birk moved as though in a dream, or in a nightmare—a nightmare where he was pursuing something he wanted and could never quite catch up to it—or where something was chasing him and he could not move fast enough to escape. In this case, he would not have been able to say which simile was more correct.

He stood silently in the bedroom while Arthur scanned his wardrobe and made the appropriate selections. Birk, moving more like a robot than Arthur did, raised his arms to get the shirt on over his head, and lifted each leg mechanically as Arthur helped him put on his trousers. Arthur took his boots and led Birk up the stairs to the roof again, where the delta was waiting for them. "You can put your boots on while we're flying," the robot said. "I just received a report from the medic team. They're nearing the site, and the crash looks like a bad one."

Birk slid into his seat in the delta, and the triangular craft lifted off the roof even before the plastic bubble had fully closed over him. Arthur, at the controls, spun the craft around, and Birk was pressed back against his seat as the delta took off. He sat stiffly, holding his boots in his hand until Arthur reminded him to put them on.

The world around them was in blackness, the only light being the dim green glow from the instrument panel. There were no stars, there was no moon, and the cities of this world had not been lit at night for two thousand years, except on those few occasions when Birk had specifically requested it. Sky and ground merged into a uniform darkness, as though Birk had been shoved into a sensory-deprivation chamber. The delta had a searchlight on its underside that could have illuminated the ground below—but Arthur didn't need it and Birk didn't think to turn it on.

The delta flew with silent efficiency, with but a subliminal hum and a few half-felt quivers to let the occupants know it was moving. Once it reached maximum speed Arthur kept it at a steady pace, and even the press of acceleration disappeared. With no scenery to watch gliding past, all sensation of motion vanished; the delta and its occupants could have been holding steady, suspended in a starless void for all eternity.

The darkness and the silence were restful, and Birk needed

that right now. They covered him like a security blanket, cushioning his psyche from the shock of tonight's event. For a few minutes, his mind could relax and flow with the solitude once more.

People. The thought was both entrancing and repellent. *Other people, other voices, other ideas. It's been so long. What could I say to them? What will they want from me? What are they doing here? What if they came to get me . . .?*

Be reasonable, the small, cold part of his mind told him. *It's been eleven years. They think you're dead by now—that is, if they even think of you at all.*

Arthur said it was a bad crash. Maybe everyone was killed. Then I wouldn't have to worry. That thought warmed him somewhat. It wouldn't be his fault if there weren't any survivors. Just rotten luck, that was all. He could mourn them more deeply than anyone had ever been mourned before, regretting the lost companionship they could have provided him. He straightened up in his seat, already consigning their souls to the land of the dead and planning some memorial he'd have the robots erect in their name. He was starting to feel almost himself again.

There was a point of light below them now, near the horizon, and Arthur dipped their craft's nose toward it. As the delta sped closer, Birk could see the point of light expand until it took on a definite shape—a lopsided ring of fire surrounding a darkened patch that glowed feebly, like an ember about to die. Then, even as he watched, the center of the ring grew brighter as the medic robot team set up its own floodlights to aid the rescue operation.

The story laid out before him was obvious. The ship had crashed into the hillside with devastating impact. The heat of its passage ignited the brush around it, and the fire began spreading out from the point of impact in all directions. The fire did not burn evenly because of a slight breeze that retarded its progress up the hill, leaving a lopsided, squashed-in appearance to the fiery circle. The robot rescue team arrived and immediately doused the fire near the ship so that it wouldn't hamper their operations. They did not care about the rest of the fire; what did it matter whether a thousand hectares burned, or even a million? The planet's history could hardly be affected by such minor details anymore.

With the gentlest of bumps, Arthur landed the delta inside the fire circle. The plastic bubbles over the passenger compartments swung upward, and both man and robot slid off their seats to stand beside their craft. Arthur moved hastily, running up the charred hillside toward the twisted wreckage of the spaceship. Birk merely stood beside the delta, watching all the frantic activity in the rescue area before him.

The rescue floodlights shone with an intense yellow glow. They provided plenty of illumination, making this portion of the hillside look as bright as day; but the color made the scene seem washed out, faded like an overexposed photograph. The rapid movements of the robots as they went about their tasks seemed in direct contradiction to the lighting. There was a feverish quality about the place, a heat emanating from the rescue site having nothing to do with the fire raging around it.

The ship itself was a total wreck. Strangely, it seemed to have impacted on its side rather than either nose or tail first, as though the attitude controls had been misbehaving. The style of the ship was unfamiliar, but that wasn't surprising—he could hardly have expected designs to remain as they'd been eleven years ago. The name *Thundercloud* could be read on the twisted metal of the hull. This was a human ship, all right—not that he'd had many doubts about it. Humanity had never encountered any evidence of other intelligent races in its short history of galactic exploration.

Except for the Makers, he reminded himself. *And they don't really count because I'm the only one who knows about them.*

The ship had been a big one, nearly forty meters long, but whether it had been military or civilian he couldn't hazard a guess. Depending on its mission, Birk estimated it could have housed as many as a hundred people—and under no circumstances could it have been run by less than twenty. That gave Birk at least a feel for the magnitude of the problem he was facing.

The rescue robots had come prepared for heavy work. Their machines were already ripping the ship's hull apart to allow medical teams to search for survivors. The din was almost deafening; the hissing of laser welding torches burning through the hull, the squealing of tortured metal being bent out of the way, the clanking of the big machines as they pulled the broken ship to pieces. Only one sound seemed to be missing, and it took Birk a few seconds to pinpoint what it was. In a human rescue operation, the rescuers would be yelling back and forth at one another, calling for assistance, coordinating their actions and giving advice or reassurance. These robots moved silently among the wreckage like gray metal ghosts. If they chatted among themselves at all—as they had to if they were to maintain any coordination—it was all in radio frequencies that Birk could not hear.

The smoke from the fire tickled his nostrils, and he sneezed twice. The sneezes broke his reverie, and he started walking slowly up the hill toward the center of all the activity. Even as he walked, his mind was analyzing the situation.

No one could have survived a crash like that, he thought. *The ship must have been traveling at better than three hundred kilometers an hour when it hit—and if the attitude controls were out, the people couldn't even have been braced properly.*

But apprehension was growing in another portion of his brain. *There could have been a hundred people in there. Some of them may have been lucky. The ship hit on one side; people on the other side had a chance. What are the odds that some of them are still living?*

He froze again as the thought triggered a memory—a memory of a thousand nightmares, but also a memory born of real life. He looked at the twisted pile of wreckage and thought of the twisted, broken bodies that must lie within it. *What are the odds, Birk? What are the odds?*

"Offhand, I'd say they're lousy. I'm open to better suggestions."

Gonzales scowled at him. He looked as though he wanted to spit, had such an action not been so unthinkable aboard a spaceship. "So we're stuck with that, eh?"

"It's like the old joke that we've got two chances, slim and none. I'll opt for slim any day."

"We could go back." Birk never knew the name of the black man who made that suggestion.

"No, we can't," he sighed patiently. "I told you that a week ago, when we passed the point of no return. We haven't the food, water, air, or fuel to make it back—and we all agreed then that we didn't want to try."

"But you've never landed a ship before," Gonzales reiterated.

"I'll try to learn fast."

But then he was at the control panel, and the ship was coming down, and his hands were sweating, and nothing was going right. Piloting the ship through a vacuum and charting a course through the convolutions of p-space were child's play compared to maneuvering through the vagaries of a thick, resisting atmosphere.

The engines were a torch beneath them as the ship slammed downward toward the planet's surface. He had confidence in the engines; he could have taken them apart blindfolded. But the engines were working perfectly; it was pilot performance at stake here, and he had no confidence at all in the pilot, himself.

The ship was shaking. It had been a slow, negligible rattle to start with—but as the whine of air rushing by became loud enough to hear even inside the hull, the vibrations grew in intensity. Now it was a bone-jarring shudder that rocked the whole ship as though the vessel itself were quaking with a premonition of doom. Birk was having trouble holding his hands steady on the controls—even assuming they were the right controls to begin with.

Then the ship started tilting as the wind currents and jet streams in the upper atmosphere buffeted the falling vessel. The attitude dials were going crazy; the ship's nose was wobbling back and forth too fast for them to keep up with it. In desperation, Birk turned the autostabilizers back on, even though everything he'd read about landing procedures advised against using them.

The mistake was obvious immediately. The stabilizers activated the correcting jets around the ship's hull the instant any tilt went beyond a given point. But the ship was tilting and bucking so rapidly that the jets could not keep up. Their compensations were out of synch with the ship's movements, adding to the chaos. The ship's wobble became even worse, and the computers were going crazy trying to correct the imbalance.

Birk tore his attention away from other matters to deal with the berserk wobble. He fumbled at the switch for the autostabilizers, and finally managed to shut them off once more. The insane back-and-forth jerking motions stopped, but the ship was almost on its side and plummeting like a stone. Forcing his brain to remain calm and his hands to remain steady, Birk patiently fought the air currents to bring the ship back to an upright position. But that effort required his full attention for more than fifteen seconds, and was at best a pyrrhic victory.

Descent was much too fast. Ground level was coming up faster than they could resist it. Birk turned the engines on full and felt the kick push him deeper into his couch. And even then, glancing at the numbers on the readout screen, he knew it was not enough. The engines were giving him all the power they'd been built for, and then some—and still it wasn't enough.

27

And while he was checking their speed, the rocking began again.

There was screaming below decks. The men could feel what was happening around them, and they were scared. They couldn't see Birk panicking at the control panel, but still they were scared. Birk could hardly blame them. He was the most frightened of the lot. He knew they were going to die.

The control panel became a blur to his vision. He had no idea what his hands were doing any longer as he moved them with great effort over the board. The shining numbers on the screen, changing with growing rapidity, were gibberish. The piercing howl of the wind stabbed at his mind, blending with the harsh curses and shouts of the men in the ship below. Someone was screaming here in the room, and only hindsight let him realize that it was him. The sweat of his stinking body mixed with the scent of urine as his bladder emptied itself, and he was crying and retching at the same time.

Then the sharp black pain, the ultimate end of all nightmares, the dissolution of self into a million shining pieces of nothingness. Gasping, pressure, pain, silence, heat, everything bad in dreams, everything painful in fear—these and more were Birk Aaland. Dark, oppressive pain, a pain so intense it transcended sensation; it was a fire through his soul, and he knew he'd discovered the depths of the Hell he'd never believed in, Then . . .

"They've found some bodies, sir."

Arthur's gentle voice sliced through the black haze of memory/dream and yanked Birk back to the present. He was standing on the hillside with the newly crashed ship, staring with glazed eyes as the robots worked frantically to rescue the occupants. He could have been standing here for five seconds or five minutes, it was hard to say. His body was hot far beyond the heat of the fires around this spot.

He forced words up through his throat. "Are . . . are they alive?"

"Not any of the ones found so far. But they've only found four, and there must be more in there somewhere. We thought you'd at least like to see these."

Birk nodded slowly and pulled himself together. With a deliberate effort, he broke out of his paralysis and started once more up the hill. With each step he took, the ship seemed to repel him more strongly, as though he and it were

28

identical magnetic charges; but he forced himself to continue despite the pressure in his mind telling him to turn and flee.

He at last reached the side of the ship, and the wreck loomed over him like a beached metal whale. He reached out to touch this, the first human artifact he'd seen in a decade, but Arthur stopped him. "The hull is still too hot for you to touch," the robot warned. "If you'll come around this way, they've lined the bodies up for your inspection."

Birk nodded and followed Arthur's lead, around the wreck and up the hill to a point near the top where the medical robots had dragged the corpses out of the debris. The bodies were recognizable as human, but only barely; smashed and bloody, they were twisted out of shape in grotesque postures. Birk felt his stomach churning, and looked quickly away— but not quickly enough to stop the gag reflex that sent him into a choking fit. He managed with difficulty to keep in his stomach what was left from his dinner six hours before; then, bracing himself, he turned to examine the bodies again.

He tried, as much as possible, to avoid looking at the torn and pulverized flesh. Instead, he studied the clothing the corpses were wearing. Though the cloth, too, was usually torn—and so smeared with blood and dirt that its original color was impossible to determine—the cut of the clothing and the similarity from body to body could mean just one thing: the people aboard this ship had been wearing uniforms. This was a military ship.

Birk clenched his teeth until his jaw ached. Why had a military ship, of all things, crashed here?

The robots dragged more bodies out of the wreckage as the minutes passed, and their work went on ceaselessly. Some victims were in even worse shape than the first ones, while others looked barely touched by the catastrophe. But all were equally dead. As the casualty toll mounted past ten, approaching twenty, Birk felt the constriction easing in his chest and his breathing becoming easier. There would be no survivors, after all. It was a pity, of course, but in a way he felt strangely relieved. There would be no one, now, to upset his comfortable routine, no one to fight with, no one to make demands on him. There were only the robots, and he could have their company or tell them to go away, as he chose. They would never force themselves on him, as real people would.

A body was dragged from the wreckage, bearing on the shoulder of its uniform the twin clusters of a major. Birk

29

gritted his teeth as he stared at the tarnished clusters, remembering

a rubber truncheon striking hard at his left cheek. He turned his head at the last instant, hoping to dodge, but he couldn't avoid all the impact. The truncheon hit with a glancing blow, stinging the cheek even more painfully, perhaps, than it would have had it hit directly. Birk could feel blood in his mouth from where the inner lining of the cheek had cut against his teeth.

He squinted out from puffy, swollen eyes at the twin clusters on the major's hat. He wanted to spit the blood straight into his tormentor's face, but he lacked the strength for even that simple act of defiance. It wasn't worth it. None of it was worth it, not since the beginning of this whole stupid mess.

"I usually do this to extract information," the major said conversationally. "But you don't have any secrets we need to know. This is just for practice, for fun."

The major raised his arm again and brought the truncheon down. . . .

Birk shuddered as the shadow-blow never came. Even after a dozen years, the memories remained too close to the surface, too easily dredged up to haunt his dreams—and now even his waking life. He knew he'd never exorcise it completely, but he had hoped he'd buried it better than that.

He gave the dead major's face a hard kick with his right foot, and was rewarded with the sound of a crunching cheekbone. But this major was beyond pain, and the action brought him no satisfaction. Birk turned away disgusted with himself.

"Sir!" Birk looked up to see Arthur waving to him from across the wrecked area. "We've found one who's still alive!"

A chill started in Birk's stomach and spread in an instant through the legs and arms. It never reached into his head, though. "Coming," was all he said as he started around the wreckage to the point where Arthur stood.

Birk could only catch a glimpse of the body as a group of robots swarmed around it and carried it gingerly to their mobile med unit. The victim was a young black man, looking in worse shape than some of the corpses Birk had seen. Both his legs had been crushed and his chest was smeared with blood, which was a strangely washed-out orange color under the yellow glare of the floodlights; his eyes, wide open, stared unseeingly at the robots as they lifted him into the back of the van and out of Birk's sight. There, Birk knew, they would connect the man to a host of specialized gadgets in an effort to

30

keep him alive. These robots, he reminded himself, had plenty of experience with battlefield casualties. But it had all been centuries ago and, with one notable exception—himself—they'd had no success with human beings.

The young man was alive for now—but how long could he remain so in that bad a shape?

Several more corpses were discovered and dragged out of the wreckage before the next survivor was found. Birk's heartbeat quickened as he raced over and saw that it was a woman—tall, well-proportioned, and blond. His first thought was *Reva!* But of course it wasn't Reva, merely some other woman who bore a superficial resemblance to her. She was in almost as bad a shape as the first survivor. With the blood smearing her body and her stringy hair obscuring her face it was difficult to say whether she was at all attractive, but the thought of a living woman, another Reva, brought Birk to a cold sweat. If she lived, perhaps he could correct whatever mistakes he'd made with Reva and restore that missing portion of his life once more. He instructed the robots to take extra good care of her as they carried her into the waiting van.

In all, a total of six survivors were found in the wreckage of the spaceship. Three more were men, one Caucasian and two Oriental; the last was another woman, also Oriental—short and dumpy, her hair in braids, looking nothing like Reva and not nearly as appealing as the first woman. She was still a female, though, and a precious commodity to Birk; he ordered the robots to give her special attention as well, though he was sure the robots operated at a single level of efficiency for all their patients.

When the wreckage had been combed thoroughly to make sure there were no other survivors, the rescue van took off back toward Beta-Nu with its precious cargo of six living humans. Birk, Arthur, and a small number of robots were left behind at the crash site. "What do you want done about the bodies?" Arthur asked Birk.

What indeed? After recovering from his own crash, Birk had had the robots dismantle the ship completely and bury the bodies of his comrades, leaving no trace that the vessel had ever been here. There'd been good reason for that then; there was always the fear lurking in the back of his mind that his course might have been traced, that the authorities would come tracking him down. He'd wanted to make certain that they had no clue he'd ever been here, much less survived in a reasonably grand style. That fear had disappeared slowly over the years, surfacing again only briefly tonight. He realized he was not important enough to warrant a major search; they had probably written him off as dead years ago.

This ship tonight was another matter. It was military, probably on an official mission; there was little doubt it would be missed, and even less doubt it would be searched for. Its appearance here was a mystery he would have to solve before knowing how to proceed. If it had been lost and well off course, he might still be safe; but if it had been coming in this direction intentionally, headquarters would know approximately where to look. Despite the density of this region's obscuring nebulosity, they would find this world eventually.

Even if he were to conceal all evidence of the crash, the planet itself would intrigue the army once they found it. They could land anywhere, at any time, and send out teams in all directions. If they happened to land on the other side of the world, he might not even know about it until he'd given his presence away—and then it would be too late.

But if he left the crashed ship here, in plain view, this would be the first place they'd come. They'd still want to explore the rest of the planet, but he'd know where to watch for them. He could be warned in plenty of time to cover his trail; with an entire planet at his disposal—and with the army not even knowing he was here to be searched for—he could remain undiscovered for the rest of his life.

"Put everything back the way it was," he told Arthur. "Put the bodies back where they were found and do what you can to restore the ship to the way it looked when we arrived."

Birk knew it was impossible to do a perfect job of camouflage. Anyone examining the crash closely would see that things had been disturbed, the ship cut apart and crudely patched together again. If the army did check that carefully, they would have a minor mystery on their hands—although they might in the end assume that the city robots had merely exercised some unexpected curiosity and then tidied up after themselves. He was hoping, though, that the facts of the crash would be so obvious that the investigators would not pry more closely into the matter.

Arthur accepted the orders without question; that was one of the qualities Birk liked best about him. The remaining robots began the task of restoring the scene to its previous state while Arthur and Birk returned to the delta and began the flight back to Beta-Nu.

"I want Beta-Nu's defensive scanners turned up full," Birk said as their craft sailed once more through the darkness. "I want the alarms going off if anything larger than a batbird lands within a thousand kilometers, understand?"

"Perfectly, sir," Arthur said.

"And make preparations for tomorrow. I'd like to take a trip to Alpha-Xi to make sure it's all set—just in case this ship was only the forerunner of more to come."

"As you wish, sir."

"Tell me," Birk said, swiveling in his seat to look more closely at his companion. "What do you think the chances are that any of those suvivors will pull through?"

"Not very good. I think it would be a miracle if any of them lasts more than two days."

Birk sighed. "That's what I was afraid of."

"It's exactly the same thing I thought, in fact, when we found you."

Birk sat through the rest of the flight in silence.

THREE

Birk arrived back at his tower to the news that one of the survivors had died en route to the city. He looked at Arthur in alarm. "It wasn't . . .?"

"No, sir, it wasn't one of the women," Arthur answered quickly. It was at times like this that Birk suspected the robot might be telepathic; but then he realized Arthur had merely sensed his extra concern for the women as they were loaded into the van, and correctly judged his master's emotions. To a man alone for eleven years, the women were quite important. As an added bit of news to ease Birk's troubled mind, Arthur went on, "Their condition remains unchanged."

Birk sighed with relief, and immediately felt guilty for doing so. "Look at me," he said, half to himself. "I'm actually glad some man I don't even know is dead, just as long as it isn't one of the women. For all I know, both those women could be nasty-tempered bitches and there fellow an absolute saint—but just because they're female . . . ."

"You're under a great deal of strain, sir," Arthur soothed. "So much has happened so quickly. You can be excused a great many things."

"Just what I needed," Birk said bitterly, turning from Arthur and walking into the building. "Absolution from a machine." His dissatisfaction with himself had to be vented on an external target, and Arthur—as always—was the only one at hand.

The survivors had been taken to Beta-Nu's main hospital, which was several blocks from his tower. Birk debated going there to keep an eye on things, but decided against it. He had no medical training and therefore had no place in a hospital except as a patient. He knew from his own experience just how thorough and complete the Makers' hospitals were; there would be hundreds, if not thousands, of robots there to tend to the survivors' conditions—robots that had been out of work for centuries, who would relish nothing more than the chance to fulfill their functions again. Even if human physiology was different from what they were used to, he'd found they were very clever and remarkably adaptable. If those people could be saved at all, the hospital robots would do it.

He went to his bedroom, but could not sleep. The thought of this new Reva haunted all his thoughts. He had too much random energy to work off, so he paced the room like a caged beast. There was nothing he could do, and that frustrated him. Arthur came down to be with him and to watch over him, but did not speak unbidden. Occasionally Birk would ask him for status reports, and Arthur would relay the radioed message he himself received from the hospital: conditions of the patients remained unchanged.

It wouldn't be so bad, Birk thought, *if the matter could be decided one way or another. If they all die, things will go on as before. If any of them pull through, I'll cope with that. But waiting and not knowing is driving me crazy.*

He knew he should be making contingency plans in case any of the victims did survive. One or more new people could be a great relief—someone to talk to, someone to share things with, someone to relieve the unbearable tedium of his solitary existence. But, on the other hand, other people could be an intrusion. He had built himself a lifestyle that was comfortable, if not exciting. Other people might fight with him,

34

something Arthur never did. Other people might laugh at him, or dislike him—and he'd lost the ability, through a decade of disuse, to cope with that.

Birk did his best to push the matter from his mind. These were things he'd deal with when he had to, not before. Right now the situation was in the lap of the Fates; there was no point in disturbing himself with needless worries. All he could do was wait—however frustrating that might be.

At last the activities of the evening took their toll of him. He stopped pacing and sat down in one of the chairs beside his bed. Sleep finally took him two hours before dawn—a gray, swirling sleep, overcast with clouds that hid his dreams and kept them forever after from his memory.

He woke suddenly and jerked himself upright in his chair. From the amount of light in the room, the sun had been up for quite some time. "Arthur!"

"Right here, sir," the robot said from across the room.

Sleeping in the chair had made his whole body stiff, particularly his neck. Birk began massaging it and moving his head around in a slow circle, stretching the painful muscles. "Why did you let me sleep so late?"

"You had so little sleep last night, I thought you might need it."

"I'll decide that. Give me a status report."

Arthur hesitated for the briefest of instants. "Another of the people died, just thirty minutes ago—one of the women."

A chill ripped through Birk's body, the same sort he'd experienced when he'd first been told there was a living survivor. Of all his hopes, the most fervent had been that the women would survive—and the chances had just been cut by 50 percent. "Which woman was it?" he asked, scarcely daring to breathe.

"The taller one with the lighter-colored hair."

Birk closed his eyes to hold in the tears. He'd lost her again—his Reva. Even though he had no idea what this woman was like as a person, he'd hoped from his first glimpse of her that she could rekindle the love he'd known with his ex-wife. Now he'd lost Reva all over again. Fate was playing another of its cruel jokes, stealing his heart twice in the same way.

"Of course," he muttered aloud. "I should have known it would be her. That leaves me with the short, dumpy one,

35

doesn't it?" He stood up slowly, grimacing as he stretched the muscles strained from a night's sleep in an awkward position.

Arthur had long ago learned to distinguish rhetorical questions, and did not bother to answer. Instead, he moved to Birk's side and helped the man over to the table. "I've had breakfast all prepared and waiting for you, sir," he said helpfully.

Birk sat down and looked at the array of food the small helper robot brought in from the adjoining room at Arthur's silent summons. All were dishes that he normally liked—a rich fruit compote, lightly toasted brown rolls, and a tangy protein custard, all served in large quantities. Arthur had gone out of his way to please his master this morning, but right now nothing looked appetizing. Birk listlessly pushed the food around on his plate and took a few dutiful bites before putting down his utensils and standing up again.

"Thanks, Arthur, but I'm just not hungry right now. I have to go out, get away from here for a while."

"Yes, sir. I've made all the preparations for your trip to Alpha-Xi."

Birk had forgotten he'd ordered that last night. "Uh, that's very important, yes, but I'll tend to it later. For the moment, I just have to be alone to . . . to gather my thoughts."

"As you wish, sir."

Birk left his tower a short while later, brooding about the ironies and idiocies of life. *Why the blonde?* he wondered. *Why Reva? Why did she die rather than the other one?*

He had seen her for only a few fleeting seconds in that strange yellow light: bedraggled hair obscuring most of her face and blood covering the rest of her body. But wherever his memory lacked for detail, his imagination was quick to supply it. She had become, in his mind, a duplicate of Reva—a tall, willowy Nordic beauty, agile of body, quick of smile, and proud of spirit. Her blue eyes were filled with intelligence and wit, and she could love a man with a passion that would consume them both. She was gentle, yet firm when she wanted her own way, a tawny tigress with a thousand and one secrets for pleasing men. All of that would have been his for the asking, and he knew he'd never lose that image of her: Reva, the perfect woman, the ideal lover—cruelly stolen from him twice now.

And what was he left with? A short, stocky Oriental woman with dull black braids. He had seen no more of her than he had of his blond Reva—but how could this one possibly measure up to the standards the other had set?

Of course, he might not have her, either. Arthur had said it would be a miracle if any of the people survived. At the rate they'd been dying so far, it wouldn't be long before he was alone again—the sole intelligent living creature on this entire planet.

He existed in a world of phantoms. It was obvious when he looked about himself at the brightly colored stone towers, at the wavy mosaic patterns of the walkways, at the army of gray maintenance robots who moved through the streets like ghosts, keeping Beta-Nu and all the other cities as perfectly preserved cemeteries.

"Death!" he yelled to no one in particular. "That's all anything is around here—death!"

His new Reva was dead. The Makers were dead. This city was dead. The whole damned world was dead. Everything that came here died. He suddenly was aware of a slow suffocation of his soul. He was the only thing here that hadn't died—and perhaps even that statement was arguable. Was he the sole living caretaker of this mausoleum—or was he merely another of the ghosts, slightly more substantial than the rest but equally as dead and useless?

His wanderings had taken him, quite without conscious thought, to the city's major armory. Beta-Nu may have been a small city, priding itself as an artistic center, but its citizens had never stinted in stockpiling weapons for their own defense. As with all the cities on this world, Beta-Nu was always prepared for war. To be otherwise was to invite destruction.

Birk entered the cavernous building and walked up and down the aisles, surrounded by enough potential devastation to destroy this continent several times over. When it came to warfare, the Makers never did anything by halves. There were automated weapons here that flew, ones that crawled, ones that swam; there were "guns" small enough to be held in one's hand, and others so large it took two huge vehicles to tow them into position. The Makers' ingenuity for mass destruction put even the human mind to shame.

Birk went first to the power-storage room and picked up a bulky power pack for a land vehicle. It was heavier than he expected, and several times he was tempted to call for one of the arsenal's robots to assist him; but he finally managed to stagger into the appropriate storeroom, carrying his heavy load and placing the power pack into one of the large armored

37

tanks. He could almost hear the vehicle sigh as it awoke instantly from its centuries-long nap.

The tank was a monster—twenty-five meters long, seven wide, and five high. Instead of having one big turret, its top was bristling with a dozen different guns of varying sizes and ranges. The tank was a dismal gray-green color and moved on one wide tread along the underside. It was a ponderous vehicle, carrying as it did a heavy load of death and destruction.

Climbing inside was awkward. It had been built for the tall, thin bodies of the Makers; the handholds were a little far apart and the entrance hatch was a bit too narrow for easy access. Birk squeezed himself inside the cramped control cabin and spent a few minutes familiarizing himself with the layout of the instrument panel. Satisfied at last that the power was indeed on and that everything worked as it should, he started the tank and rolled it majestically out of the arsenal, into the street.

Birk had to pick his route carefully, for the big machine was too wide to travel along some of the smaller thorough-fares. It moved at a surprisingly good speed, however, and in less than an hour he had reached his destination. This was in the north quadrant, the only portion of the city he'd explored thoroughly so far. This particular neighborhood was devoted largely to industrial activities, with tall apartment buildings along the fringe. There was nothing here that would be of great use to posterity—but it would be a lot of use to him.

He set his jaw tightly and peered through the viewfinder until he had a large, blocky warehouse squarely in his sights. He switched on one of the smaller energy cannons and depressed the firing button, smiling grimly as the charge of blue energy burst forth from one turret. The bolt hit the warehouse perfectly, and the building collapsed in a long, slow moment of rumbling destruction, sending a cloud of gray-white dust into the air.

Not spectacular enough, Birk decided as he swiveled his sights around in search of a new target. Ninety degrees away he spotted an apartment complex, at least fifty stories tall and covering an entire city block. A predatory smile spread slowly across Birk's face as he lined up the range in the viewfinder. He ran down the list of weapons at his disposal, and decided on fireballs. Perhaps they would have a more satisfactory effect.

He launched two fireballs, one after another, at the upper stories of the building. The twin explosions as the energy missiles hit were most gratifying. Loud booms rocked the ground, windows shattered, and bits of rock and brick flew through the air, to land sometimes hundreds of meters away. The top four stories of the apartment complex were gone, leaving but a ragged silhouette against the blue sky.

Eleven years, Birk thought as he gripped the controls tightly. *Eleven stinking years on this asshole of a world. Eleven years with no one to talk to but those goddamn robots. I like Arthur, but God, he can be a pain in the ass. Why does he always have to know what I'm thinking? Why does he keep pushing at me? Why can't he just leave me alone sometimes so I can be miserable in peace?*

Even as he was thinking, spewing out the thoughts that had been festering in his mind, he lowered his sights and took aim at the next few stories of the apartment building. He launched two more fireballs on their way, and watched with frozen glee as they did their damage.

Why did she have to die? It isn't fair! After eleven lousy years I had a chance to correct my mistakes with Reva, and they take her away. Nothing ever works out right. It isn't too much to ask for one fucking break in eleven years, and they won't even let me have that.

A volley of fireballs streamed from the tank's turret, their explosions rocking the still air of Beta-Nu with a succession of magnificent explosions. The apartment building was brought down to twenty stories, and the ground around it was littered with debris. Birk kept firing his hatred at the ruin, a salvo of vehemence and pent-up frustration.

Death and destruction, that's what it all is. That's what this world is all about, isn't it? Everything around me is going to die. I'll never leave here; I'll never talk to another person as long as I live. I'm going to die just like these new people are dying, just like the Makers died, and in the end no one will care. It'll take me a little longer, that's all. But if I die, I'm taking something with me. You're coming down too, you goddamn city! What right have you to outlive me? You can take my Reva away from me, but I'll see that you pay the price!

The tears in his eyes were making it hard to aim through the viewfinder. He was pointing his launcher out of instinct, as round after round of fireballs burst into the empty apartments, demolishing them beyond all recognition. He fired until there was no response, and the indicator told him the tank was all out of fireballs; then he switched to other targets and other weapons, leveling the neighborhood

39

around him with a concentrated barrage of hatred and destruction.

Two hours later, the shooting stopped. The tank's power pack and ammunition had run out, leaving it as lifeless as it had been in the arsenal. Around it for seven hundred meters in any direction were shapeless piles of rubble, some still smoldering from the heat of the blasts they had received.

Birk climbed out of the vehicle and looked around at the devastation he had caused. He felt weak, but strangely cleaner, purged of the poisons that had infested his mind for the past day. The hatred, the insecurity, the frustration were all gone, at least for a while, and he could deal with his problems again in a rational manner. The price paid in archeological terms might have been high—but it was the only coin Birk had, and he felt it well worth the bargain.

Climbing down from the top of the tank, Birk started making his way back to his tower. He was even whistling as he skirted the larger piles of rubble in his path, and wondered what Arthur would have ready for his lunch.

Arthur had to have known about the destruction Birk had caused on the north side of town. He couldn't have missed hearing the loud reports and the crashing of stone, and the maintenance robots would have radioed him a complete report about the bombing. But the chief robot said not a word on the subject as Birk returned home. Perhaps, Birk reasoned, it was because Arthur already knew him too well; he would probably just give the maintenance teams a silent order to clear away the debris and return the tank to its previous place in the arsenal, and the subject would be closed forever.

Arthur was surprisingly silent as he served lunch. Birk, too, felt subdued by his activities of the morning and spoke but little as he ate. His cathartic attack on the city, coupled with the strain of last night and his skipping breakfast this morning, had given him a ravenous appetite. He wolfed down the food set before him and called for second helpings.

Only after he had satisfied his bodily appetites did he dare broach the subject that had been hanging over the room like a shroud. "How are the survivors doing?"

"Two more of the men died while you were out this morning."

"I see." Such news no longer inspired the waves of anxiety he'd felt earlier; his few hours of destructive frenzy had exorcised those particular demons, and he was able to assimi-

40

late facts in a much more rational manner. *Let's see, one died in the van on the way back last night, Reva died while I was sleeping, and now two more this morning. That leaves a man and a woman.* "How are the other two?" he continued aloud.

"Not very good," Arthur said. If he'd had a head, he probably would be shaking it now. "Both are very seriously injured, although the medical robots tell me there's about an even chance that they can save one of them."

"Which one?" Birk asked, trying to pretend it didn't matter to him.

"That's apparently up to you, sir."

"Me? How? I'm not a doctor; there's nothing I can do to help anyone get better. I can barely bandage a cut finger."

"They tell me you have a choice." Arthur moved over to stand directly in front of Birk's seat. "You see, both survivors have suffered damage to their internal organs—damage that will probably prove fatal to each within the next day or so. But the damaged organs in each survivor are different. By replacing the damaged organs in one with the working counterparts in the other, it may be possible to save at least one of the people. The process is equivalent to scavenging parts from one robot to keep another working."

"A transplant," Birk said softly.

Arthur assimilated the new term. "That would seem to be the proper word, yes, sir."

"And you want me to choose which is to be the donor." It was more a statement than a question.

"Yes, sir. With the exception of the two wounded people, who are both unconscious, you are the person most strongly affected by the decision; it's only right that you should make it."

Birk's palms were sweating. His body knew the choice, but his mind was not yet ready to face it. "There are all sorts of problems, I hear, with transplanted organs. There's blood-type factors, and making sure everything if properly connected, and the big problem of rejection. . . ."

"The medical robots are aware of all these problems, and more. Our Makers also used the transplant procedure, and they had ways of dealing with these things."

"Human beings are so different from the Makers. . . ."

"Our doctors are aware of that, too, sir." Arthur's humor—if it was meant to be humor—was drier than sand. "They don't guarantee success. Far from it, in fact. They only say that there are enough similarities to make the risk worth

41

taking. The odds would be no better than fifty-fifty in either case; but if the transplant isn't attempted, the odds of either person surviving past another day are essentially zero."

Birk stood up from the table and walked around the room, his back deliberately toward the robot. "You're asking me to play God, Arthur. You're asking me to decide whether one person has more right to live than another. That's an enormous responsibility."

"I could make the choice for you, if you prefer."

"That's not the point," Birk said quickly, and realized even as he spoke that it was exactly the point—whether he was willing to take responsibility for this act. So far he had been able to drift and let events take care of themselves. The robots had gone out to the crash site automatically, as they'd done when his own ship crashed; he had not had to judge whether their action was right or not. Survivors had been carried back to the city and, despite the best medical efforts available, four out of six had died. That had been fate; Birk could hardly be blamed for that.

But now the responsibility *was* his, and the choice he made would affect the lives of two total strangers. The other deaths weren't his fault, but by making a choice here he would be deliberately killing one person in order to save another.

"The point is," he continued, trying to salvage his statement to Arthur, "that I must make the best, most enlightened decision I can."

"Of course, sir."

"You say both people will die unless this transplant is performed?"

"Undoubtedly."

"Then it isn't really a question of killing one to save another," Birk mused aloud. "They're both equally dead right now. It's merely a question of which one I should try to resurrect."

If Arthur had any opinions about the value of Birk's semantic argument, he kept them to himself.

"Would one of the patients require less transplanting than the other?" Birk asked.

Arthur was silent for several seconds. He was probably in radio conference with the doctors to find the answer to that question; but always, in the back of Birk's mind, there was the suspicion that the robot was trying to analyze Birk and figure out which answer his master *wanted* to hear. Arthur, he had learned, could be subtly devious when the situation warranted.

"The woman would require slightly less work," Arthur said at last.

Birk, his back still turned to the robot, closed his eyes with relief. *Something* had finally worked out right. Now at least he had a rationale for making the choice he'd wanted to make all along.

Turning around again to face Arthur, Birk said with an air of authority, "Have them try to save her, then. Let them take what they need from the man."

"Very good, sir," Arthur answered. And the die was cast.

FOUR

Birk considered going to the hospital and watching the transplant operation personally, but Arthur talked him out of it. Birk could do nothing to help, and his presence might only be a hindrance, the robot pointed out; he also hinted broadly that Birk could become emotionally involved in the process if he came too close, and it might then be a more serious blow to him if the woman should die despite the doctors' best efforts. Birk weighed these arguments and agreed to their validity; he would stay away from the hospital, and Arthur would keep him informed of any developments that might occur.

It was by now too late to visit Alpha-Xi, as Birk had originally intended; that was an all-day task he would have to put off until tomorrow. On the other hand, there was little Birk *could* do to pass the time constructively while the tense transplant operation was being performed, and he quickly grew tired of pacing about his room like an expectant father. Arthur finally suggested a walking tour, and Birk leaped at the idea. The two roamed the streets of Beta-Nu with Arthur pointing out places of interest—but Birk remembered almost nothing of what he saw that afternoon. His mind was far away, hovering near the operating theater where the crucial operation was occurring.

As the sun was setting and the two began making their way back to the tower headquarters, Arthur suddenly cut short the remark he'd been making and said, "The operation is complete, so they tell me."

"How did it go?"

"The medical robots are satisfied at the moment. The donor, of course, expired. The connection of the organs into the woman went without major incident, and she was still alive when they closed her up. Her vital signs, as best we can monitor them for a human, are weak, but steady. She will be kept under continual observation for the next two days; if she can survive past that, the doctors feel she will have a good chance of living through the ordeal."

Birk nodded. "Keep me posted on any change in her condition, no matter how slight."

"Of course, sir."

Dinner that night was a banquet, seven courses of Birk's favorite native foods ranging from a hearty vegetable broth through a sticky-sweet fruit-and-pastry dessert. *Maybe I should arrange for a ship to crash every day,* Birk mused. *It really does wonders for the cook's repertoire.* He knew that the reason was really Arthur's concern for his mental health, and he was amused that the robot thought psychological problems could be assuaged by a pleasing diet. It was, at best, an external remedy—but he saw no point in explaining these finer points to a robot that neither ate nor had psychological dysfunctions.

He left orders to be awakened early in the morning for his inspection tour of Alpha-Xi, and retired early. Sleep came only with difficulty, and he was bothered by a fantasy of a man's ghost accusing him of murder. Before the ghost could harm him, though, a dream-Arthur came and gently touched it. The ghost blew away like a punctured balloon, and the rest of Birk's sleep was dreamless.

As ordered, Arthur woke him at dawn to begin their journey. The woman's condition remained unchanged, which the medical robots considered a positive sign; the longer her new organs remained stable, the more time her body had to adjust to them. There was still no prognosis, but the fact that she had survived this long was promising.

After a simple breakfast, Arthur and Birk took off in the

delta for the distant city of Alpha-Xi. It was on this same continent but at the southeasternmost tip, nearly seven thousand kilometers away. Arthur again took up the piloting duties, giving his master a chance to watch the scenery below them. Birk could feel the edges of frustration creeping in on him again, and he ruthlessly quashed the emotion before it could spread. True, there was nothing he could do to increase the woman's chance of survival, but he was not being idle. This trip had a very important survival function and was not merely a time-filler.

Alpha-Xi was Birk's ace in the hole, his insurance against discovery should any human ship land here and send out a survey expedition. It was a town built entirely underground, hidden away from inquisitive eyes. Located more than a hundred kilometers from the nearest city, Alpha-Xi had only one entrance, hidden and easily defendable. The majority of robots in the major cities didn't even know of its existence; Arthur had known about it only because one of his previous owners had been an architect involved in building the city, and had died in an accident before he could erase the memory from Arthur's brain.

The principle behind Alpha-Xi's origins was simple. Some of the richest and most influential of the Makers from many separate cities did not like the trends they saw in the ever-escalating warfare around the planet. Secretly, they planned a hideaway for themselves if ever the final war should come upon the world—a place where they, their families, friends, and servants could congregate and wait out the battle raging on the surface above. Then, when things had quieted down and the world was at peace again, they would re-emerge and take their place as society's natural leaders.

That, at least, was the theory. In practice, like so many other fine ideas, it had not worked out. Alpha-Xi had been built in total secrecy, but the city had never been used. The planners and builders, those forward-looking individuals, had not even suspected that the final conflict on their world might be bacteriological in nature. They died of that last, hideous disease before even one of them could reach this splendid sanctuary.

Birk hoped to have better luck with it. His constant fear of discovery, particularly during his first few years here, had finally prompted Arthur to suggest establishing a hidden base in the secret city. Birk had explored the place and eventually found it acceptable—but there were many changes that had to be made before it was livable again.

In the many centuries since its construction, Alpha-Xi had deteriorated badly. Unlike the cities on the surface—which either mined and processed their own nuclear fuel or else obtained their energy from the sun—Alpha-Xi had to be self-contained. Solar collectors would have made the city's location too obvious, and mining operations were out of the question. The designers had stored away energy power packets in container forms, similar to the packets that ran the tanks and other vehicles. Enough energy had been set aside to last the inhabitants a hundred years—long enough, they reasoned, to outwait any conceivable holocaust above them.

Alpha-Xi lasted its planned century; its maintenance robots—like their counterparts in the cities above ground—kept the place clean and orderly for the anticipated return of their masters. But when the power ran out, all maintenance ceased. The little gray robots slowed down and came to a stop in midaction. Dust gathered—a year's worth, a decade's, a century's, a millennium's. Insects swarmed through the city, building their hives and nests in its recesses, adapting their lives and their ways to a totally underground existence. Small animals burrowed in and found the food caches; with such a bonanza waiting for them, they multiplied beyond bounds until the streets were running with small bodies and the air stank of musk and manure. Earthquakes and decay caused some buildings to collapse and windows to shatter; spontaneous combustion caused a few fires, though a lack of decent air circulation kept them contained to small areas. Some water mains burst, flooding sections of the city for years before finally evaporating; in other places, water seepage from the earth around the cavern caused major damage.

And over everything reigned the darkness, the complete absence of even a single ray of light. Night held Alpha-Xi securely within its bosom, a night that was two thousand years long.

Those were the conditions Birk and Arthur found when they first came to Alpha-Xi. The vaunted defenses, designed to withstand the onslaughts of whole armies, were literally powerless to resist the simple efforts of the two explorers. At first the noxious odors and the still, dead air overpowered Birk, and Arthur had to carry him outside to revive him. Even with an improvised gas mask and a powerful searchlight, Birk could feel the oppressiveness of the dark closing in

46

around him. It was a powerful hand in a black glove, about to squeeze his soul from his body. Alpah-Xi, as perhaps nowhere else on the planet, personified the death and decay that was this world.

He would have given up on the project right then were it not for Arthur's insistence that the city could be restored. Their first task was to replace the power units and bring Alpha-Xi back to life. Despite the centuries of decay and neglect, the city reacted to the reinstatement of power better than Birk expected. Many circuits had been broken or eaten through by time and the gnawers, but lights sprang to life nonetheless all over the city, dispelling the pall of darkness.

In some ways, Birk discovered, the darkness had actually been a blessing in disguise—it had covered the magnitude of the problems now facing him. With light restored, he could see just how formidable a task the city's rebirth would be. Most of the original maintenance robots were useless, serving only as nests for insects and small animals. Again he was ready to give up—and again, Arthur's insistence prevailed.

New maintenance robots were brought in from cities all over the continent to help with the clean-up and repair chores. Birk had only one stipulation, to which Arthur readily agreed: No new robot brought into Alpha-Xi was ever to leave it again. The secret of the underground city was to remain secure; if other humans ever landed on this world, there would be no one to point to his hiding place.

Slowly, thanks to the tireless work of thousands of robots, Alpha-Xi became livable again. The animals and insects were exterminated or driven from their burrows. The air-circulating ducts were then cleaned out and fresh breezes once more stirred through the cavern. Streets were swept clean of filth and debris. Inoperable circuits were tracked back to their breaks and repaired; even the ones that were working were checked to make sure they would stay in that condition. Rubble was cleared away, leaving only empty lots to show that there had been any damage. Working from one end of the city to the other, an army of maintenance robots renewed their perennial battle against the dust that had heaped high everywhere, inside the buildings and out. Six months after first coming to Alpha-Xi, Birk and Arthur returned to find the city changed almost beyond recognition. The city's stores were restocked with plenty of food and Birk—after thanking Arthur for persevering in this matter—

proclaimed that he was pleased with Alpha-Xi as his personal retreat if the planet should ever be discovered.

He had visited the city every six months, at first, always checking to make sure his sanctuary was still in perfect order and ready to shelter him at an instant's notice. But as the years went by and it became increasingly obvious that no one would ever find him, his anxieties slowly diminished. Now, as the delta settled gently down outside the forest that hid the entrance to Alpha-Xi, Birk realized it had been almost three years since his last inspection tour. He was half afraid he'd discover the city sunk back to the mess in which he'd first found it, even though he knew that was ludicrous; he'd left enough power packs to fill the city's needs for another century—after which he figured he would no longer be interested in it, anyway.

Birk and Arthur left the delta and began walking through the woods. It was a pleasant morning hike through a tree-shaded lane, the air smelling fresh after a recent rain, and small animals scampered about at the corners of his vision. Even knowing about the city beneath this forest, Birk could not spot any telltale signs of its existence. He knew that he and Arthur were being monitored by Alpha-Xi's automatic defenses, but even so there was no giveaway. Birk was pleased that everything looked so natural.

They stopped in front of one particular tree that grew in two parallel trunks from a peculiar crotch near the ground, as though it had once been struck by lightning. Birk faced the tree and said, "Birk Aaland. Open sesame."

The whimsical code phrase, matched to a recording of his own voice, triggered the door to open. In a clearing just beyond the split tree, a large grassy section of ground slid back to reveal a steep broad ramp leading downward into the earth. Birk and Arthur strode down the slope, and the cover slid back into place over their heads as soon as they'd passed. The two continued down the ramp until they were ten meters below ground and their progress was stopped by a heavy metal wall in front of them.

If they'd been unwelcome intruders, the city's defenses could have disposed of them in a number of ways at this point; the methods ranged from poison gas to energy explosions. Birk merely repeated his name aloud, though, and the heavy wall slid aside to allow the man and the robot to pass. In all, they went through three different sets of locks, each designed slightly differently to slow down an invading force,

48

if not stop it altogether. After they'd passed the last wall, they came to an open elevator shaft to take them down to the level of the city itself.

Birk called for the elevator and once again the city responded to his voice. The elevator—large enough to carry both heavy earth-moving equipment for the original construction of the city and hundreds of intended survivors of a worldwide holocaust—rose and transported them rapidly down to Alpha-Xi. An invading army would not be so lucky; it would have to find some way of lowering its men and equipment more than two hundreds meters down a darkened shaft, with boobytraps located every five or so meters.

At the bottom of the shaft there was one more door to be opened, and then Birk and Arthur found themselves entering the city of Alpha-Xi itself. Birk slowly let out the breath he hadn't realized he'd been holding as he looked around and saw that Alpha-Xi was as beautiful as ever.

Far above their heads arched the ceiling's dome, carved from naked rock but showing no traces, now, of its origins. Every square centimeter was covered with lights, changing in color and brilliance, rippling in patterns that were sometimes designs, sometimes surreal light flows. The cavern's "sky" could even be used as a message board, spelling out anything the city's leaders had to say. The constantly changing patterns of the ceiling caused odd shadows to flow and dance across the buildings and the ground so that the city, even though as dead as any of the others on this world, gave the perpetual illusion of life and motion. The sky dimmed at night to a restful dark blue, but never went completely to black. The builders did not want to invoke feelings of claustrophobia.

Beneath the dome, spread out before Birk like an illustration from a child's fairy book, was the city itself. Alpha-Xi still maintained a quality of unlived-in virginity, despite its centuries of despoilation. Tall needled towers, the highest fully fifty-five stories, pointed imperiously toward the blazing sky. Interspersed among the towers were shorter buildings, but none of these were rectilinear. There were domes, ovals, structures with sweeping curves, but no straight lines to lend harshness or artificiality to the setting. All the designs within Alpha-Xi flowed easily along the eyes, and the colors were pastels in pleasing hues; happy and light was the feeling the city conveyed, and the scent of berrybuds wafted tantalizingly through the air.

The designers of this underground sanctuary had been among the richest and most powerful members of the Maker's society. They had not envisioned a Spartan survival as their only existence after the coming holocaust. They were used to lives of wealth and luxury, and they saw to it that their glamorous lifestyle would continue unabated. Alpha-Xi was a fairy city, a Xanadu, a garden of earthly delights to occupy the heavy moments of the world's richest and most famous survivors. Parks abounded, and buildings alternated with the open areas of greenery; these parks had all been replanted and restored since Birk's renewal project had begun. There were also theaters and concert halls, amusement parks and promenades; the people of Alpha-Xi had not intended to lack for any civilized comforts.

And now it had become Birk's private paradise should life outside grow suddenly hostile. The world turned, but functions remained the same.

Birk wandered down the streets—his streets—with Arthur by his side. In all the other cities, Birk felt more like a curious tourist than a conqueror, but Alpha-Xi was *his*. He had rescued it from the darkness; he had ordered it rebuilt and restored to grandeur. Alpha-Xi was his, and the feeling was reflected in his walk. He strutted through the streets with small nods of his head to acknowledge the silent cheers of a grateful populace.

One by one, he and Arthur visited the major points of the city. They checked the control areas to establish that every component was functioning normally; they checked the military complex to ensure that the city's defenses were capable of withstanding enemy assaults; and they checked the food and supply depots to see that there were no shortages or inroads by scavengers. Birk did not intend to leave such details to chance—particularly not with the current threat of more human ships arriving to search for the lost one.

Everything checked out perfectly. His city was ready and waiting for his occupancy. Birk had lunch served to him in one of the "outdoor" plaza restaurants as he leisurely contemplated his domain before deciding to head back to Beta-Nu.

As he sat there, Arthur announced. "The doctors have some slightly encouraging news. The woman's vital signs appear to be gaining slightly."

"Is there more of a chance that she'll recover, then?"

"I can't force the doctors to commit themselves to an opinion. They merely say they are slightly encouraged."

Birk finished the last few bites of his meal hastily and stood up. "Perhaps we'd best be heading back, then," he said. "We've accomplished all I meant to do here, seeing that the city's in working order. I'd feel more comfortable now back in Beta-Nu, right at hand in case anything should happen."

"Certainly, sir."

The city locked itself up behind them as they climbed the ramp to the surface. Birk's pace was faster this time; the man took long, purposeful strides through the forest back to the delta. The robot easily kept pace with his master, but scarcely a word was spoken between the two.

Birk insisted on taking the controls for the return trip himself. He could feel the pace of his life accelerating, as though whatever was going to happen would happen soon. Now that he'd taken his precautions he had to get back. Like Cinderella, he had to be at home when the change hit, or his whole world might vanish around him. He flew the delta at top speed, and still it wasn't fast enough.

As they approached Beta-Nu, Birk asked whether he would be permitted to look in on the patient. Arthur put in a quick radio call to the medical robots and was informed that Birk could pay a short visit to her room, but that he must be careful not to come near her or touch anything; contamination and infection were still great dangers at this stage of the recovery process.

Birk landed his craft on top of the hospital and Arthur escorted him downstairs. As they neared the door to the ready room, Birk could feel his plams growing sweaty. He had only seen this woman once before, for a period of less than a minute, under the most unflattering of circumstances. She had been in a state of shock, her hair braided unattractively and her body covered with blood. The harsh yellow emergency lighting had made her Oriental complexion look sallow—and, he had to admit, his own mind was not thinking too clearly that night. Both his memory and his senses were being bombarded by hasty and conflicting impressions. Now he would see her much more as she really was, and he was frightened. So much depended on this; he sensed instinctively that his entire future would be affected by the woman lying unconscious in that hospital bed.

In the ready room, the medical robots dressed him in an ill-fitting sterile robe that was designed originally for the Makers, and had been awkwardly adapted for Birk's use. The gown was much too long, and was gathered behind Birk like

51

a train, while the gloves were so oversized that his hands flapped around loosely inside. He could not have handled anything if he tried; but he was only here to observe, not to operate, so it really didn't matter.

Then the door to the woman's room was finally opened and Birk was allowed to enter. The light beyond was dim, and the bed was so completely surrounded by monitoring machinery that at first he could barely make out the woman's body lying on it. Birk approached slowly to obtain a better view, but was stopped by one of the medical robots while still a couple of meters from the bedside. This was as close as they dared allow him to come at present. He would have to watch her from here.

The woman's body, covered only by a thin sheet, was as short as he remembered; if she were standing, she wouldn't even reach his shoulders. Only her head was readily visible; her hair was unbraided now, flowing freely down her back and making a black frame around three quarters of her pale, sleeping face.

As Birk peered forward, trying to make out more details, he could see that the woman was not as homely as he'd first feared. She was of Japanese heritage, with a round face, full cheeks, and a small nose and mouth. There were hints of roundness to her entire body as outlined by the sheet, but Birk could see now that it wasn't fat, just stocky construction. The face had a quality of serenity that carried with it some degree of attractiveness—and she was young, too, probably in her twenties. She was not beautiful, not in the same sense that his lost Reva had been, but she was far from the fat old *mama-san* he'd half expected. As he looked at her, he felt an erection growing inside his trousers; even though there was no one else to notice or care, he turned away, embarrassed.

"She looks okay," Birk said to Arthur, his voice cracking slightly despite his best efforts to keep it level.

"The doctors still cannot promise she'll pull through."

"Did she have any kind of identification? Maybe a tattoo or a necklace or a bracelet. . . ."

Arthur took a second to converse silently with the medical robots, then turned back to Birk. "Yes, there was a small tag around her neck. It is being brought here now."

A robot entered moments later carrying the necklace, and handed it to Birk. The man held it gingerly as though it were made of butterfly wings, bringing it close to his eyes to read

52

in the dim light. The letters said, "LT. MICHI NAKAMURA, 97426328."

"Yes, that should be sufficient for now," Birk said. "At least until she comes to and can tell me more about herself personally." Still slightly embarrassed by his body's automatic response, he turned and walked out of the room with Arthur following, as ever, right behind him.

Lieutenant Michi Nakamura, he thought as he stripped off the sterile robes outside the room. *Not bad. It flows well. It's a name I could get used to, I think. We'll drop the "lieutenant," of course; her military career was over the instant her ship crashed.*

He gave no consideration to what the young lady thought of dropping her title. She would have to agree with him eventually—because he knew that she, like himself, would never leave this planet again.

FIVE

Birk endured four more days without significant change taking place in the woman's condition. The medical robots looked on that stability as a positive sign, but it only served to make Birk edgy. He went on wide-ranging food expeditions, even though the larder was currently stocked. He excused it by saying that they would need more food on hand when the woman recovered, and Arthur did not challenge that statement.

At least twice a day, Birk would go over to the hospital and stand in the woman's room, looking at her as though she were on display in a museum. Her facial features became more and more familiar, and he began to realize how harshly he had judged her the first few times he'd seen her. There *was* beauty in her face; not the Nordic type he was use to, not Reva's beauty perhaps, but there was a full, sensual quality not to be denied. He'd seen so many pictures of the Makers in the past decade—while the only human image was his own in a mirror—that the tall, slender form had become much more a standard than he would have believed possible. Short and solid jarred with everything around him. The maintenance robots were built that way, and they were made to be ignored; Arthur was a tall, slender cylinder, and he commanded respect and friendship. But once Birk forced himself to look past his prejudices, he had to admit that Michi Nakamura could be considered attractive—perhaps even beautiful.

In any event, he had little choice. If she lived, he was stuck with her exactly the way she was. He might as well learn to like it.

He found himself masturbating even more frequently, with Michi Nakamura becoming the focal point of his fantasies. He remembered all the myths about the secret sexual knowledge of the Orient, and convinced himself that Michi—as he was already calling her—was a living repository of that lore. She would come into his desert and make it bloom again, fulfilling him beyond his wildest expectations.

On the second day after his return from Alpha-Xi, he went into her room and asked the medical robots to remove the sheet covering her body so that he could examine her better. The robots knew nothing of propriety and, since the sheet was not absolutely necessary, they whisked it off. Birk found himself staring at the woman in her full naked glory.

Surprisingly, the first thing he noticed was her hair. He hadn't realized until this moment just how long it really was. It flowed down the bed almost to her thighs, a black silken curtain against the white sheets and her delicate golden skin. Strands of it in casual disarray modestly covered one breast, and as Birk's eyes tracked down the stocky body he followed one long strand which curved, in all innocence, right at the top of her pubic triangle.

His head was swimming, and he had to remind himself to breathe. She lay before him soft and helpless, and there was nothing he could do. To touch her now might be to kill her—yet a dozen years of deprivation made his body scream out its need. His flesh was pulsing with desire, and he finally had to run from the room in a cold sweat. Never again did he ask the robots to uncover her for him—but the image stayed with him, burned into his memory and haunting his deepest dreams.

And there were other ghosts demanding attention as well. An image returned from the recent past, an image of the "window" in the art museum. The two figures came into his sleeping mind while he was defenseless against them—the one on the ground, pleading for aid or mercy, and the one standing with its back turned, scorning its fellow's pleas. At first, he would find himself viewing the scene dispassionately from the outside; but abruptly he would be a part of it, lying on the ground, his body twisting upward with arm outstretched and begging for the help he knew the other could give. In front of him, the other figure stood with cold indifference. It was impossible to tell from the back who it was, though he suspected from the stance and the shape that it was Reva, betraying him yet another time. But then, even as he watched, the figure changed, shifted, became shorter, rounder, stockier. . . .

He always woke himself up at that point, driving the feelings from his mind. He did not want to face what that image might become, did not want to admit there could be more rejection ahead of him. In some ways, that was harder to face than the prospect of being alone the rest of his life.

On the fourth day after his return from Alpha-Xi, Arthur gave him the news: Michi Nakamura would apparently live. For four days, ever since her transplant operation, she had been lying comatose, barely breathing without artificial assistance. Now her vital signs were definitely on the increase, gaining strength; she no longer needed machines to keep her blood pumping and her lungs expanding. No longer did she lie still in her bed; though drugs still kept her unconscious, some of the pain was seeping into her mind. She writhed gently under the sheet, moaning occasionally. Slowly, her mind was becoming aware of itself once more, and cognizant of the fact it had survived.

If the waiting before had been unpleasant for Birk, it now became unbearable. He watched from his tower on a vision monitor as Arthur relayed the scene to him. He saw Michi twisting on her bed, and he squirmed in his own chair as the sympathy pains built to intolerable levels. Her low moans were the wails of a banshee to his ears; even after he turned off the set, the sounds and the images persisted in his imagination, leaving him without peace.

That night he dreamed of the window again and of the two figures within it. Once more he was on the ground, begging for help. Once more the other figure scorned his pleas. The other then began to move, turning as if to face him, and Birk quickly averted his gaze. He did not want to see who was

55

treating him this way, who was rejecting him so terribly. In this case, fear of the unknown was definitely preferable to knowing the face of his Judas.

He awoke with a startled cry and sat bolt upright. Arthur, standing faithfully in one darkened corner, moved quickly to the bed to comfort him; but this had not been one of *those* nightmares, and Birk did not need the robot's assurances. He waved Arthur away, feeling very much in control of himself. In a cold, level tone he said, "Have the delta fueled and ready for me tomorrow morning. I'm taking it out alone."

"As you wish, sir. May I ask where you'll be going?"

Birk barely hesitated. "The Black City," he said.

Of all the towns Birk had so far explored, there was only one to which he'd given a name rather than merely a Greek-letter designation. This was the Black City, half a world away from Beta-Nu on another continent, across a vast ocean. The flight would take him over four hours, even at the delta's top speed. It was not a journey he undertook lightly, and certainly not without trepidation. He had vowed once before that he would never return there; but now there were some particularly savage spirits that must be exorcised; and the Black City drew him like a magnet.

Arthur, once he heard Birk's intended destination, begged to come along. The delta would require refueling in the city for the return trip, and even if Arthur remained with the vehicle he would be there to pilot the craft home if Birk's emotional state was adversely affected by his experiences there. But Birk refused. This was something he had to face alone; Arthur's presence would only serve as a distraction. He did, however, agree to let Arthur radio ahead and tell the robots of that city to accept Birk's orders and refuel the delta while he was out on his crucial errand.

Birk ate a hearty breakfast before taking off. The weather had been clouding up as he departed, and his course took him into the teeth of the storm. The delta could not fly high enough to rise above the clouds, so Birk had to grit his teeth and plow ahead through the driving rain. The delta shook as he bucked the headwinds, and lightning bolts flew all around him. There were moments he wished he *had* let Arthur come with him; the robot was a surer, steadier pilot. But he knew he'd done the right thing, and flew as best he could alone.

He passed through the back edge of the storm when he was midway over the ocean, and from that point on had only clear weather ahead of him. The endless expanse of water gave him a boring vista as he flew, but he was not making this trip as a sightseeing tour. He placed the craft on autopilot and settled back in his seat until his instruments informed him that the new continent had been reached.

Inland he flew, over land every bit as wild and overgrown as that around Beta-Nu. Without the incursions of the Makers, wildlife flourished everywhere; the open plains were filled with grazing herds of beasts. *Maybe intelligence is a parasite on the face of planets,* Birk mused. *Things certainly look much more peaceful without sentient beings spoiling the landscape.*

But then, he countered, *without intelligent beings around, there's no one to notice how peaceful things are.*

Three hundred kilometers in from the shoreline rose a mountain chain. Birk checked his coordinates and banked toward the north to parallel the range. After another few minutes of flight he spotted his destination. The Black City was situated on a plateau within these mountains, one and a half kilometers above sea level. Birk brought his craft down atop the building he'd used as his headquarters when he originally explored this place, and the delta was immediately surrounded by robots eager to obey the radioed commands they'd received from Arthur. Birk left the vehicle and set out alone on foot.

The Black City was exactly that—dark, morbid, mysterious, and perhaps even a little menacing. Unlike most of the cities on this world, this one was built low; no structure was over thirty-seven stories tall, and the shapes were broad and flat rather than needlelike as elsewhere. There was a massive, brooding quality to the architecture here, the squat style like heavy, slow spirits of the earth.

But even more than the architecture, it was the color of the place that set it apart from all the others. The rest of the Makers' cities were decorated in bright pastel colors—colors that made the viewer feel alive, or stirred him to a calculated emotional pitch. The effect here was carefully calculated, too, but in other directions. All the colors were dark, somber tones, with black the dominant influence. It weighed on the soul and depressed the spirit, dragging a person's thoughts down to the ground and below. This was a city in mourning, a city in love with death and morbidity, a city fashioned in despair and dedicated to decay. The Black City, more than any other single locale, represented the tragedy of what this world had become.

According to Arthur, the Black City had been constructed as a town of remembrance and memorial. War, destruction, and death had become so ingrained in the Makers' character that it was only natural for a place to be set aside exclusively for grieving. The Black City was where people from all over the world who'd lost loved ones could come to experience a healing catharsis. Here they were cared for and received sympathy, both from fellow mourners and from the local inhabitants who survived off others' grief. It was the most bizarre form of tourism Birk had ever heard of—but it had fulfilled a need in the Makers' collective psyche, and the Black City had thrived, in its day.

The narrow streets and the somber atmosphere did little to improve Birk's spirits as he walked alone toward the amphitheater that was the object of his pilgrimage. There was a brisk wind at his back, ruffling his long hair. There always seemed to be a wind in the Black City, vibrating the buildings and singing a dirge for the entire world. The song had never sounded sadder than it did right now—a quiet, tuneless sigh at the injustice of the Universe and the nobility of death.

After half an hour's walking, Birk reached his destination. Near the center of the Black City was an open, diamond-shaped plaza that stretched ten city blocks on a side. Part of the plaza was landscaped with trees and flowering bushes pruned to absolute symmetry by the tireless robots. Shaded lanes wandered through the lovely garden, some paved, others pebbled or "natural." Closer to the center of the plaza, the landscaping ended and the ground was completely paved over, becoming a garden of art and sculpture instead of greenery. Elaborate fountains sprayed water in geometric patterns while figures of black marble brooded in their niches.

But it was the structure at the very center of the plaza that attracted Birk's attention, as it was designed to do. It rose out of the ground like a volcano, dominating the entire scene—a cone of white stone, the only white Birk had found in this whole city. It had a base diameter of more than a hundred meters, tapering off to twenty at the top, thirty stories above the ground. Rows of windows were set around the perimeter every three stories up the side—large, prismatic windows, reflecting rainbows of light through the gardens around the plaza.

This, then, was the Hall of Remembrance, prime attraction the Black City offered its visitors. To Birk, it was a place of pain and fear—and the alternative to masturbation he had forbidden Arthur to mention. It was the magnet that had pulled him today halfway around the world from Beta-Nu.

Despite his intention to walk slowly and calmly into the hall, Birk found his pace increasing the closer he came to the artificial mountain. The pristine structure towered over him as he approached, and once again he could not help but be awed by what the Makers had wrought here. There were taller edifices on this world, and even within this very city, but none that evoked so much awe as this one.

There were series of doors all around the base of the cone. Birk entered and walked through wide, high corridors that echoed the hollow sounds of his footsteps on stone flooring. There was a time when this building was crowded at all hours of the day and night, with hundreds—or even thousands—of people jamming its hallways. Now there was but a single pilgrim, coming to mourn not for someone else's lost life, but for his own.

He reached a concourse where ramps led to the upper levels, spiraling along the inner walls of the cone. These went to seating sections in the main amphitheater, where mass memorial services had been conducted around the clock and mourners could indulge in group catharsis to relieve their grief. Birk ignored the ramps and walked straight ahead. He was interested today in the more private methods of therapy available here.

Ahead of him was a ramp leading down into the building's subterranean levels. At the bottom were signs in one of the Makers' languages, offering directions and various services. Because he always had Arthur to translate, Birk had never bothered to learn the native tongues, but it didn't matter—he remembered quite distinctly where he had to go.

He walked resolutely over to a series of cubicles, opened one door and entered. The room was dark and cool, with just enough light for Birk to make out the sole furnishing—a reclining lounge chair in the center. He hesitated just for a moment, then walked to the middle of the room and lay down where he was supposed to. The chair had been designed to fit the contours of the Makers rather than those of a human, and it was slightly uncomfortable, but Birk forced himself to relax and let the peace and stillness of the room wash over him.

Arthur had admitted he didn't know the principle behind the Remembrance Booths, and Birk had been averse to tearing one apart to find out; all he knew was that they did work. Two different explanations came to mind, but he could prove neither. One was that a drug was somehow introduced into the subject's body, inducing the desired hallucinations and making the experience so completely believable that the subject came away convinced it had all been real. The other was that the subject's mind was telepathically scanned for sufficient information, then some sort of robot was fashioned based on the subject's memory.

Both theories had their flaws. Birk couldn't believe in a drug that would work identically on both the Makers' minds and that of a human; the two races were sufficiently different to make such a hallucinogen unlikely. On the other hand, the Makers' technology showed no other indications of a telepathic process; if the Makers could indeed look into someone else's mind, the entire structure of their society would have been markedly different from what he found here.

The question of *how* was irrelevant. All that mattered was that it *did* work. Birk had found that out already, much to his chagrin.

Birk lay still for half an hour, breathing lightly and barely moving. He tried to make his mind as blank as possible, even though Arthur had assured him the first time that no special mental discipline was required. Then, just as he was getting used to the strange curvature of the couch, a door opened at one end of the room and the faraway sound of a chime was heard. Birk got awkwardly up from the couch and walked through the open door.

He was in a small antechamber, with cool fluorescent light coming from tubes near the ceiling. There was a single garment hanging from a rod—his old white satin dressing robe. Ingrained habits gripped him as though the intervening years had never occurred, and he slipped the robe on in place of his current clothes. He knew he shouldn't enter the next room without the proper attire.

Set at last, he walked out the door at the far end of the dressing room and found himself in Reva's bedroom in their old house back on Earth. The plush white carpet under his feet was dotted with flecks of pink; the double bed, overhung by a canopy of white lace, was draped with a bedspread done in shades of pink and covered with half a dozen small pillows trimmed with more white lace. Rows of expensive bottles and jars were lined neatly along the top of the pink-and-white dressing table just in front of the mirror.

Birk shifted his weight nervously from foot to foot. He had never been truly comfortable here. The room was uncompromisingly Reva's, from the choice of the color scheme to the perfume that constantly wafted through it. Birk could never be more than an interloper.

The far door that he knew must lead to the bathroom was open, light from beyond spilling into the darkened bedroom. As Birk stood waiting, there was a faint sighing sound—and then she entered from the bathroom.

"Reva." He was hardly aware he had whispered the name aloud as he stared across the room at his wife. She stood there in the pink glowcloth negligee he had always loved, which covered her with shimmery translucence from armpits to midcalf. The glistening fabric clung with just the proper amount of erotic suggestion to her breasts, waist, and hips, emphasizing her rich sensuality. Reva's blond hair was fashionably set, curling down to her shoulders with a naturalness that only a top hair stylist could achieve. His eyes traveled down her body, down below the negligee to her long, shapely legs and her pink-slippered feet. Then his gaze was back up at her face—that beautiful face with wide-set eyes that were a deeper blue than any he'd ever seen in a human being. There was a glistening in her eyes as she looked back at him; could they be tears, perhaps? Her face was aglow with love and alive with passion, the stuff of a million fantasies and a host of lost, lonely dreams.

Birk wanted to rush across the room and take her in his arms, but his feet felt nailed to the floor. Reva looked back at him, and reached out a hand with her own little peculiar turn of the wrist. "Birk?" she said. "Oh, Birk, I'm so glad you've come back. It's been so long, too long. . . . I'm glad you're here now. I need you."

With great effort, Birk pulled one leg free of its paralysis and slid it slowly forward across the floor. An equally great effort was required for the second step. After that they became a little easier; he concentrated on making them into a series, first one then another until he found himself actually walking across the room, around the perimeter of the bed and to his wife's side. Reva stood where she was, watching him invitingly until he was only a few steps away. Then she too stepped forward, closing the gap until finally nothing was between them.

Their arms were around one another, and Birk was squeezing her so tightly he was afraid of breaking her ribs. Reva didn't notice, though; her passion was fully a match for his. He could feel the warmth of her skin as she pressed herself tightly against him, the soft and vibrant quality that had always been Reva. One part of his mind marveled that she was not a day older than he remembered, while he had aged a dozen years; then he chided himself with the knowledge that she couldn't age—she was only a memory.

He ruthlessly killed all traces of the thought. This was more than some idle fantasy; Reva was warm, she was real, she was alive and willing and loving. Her hair smelled faintly of honeysuckle and her breath was of wintergreen as she opened her mouth to return his kiss. Her hands were clutching tightly at his shoulder blades, and her body was grinding sensually against his in a suggestive motion that had his manhood rising in response. This was as real as he could ever hope for, and any thoughts to the contrary were merely semantic quibblings.

His hands caressed her body, his fingers exploring once more the sleekness of her skin as they slipped easily inside the material of her negligee. Her own fingertips stroked his body lightly while her mouth pressed to him in a long kiss of passion. Birk fidgeted for a moment with the fastening at her back, and then her negligee slid silently to the floor.

"Oh, Reva," he moaned softly, pulling his lips away from hers. He tilted his head to kiss the side of her neck, then began working his way slowly down her body to her naked breasts. The nipples were firm with desire, yet even as his tongue played across them he could feel something change within the moment.

He pulled back slightly and looked directly into her eyes. "Darling? Is something wrong?"

"Why should anything be wrong? We're together again, aren't we?"

But her face belied her words. Her eyes were not glistening with unspoken passion and her body, too, was tenser, more distant. Birk tried to think, tried to analyze what had gone wrong. In a split second, and for no apparent reason, everything between them had changed. The difference was subtle, but unmistakable.

"I . . . well, it all feels different, somehow. You seem to have lost interest."

"No, I haven't," she answered stubbornly, her lower lip

62

going into its all-too-familiar pout. She spread her arms apart and stepped back a pace so he could see her full length. "Here I am, all naked and willing. Come on, it's your turn." She jumped onto the bed and looked up at him. "What are you waiting for?"

Birk could feel his desire fading fast. "Why, Reva? Why are you doing this to me?"

"I'm not doing anything," she said, wiggling her hips on the bed. "You're the one who's backing out."

He recognized that tone all too well. It was an impatience that hid an anger boiling up just below the surface. He glanced around the room as though looking for the way out once more, then closed his eyes tightly. *It's not supposed to be this way. Why isn't it working right?* "Now you're sounding spiteful."

"Spiteful? Me? What have I got to be spiteful for?"

Birk turned away and opened his eyes again. He did not want to look at her painfully beautiful body. "There's a coldness to you that never used to be there."

He could hear Reva get off the bed and walk around to face him. "If there's a coldness in me, you put it there."

"You always used that tactic, blaming everything on me. Some things are your fault, too, you know."

"Not this time, Birk, not this time. I'm just a creature of your mind, a compilation of your memories, dreams, and desires. I function the way I'm programmed to. If there's any coldness in me at all, it's because you put it there."

Birk was shaking his head in astonishment. "That's not it. You've got it wrong. That's not it at all."

"That's exactly it, and you know it." Reva stepped closer to him, forcing herself into his personal space. "You're the one who detected the coldness; you're the one who makes me act the way I do."

"This is ridiculous," Birk said, starting to turn away. "I'm arguing with an illusion, some living memory without heart or mind or . . ."

"Why, Birk?" Reva insisted, grabbing him by the shoulders. "Why did you want me first hot, then cold?"

Birk's temper suddenly exploded. "You've always been cold, you goddamn bitch! I didn't want it that way. It's my memory of you, that's all. It all started out warm, our first few years together, but then I saw the coldness, the selfishness behind you. You weren't any creation of my mind then.

63

You deserted me, Reva, just when I needed you the most. After all the love we shared, for you to treat me that way . . ."

"Is that the way you think it is? Has it ever occurred to you that you actually deserted me long before any of that ever happened?"

"Did I let you rot in prison without visiting you? Did I denounce you in public? Did I testify against you in court, spouting any lies they wanted to hear? Did I file for the divorce, charging you with all sorts of things that never happened?"

"There are all kinds of ways to desert a person," Reva said. Her voice was maddeningly level. *Why doesn't she shout back at me?* Birk wondered. *Why doesn't she fight fair? Why does she have to be so goddamn cool about it?*

"I loved you, Reva," he said, a sob catching at the back of his throat. "Even after you did all those things, I still loved you. I never . . ."

"You loved yourself and your own pristine principles," his wife accused. "If you'd loved me, you would have cared what happened to me. You'd have had a sense of responsibility about *us*. You'd have given some thought to my feelings before barging ahead with your crusade. I didn't enjoy doing those things against you, Birk, but they made me. You forced me into a position where I had no other choice."

"You could have resisted, the same way I did."

"Could I? I wasn't a world-famous inventor. They didn't have to keep me looking pretty for a show trial. They'd taken you away from me, they'd taken all our money, they'd smeared your name—what did I have left? Just myself. Not all of us are cut out to be heroes. The thought of torture and prison scares me. Is it some heinous sin to want to survive?"

"And it didn't matter to you how badly I was hurt?"

Reva gave a little shrug. "Why not? You were just saying I should have let myself be hurt for your sake. You wanted me to be the one to make all the sacrifices."

"I made plenty of sacrifices. That's how I ended up here."

"Sure you sacrificed. You sacrificed *me* for the sake of your honor and your principles. Not once, Birk, not once did you think of sacrificing any of those principles for *my* sake. If you'd loved me half as much as you claim, you'd have given some thought to how your actions would affect me."

Birk was shaking his head in astonishment. He could hardly believe this was his Reva saying these things. "But those principles were more important than either of us.

We talked about them at great length, remember? You agreed. . . ."

"Correction: you talked, I listened. That was what you really wanted, an audience to hear you out so you could clarify your thoughts in your own mind. That's fine, you got what you wanted. You never really cared what I thought."

"But . . ."

"I stuck by you long after all those other so-called friends had crawled away under their rocks and left you alone in the rain. But you were the one who made the decision to desert. You just said it yourself: The principles were more important to you than I was. It was your choice, Birk, and I hope you're happy with it."

She gave a bitter laugh. "In some ways, I would almost have preferred your leaving me for another woman. At least I'd know how to compete in that arena. How could I stand up against one of your mighty principles?"

There were tears in Birk's eyes, and he shut them tightly to ease the stinging. He knew that was not the way he had felt back then. Réva was the most important thing in the world to him. He had been thinking about her; he had tried to protect her. Maybe he'd done it badly; he could see now that he'd never had the proper training to be a political activist. He was much too naïve; he should have stayed with his engineering and left the running of the world to others. But he *had* tried to protect her; why couldn't she see that most of what he did was for *her* sake?

"You don't understand," he said, and he was sobbing heavily now. "You're twisting it all around. I really did try. . . . You don't understand."

"I understand perfectly," Reva said with cold clarity. "Your principles were more important than my welfare or our marriage. You sacrificed everything you had in the name of Justice. You left me to fend for myself. All right, I fended for myself—and because of that, because I only tried to survive under conditions I didn't make and didn't want, you call me cold, you say I betrayed you and deserted you. I only hope your principles gave you more comfort than I could."

Birk had sunk to the floor, weeping openly. He was trying to think but the tears that clouded his eyes had befogged his brain as well. He searched desperately through his mind, looking for the one golden sentence that would explain all his feelings, all his meaning so that Reva would at last understand and stop hating him. He had to get her to stop hating

65

him! He had to prove that she was wrong, that he had done the proper thing, that her betrayal of him was unjustified and that she should ask his forgiveness. He would grant it in a second if only she would ask. But she had no intention of asking.

He loved her as much as life itself, and she hated him. That alone wracked him to the bottom of his soul. But for her to say he *made* her hate him—how could he possibly accept that idea and remain sane? He loved her; he would never do anything to hurt her. He had to tell her that, somehow. He had to make her believe. But how could he? What words would work? He was just a sobbing mass on the floor. What could he possibly do to convince her of his love?

He reached up a hand, stretching out to her in helpless frustration. "Reva. . . ."

She deliberately turned her back to him. "Why did you come here again, Birk? Why did you call me up?"

His mind could no longer think in straight lines. Her question barely made sense, and it took him more than a minute to answer. "I . . . I . . . needed to know why you did what you did. I needed your love."

"You didn't think much of my love when you had it before. And you now know why. Does it make you happier?"

Birk propped himself on one elbow and tried to crawl toward her, arm still outstretched. "Reva. . . ."

"That's not really why you came, Birk. You don't want to face it, but I'm the one part of you that won't allow you to lie to yourself. You came because you wanted my forgiveness, not the other way around. You want to shirk the responsibility for the entire fiasco. If I forgive you, that automatically makes it partly my fault—and it wasn't. You want absolution for what you did to me, and I can't give it. The best thing you can do is accept the facts, admit you made a tragic mistake and try to live on in spite of it. But you're not ready to do that yet, are you, Birk?"

"That's . . . not it, Reva. Not it." He could barely speak, he was choking so hard on his sobs. But Reva's back was to him, unheeding, while he reached out for her help. Eventually he gave up trying and collapsed into a heap on the floor.

When next he looked up, Reva was gone and the room around him was empty. Staggering outside, eyes red and swollen, he saw that it was well past sunset; there'd be barely enough light for him to make his way back to the delta.

It was a mistake, coming back, he thought. *I should have*

66

known after the first time. The Hall of Remembrance is no place for a person who can't afford *to remember.*

He left the building shakily, without looking back. He knew he would never return to it again.

ACT 2

SIX

For Lieutenant Michi Nakamura, the process of coming to full consciousness was a long and painful one. Breathing was a series of sharp pants, each one a stab into her chest. There never seemed to be quite enough air, and she had strange nightmares of being crushed in a cave-in at the bottom of some mine. Her skin felt on fire, a tingling she could not quell no matter how much she writhed. Her surroundings were quiet, with just occasional sounds of a machine doing its job. The only thing good was the darkness—not a total black, but dim enough to be restful. The light did not intrude on her mind until she was ready to let it.

She grew aware of motions around her, of people or things constantly going to and from her bedside. Occasionally something touched her, and it felt cold against her burning skin. She felt she should open her eyes and say something, but that was too much effort; it seemed hard enough just to keep breathing. Lower down was an icy numbness, as though her abdomen had been completely removed. Better to rest now. Easier, too. At one point she tried to sit up, but the muscles refused to obey her and she slumped back onto the bed, exhausted from the effort.

Consciousness faded in and out with annoying irregularity. She could scarcely tell from one moment to the next whether she'd been dozing between two consecutive thoughts. Since the room light was kept at a constant dim level, she could not even measure passage of days. She could only lie in bed and moan, half-wishing to die but knowing that even so simple an act was not worth the effort.

She'd been staring at the ceiling for a long time before she even realized her eyes were open. The light, as always, was dim, and the ceiling was devoid of any markings. The corners were blurry and indistinct. She blinked—a major effort—and

70

the edges began to focus. She was pleased with herself, but also a bit frightened. Should she try turning her head now, or would even that motion prove too much for her? When mere blinking culd be accomplished only with difficulty, might not the neck motions be painful?

You'll have to move sometime, she told herself sternly. *You've got your duties, and they won't get done while you're lying here goldbricking. . . .*

A sudden flash of memory shot through her mind. The invasion, the escape from New Edo, the running battle in space against the enemy cruisers, the flight into the nebula to avoid detection, the attempted landing, the crash. . . .

The crash! That very thought brought Michi alert, muscles tense. Instinctively she sat upright, but her muscles protested that action so harshly that she cried out and fell back weakly onto the bed. She lay there for several minutes, gasping deeply and trying to push the red fog of pain from her mind once more.

Around her was a sudden flurry of activity. Her cry had brought plenty of concerned help, which would have been a relief if she were in any condition to appreciate it. As it was, she could only lie panting on her bed while things went on around her.

After a while the pain eased. Her muscles, even those not directly injured in the crash or cut through during surgery, were stiff from long disuse. She found, though, that by moving slowly and carefully she could look around herself and get a good picture of her surroundings.

She was in a hospital. There was no disguising the institutional nature of the place. The pale, sterile walls and the sharp smell of disinfectant were the same everywhere. *Well, it only makes sense that I'm in a hospital after that crash,* she thought. *I should count myself lucky it's not a mortuary.*

There were machines, robots, scampering around her bed. She had seen robots before, of course, but never in these particular shapes and certainly never so many in one place. Robots were still too expensive to use so prodigiously. These were also smaller than most of the robots she'd seen before, just chest high on her—and she was barely minimum height for army duty.

She had little time for these observations, as two of the robots—one on either side of her bed—grabbed her shoulders and forced her back down in a supine position. "Hey," she started to protest, but found she could barely utter a croak.

Her throat was dry and raw, sore from the instinctive cry she'd yelled when she sat up. Fighting the robots would be too much of a strain on her still-weakened body, so she reluctantly relaxed and let them fuss over her. It was obvious after a few moments that they meant her no harm, straightening her covers, taking her pulse, and checking the different instruments like a corps of nurses. Whatever hospital she'd been taken to, the people here had a genuine concern for her welfare.

Except that, so far, she'd *seen* no people here, and even in these dizzy few first moments of wakefulness she thought that was peculiar. There had to be a real live person around somewhere to supervise all those machines; no robot she'd ever heard of was smart enough to monitor and care for a patient as badly injured as she was without some human guidance.

She tried to work up some saliva in her mouth. If she could swallow that, her throat would not be so dry, and maybe then she would be able to speak. She wanted to question these robots to find out how badly she was hurt and where exactly she was. As she thought about questioning them, a thousand more questions swirled into her mind in a dizzying array.

But her exertions had so exhausted her that she fell asleep again before she could say another word.

"The woman recovered consciousness for a brief while last night, sir," Arthur said as Birk got up from his bed.

The man froze and stared at his robot companion. "Why didn't you wake me at once?" he demanded.

"I debated that, but decided against it. There would hardly have been any point. She was conscious only for a short while, sat up abruptly and seemed startled at her strange surroundings. She lapsed back into unconsciousness, though, before anything could happen."

"She's still all right, isn't she?" Birk asked anxiously. "She didn't hurt herself or . . .?"

"Perfectly fine," Arthur assured him. "The medical robots are now predicting a complete recovery, barring any unforeseen complications. She's merely in a weakened condition after so serious an operation. She'll need some time to regain her strength, that's all."

Birk closed his eyes, and his shoulders sagged with relief. "Thank God," he sighed. "After all this time . . ."

"I imagine it's quite exciting."

72

"Exciting? Yes, I suppose it is." But it was also frightening, as frightening as anything he'd ever had to face. After more than a decade of loneliness, to be suddenly confronted by another human being, another person with feelings and moods, an unpredictable variable in the staid equation of his life—this was a challenge that made him sweat when he thought too hard about it. He could cope with Arthur; Arthur had no emotions, no surprises. The robot could be badgered, yelled at, or insulted without being personally affronted. Arthur took everything in stride, and did his job as efficiently as ever. Arthur would still be working long after Birk had died and turned to dust. Arthur was one of the world's greatest constants.

But this was another human being—and not just any human being. This was a woman, a young, attractive woman. What would he say to her? Here he was, eleven years out of touch with human civilization. He hadn't thought about his age in years, but it hit him just now that he was forty-seven years old, while she was in her twenties. The difference in their generations was a larger gap than he'd realized at first. What could he possibly offer her? What would she see in him?

"I've taken the liberty," Arthur went on, oblivious to Birk's anxiety, "of having her moved into the tower here so that she'll be nearer at hand and easier to take care of."

"Is . . . is that wise? There might be complications. Perhaps she should stay in the hospital, where there are all the machines to take care of her in case of a relapse."

"I am assured that such a thing is most unlikely. The medical robots are bringing over all the monitoring equipment they will need to measure her progress, as well as any emergency gear, but those things are purely precautionary. What the woman needs primarily is rest so that her body has time to repair itself. She can do that here as well as anywhere."

"But they will keep her under strict observation."

"Of course, sir."

Birk walked over to one side of the room and looked at himself in the mirror. As he looked, the horror of his situation seemed to compound itself. *I'm an old man*, he thought in panic. *I've kept myself in good shape, but I haven't had any of the rejuve treatments she's used to seeing. There are lines on my face, across my forehead, and around my eyes. My skin is all tough and leathery. I still have my hair, thank God, but how did all the gray get in there? Funny I never noticed it before.*

73

He ran a hand self-consciously through the dark tangle of his hair in a vain attempt to make it look civilized. His beard, too, was long and matted, though he made an effort every few weeks to trim the edges away, at least. He would have to ask Arthur for a fuller cutting this afternoon.

What if she doesn't like me? he thought in sudden horror. It was strange, but in all his previous wondering whether he would like her, he had scarcely wondered whether she would like him. And yet, it meant so terribly much. He was old, or at least would look so to her young eyes; he'd once had a certain boyish charm about him, but that had evaporated over the years until now he might even be called ugly. And he was certainly ignorant of what was happening in human society. His only companions for eleven years had been robots and ghosts; what kind of company did that make him?

Even if the sight of him didn't instantly repel her, what were the chances he wouldn't make some mistake and drive her away? Ever since the argument with Reva in the Black City, that fear hung over him like a cloud. *What if I yell at her?* he thought. He knew that his temper, after so many years of frustration and loneliness, was not what it should be. He was capable of blowing up at the slightest remark. Arthur was used to it, Arthur didn't react. Michi would. It was entirely possible that Michi would end up hating him, just as Reva did.

Being rejected by the only woman in the world, Birk thought with tears in his eyes. *I couldn't live with that. Not after all I've been through.*

"All right," he told Arthur. "Have her brought to the tower. Give her a room a few floors down from me. But I don't want to have any contact with her."

If a robot could be surprised, Arthur was just then. "I beg your pardon, sir?"

"I don't want anything to do with her. At least not . . . not right away. She'll be frightened, confused at first. I don't want to do anything to jeopardize our long-term relationship. We'll have to get used to each other gradually. Don't tell her anything about me just yet."

"If she is a normal intelligent being, she is bound to be curious about her new surroundings—where she is, how she got here, how badly she's been hurt. To tell her nothing would lead to suspicions and anxieties that would not promote her rapid recovery. We'll have to tell her something."

"Fine. Tell her something. Tell her anything you want.

74

Only don't talk about me. That will have to come . . . slowly, after she's gotten used to the idea of being here."

"Very good, sir."

Sure, that ought to work, Birk reasoned. He could break her in gradually to himself and his world. Once she understood completely that she was stuck here for the rest of her life, and that he was the only other person around, she would know better how much she needed him—how much they needed each other. Once she realized that, she would not reject him. Until then, he would have to take great pains not to do anything that would offend her.

If she's the only woman in the world, it's equally true that I'm the only man, Birk thought, a little self-confidence restored. Glancing at his reflection full length in the mirror once more, he added, *Looked at from that standpoint, I'm not half bad.*

The next time Michi awoke, she felt much better. There was still the numbness in her abdomen, still the shortness of breath, but her mind was clearer than it had been the first time. She remembered the confusion she had felt before and the mental fog that had clouded all her actions. Now it was as though she'd awakened from an ordinary sleep, and she could spend more energy to consider her problem.

Though the memories of that previous occasion were hazy, she was almost positive she had been in a different room than this one. The walls before had been—she strained to think—a pale green, and now they were yellow. The other room had been perpetually dim, whereas now there was a window with sunlight streaming in. The other room had seemed smaller and square, while this was large and more rectangular. There was still the swarm of machines around her, but the environment had changed.

Maybe they moved me from Intensive Care to a regular ward, Michi thought. *That's at least an encouraging sign.*

She cleared her throat experimentally. It was still a bit sore, but not unbearably so. Slowly, taking care not to exert herself too much, she propped herself up on her elbows and called out, "Hello? Is anyone out there?"

When there was no answer after a minute or so, she tried again, a little louder. Two robots wheeled into the room, looking like small domed trashcans; but they went about routine business, and had not come in response to her voice.

Michi thought it was odd for a hospital to be so deserted that no one could hear her. She looked around for a call signal, but there was nothing of the sort here. She leaned back in her bed again, puzzled, and tried to think.

There was something very peculiar about all this. No hospital she'd ever heard of was so fully automated that there weren't nurses somewhere to check up on the machines. There had to be some way to communicate with the people in charge. They did not answer her voice call, and there was no apparent signaling system—so Michi would have to think of another way to draw attention to herself.

By leaning all the way over the side of the bed, Michi could just reach one of the machines that monitored her condition. She flipped off a series of switches on its front and was rewarded with a loud series of wailing sounds. Satisfied, she settled back on her bed with a triumphant smile. The effort had hurt considerably, but the effect was worth it. Let the machine call its masters for her.

Within seconds, her room was filled with robots bustling busily about, running their cold metallic hands over the length of her body, examining the machine that had sent out the alarms, and routinely checking the other monitors as well. Michi was almost smothered by their attentions—but still there was no sign of a living human being.

"Hey, who's in charge here?" she asked her army of attendants. "I want to see your supervisor immediately." When that elicited no response, she tried another approach. "There's been a terrible calamity: New Edo has been invaded and captured by some unknown enemy. I must report to someone immediately."

Still there was no answer; the robots treated her as though she were merely some important but decorative adjunct to the bed she lay on.

"Didn't you hear me? This is important. There are millions of lives at stake. I must talk to someone."

The robots, having satisfied themselves that she was all right and that the machine had merely malfunctioned, were resetting the controls and starting to leave the room.

"What's the matter? Aren't you equipped for talking? Don't you have any sense at all? Why am I being treated this way?"

Almost as quickly as they'd come, the robot horde was gone again, leaving Michi alone and mystified. She lay back on the bed, trying to think through her pain and piece together as much of the puzzle as she could.

The *Thundercloud* had been, to her knowledge, the only ship to escape from New Edo. They had been pursued by the enemy and hit. With the vessel partially disabled, the captain deliberately steered into an obscuring nebula, hoping to elude their pursuers. This planet had been spotted, and the captain had decided to land here to effect repairs before trying to reach some other colony for help. The attitude controls were too badly damaged, though, and the ship crashed. And then . . . Michi knew nothing further until she woke up here. Obviously a great deal had happened in the interim—but what? How had she gotten from an undiscovered planet to a hospital on a human world? How . . .?

A sudden chill started at the base of her spine and worked its way slowly upward. She realized she was being a bit too glib with her assumptions. There was no reason whatsoever to suppose she was in a human hospital. Quite the contrary, in fact; everything she'd seen here so far had been peculiar in one way or another. The implications of that were horrifying.

What if the enemy ship had followed them in here, despite their best efforts at hiding? What if the enemy had seen the crash and picked up the survivors? She could now be at the mercy—if, indeed, they even had any—of those hideous invaders. She could be a prisoner of war, saved from death in the crash only to be tortured and interrogated.

She bit her lip anxiously. Where these invaders were concerned, there were no ground rules for treatment of prisoners. There had been no time for such niceties. The surprise attack on New Edo was quick, bloody, and effective. How could she expect any humane treatment from creatures like that? They would torture her with less concern than she would have about pulling legs off an ant.

She took in a deep, slow breath. She was First Lieutenant Michi Nakamura, serial number 97426328. They would get nothing further, no matter what they did to her. She knew her duty to Earth. She'd been raised in a family tradition steeped in military honor. She would not betray the human race to those . . . those things. If the torture became too bad, she would find some way to kill herself.

Even as her heart was flooded with those noble sentiments, her mind was rationalizing its way around them. *They went to a lot of trouble patching me up,* she reasoned. *They wouldn't do that if all they wanted to do was torture or kill me.* There was also the consideration that she knew very little they'd want to know. First lieutenants were rarely invested with crucial information about the Commonwealth's defenses. *Even if I wanted to talk,* she thought ironically, *I wouldn't have much to tell them.*

There was a movement in the doorway that caught her eye, and she turned back in that direction. A new robot was standing there, looking different from the others who'd attended her. This one was tall and slender, like a water heater with arms and legs. The metal arms around its body were waving in an almost sensual pattern. "Good afternoon," it said in a tone of pleasant formality. "I hope you are feeling better after the accident."

"Who are you?" Michi asked brusquely. She would not have been quite so hostile just a few minutes ago, but her recent train of thoughts had sharpened her suspicions.

"My name is Arthur. If there's any way in which I can be of assistance . . ."

"Arthur" did not sound like a particularly alien name, but there was still something about this situation that did not ring true. "Yes, there is. You can tell me where I am."

"You are in a room near the top of the tallest building in the city of Beta-Nu. You were recently released from the central Beta-Nu hospital after receiving several transplants, although you are still under medical observation."

"Beta-Nu? Never heard of it. What planet is it on?"

"The same planet where your ship crashed."

Michi blinked. "But that planet was unexplored."

The robot did not react.

The woman decided on a new line of questioning. "Who's in charge here?"

"At the moment, I am not permitted to divulge that information."

Michi's suspicions were instantly aroused. No one but the enemy would have anything to hide. No one but the enemy would hesitate to answer that question. "I presume I'm a prisoner, then."

"Oh no, certainly not. You will have to stay here for a short while until you recover more fully—your injuries were quite extensive—but after that there will be no further imposition. You'll be free to travel about as much as you wish."

"I'll bet."

"I detect some distrust. If there's anything I can do to allay your suspicions . . ."

"Yes. You can give me more information."

"I'll be happy to tell you anything that isn't specifically forbidden."

"Are you a representative of the beings who raided New Edo, or am I on a Commonwealth world?"

"This is a human-occupied world."

The answer's phrasing surprised her a bit, and she didn't know whether to believe it. After all, she knew of no law forcing robots to tell the truth—particularly if the robot really *was* in the enemy's service. "If this is a human world, then please let me speak to a real person."

"That isn't possible at this time."

There it was again, the same dead end. It seemed to happen every time she asked about real people. Was the enemy trying to confuse her, play some massive psychological game? Maybe she could get some results by coming at the problem from a different angle. "How many others survived the crash?" she asked.

"You are the only one," the robot said flatly.

That stopped her. There'd been better than eighty people aboard the *Thundercloud*. Was she really the only one left? How could she possibly account for such luck? Or did the enemy just want her to think she was alone, cut off from all her friends and any possible assistance?

"Then the warning hasn't been given?"

"I know of no warning," the robot said hesitantly.

Michi jumped on that opening. "That's why it's so important that I contact someone in authority. The colony world where I was stationed, New Edo, was invaded by an alien force. They took us completely by surprise and knocked out our communications. Only our one ship escaped to spread the message. I must tell someone so that High Command will know about the emergency and be prepared for the next attack."

"I don't believe it would be possible for you to contact your High Command from here, even under the best of circumstances."

"That's right, we're in the middle of a nebula, aren't we? I didn't know that would stop hyperbeams, but maybe it does. Still, we could send a ship." Michi sat up, ignoring the pain as she considered possibilities. "It's vitally important that we . . ."

"What is vitally important right now," Arthur said, "is that you recuperate from your injuries. You will be pleased, I'm sure, to hear that the doctors predict a complete recovery."

"That is good, yes. Thank you. But my duty to . . ."

Michi found herself talking to empty air. Arthur had left

79

the room, closing the door behind him. With some effort, she struggled out of bed and stood for the first time since the crash. She had to lean against the bed at first and hold her stomach with one hand to avoid the feeling that her insides were about to spill out. By moving slowly and keeping one hand at her belly while holding on to objects with the other, she managed to cross the room to the door. She was not too surprised to find it locked.

As she made her slow, painful way back to the bed, she thought on her meeting with Arthur. His knowledge of Worldspeak had been impeccable—a fact she'd barely noticed at the time, but which seemed significant now. Unless the enemy had a much better reconnaissance ability than she could believe, they would not have had time to learn the human language *that* completely. The very fluency of the robot's speech lent a certain credibility to what he'd said. But although he had given her some information, their conversation had left her with at least as many questions as before.

If this was, indeed, a human-occupied world, neither she nor anyone else aboard the *Thundercloud* had known about it when they came down. Why was there all this secretiveness by the people in charge? Why did they let robots do all their work, and why were they so afraid to show themselves? Had the *Thundercloud* accidentally stumbled on some secret base established by High Command for God-alone-knew what reason? That could explain some of the secrecy; in view of her peculiar arrival on this world, they might suspect *her* of being an enemy infiltrator.

She liked that explanation very much. She was not worried about their suspicions; she knew her identity could be checked eventually, and she would be cleared of any wrongdoing. But it would mean that she had found a safe harbor, and that her warning of New Edo's fate would eventually be heard.

Even her small exertion had totally exhausted her, and she climbed gratefully back into her bed. The robot had been right about that much, at least; she did need to recover more fully before she could do anything. She closed her eyes and lay back, hoping devoutly that her theory would prove correct. Even as she drifted off to sleep, however, there were still unanswered questions that circled in her mind and refused to light.

Michi spent the next three days dozing and waking at irregular intervals. Her periods of wakefulness were growing longer, and she could feel her strength returning. Now that she was awake more often, the doctors felt she could return to feeding herself rather than receiving intravenous injections. The food was of strange colors, shapes, textures, and tastes—but that was only to be expected on a totally alien planet. Michi found it quite edible and even developed a fondness for certain items.

Arthur was quite willing to satisfy her physical demands, and her first request was for a mirror. She had not seen her face since the crash, and despite the fact that is felt all right to her exploring fingertips, there was the lingering worry that she would be badly scarred. The mirror assured her that her face, at least, remained undamaged.

Her body, however, was a different story. An enormous red scar ran like a railroad track diagonally across her torso from just under her rib-cage on the right to her waist on the left. It seemed remarkably primitive—in most operations nowadays the openings were sealed almost seamlessly by skin welding—but this was a hospital on some unknown world, and perhaps they were not as sophisticated here. The scar itself didn't hurt much unless she touched it, though the underlying muscles were sore from being sliced through. Her biggest worry—which stayed with her no matter how often she was reassured to the contrary—was that the stitches might pop open and let her organs fall out. She developed the habit of holding one arm supportively against the stitch line whenever she moved.

When she complained about being naked, Arthur brought her a simple white toga. The garment was sideless, with snaps at the shoulders and waist for easy donning or removing in an emergency. Arthur apologized for not providing better clothing; that, he said, would be taken care of later.

Her room had its own bathroom attached. Arthur helped her the first time she had to use it, and explained some of the plumbing's peculiarities. The toilet was higher than she was used to, and most uncomfortable; Michi found her legs dangling awkwardly when she sat down. Arthur would give her no explanation for the bizarre construction, however, so she was forced to accept it as it was.

The big robot visited her frequently to check on her progress and to ask how she was feeling. He was as vague as ever about the people running this establishment, though he did at one point let slip the fact that his boss lived in this same building, a few floors up. He was unfailingly polite, though, and genuinely seemed to care about her. Michi's treatment in this place was so considerate that eventually she abandoned the theory that she was an enemy prisoner. She was, however, *someone's* prisoner, and as time went by without any sign of people she grew more and more worried about who it might be.

The door to her room was always kept locked when there were no robots going in or out and, in those first few days, she did not have the strength to test the limits of her confinement. Arthur did provide a telescreen that gave her pictures of this world's scenic wonders, and there was a window through which she could catch disturbing glimpses of a strange and exotic city outside.

She had spent some time on three different planets before coming here and had seen pictures of many others; nowhere had she ever seen a city built quite like this one. She was scarcely an expert in architectural criticism, but she couldn't believe this city had been designed by a human mind. And if this were some secret base, how had so large a city been constructed without some word of it leaking out?

She could see plenty of figures moving about on the streets below, but no cars or other mechanized traffic. From this height—seventy or eighty stories, she estimated; she tried to count exactly, once, but got dizzy looking straight down for so long—it was impossible for her to make out any details, but the figures seemed to be moving in too precise a pattern to be live people. That meant more robots. But where were they all coming from—and where *were* the people? Arthur had assured her several times that this was a human-occupied world. *Where were the people?*

Several times she caught sight of a large triangular flying craft gliding through the sky, landing or taking off from this very building. It moved with an amazing speed and gracefulness, barely making a sound; Michi had never seen anything quite like it. This place, wherever it was, seemed filled with wonders—but in her situation, she could not appreciate them. She was a woman with a very practical turn of mind; she wanted explanations, not miracles. And she wasn't getting them.

By her fourth day in this room she was getting very bored. Her breathing had returned to normal, her strength was back almost to its former levels, and the soreness of her muscles, if not totally gone, at least did not hamper her from moving about quickly and freely. She was not nearly so tired, and she stayed awake most of the day. She had asked Arthur and the other robots for some reading materials to help her pass the time, only to be informed that there weren't any. She had exactly two alternatives: She could lie in bed and stare at the telescreen or she could sit by the window and stare out at the beautiful, mysterious city below her. She had plenty of time to ponder her dilemma, but without hard facts she could not reach any satisfactory conclusions.

A decision had to be made, and she finally felt well enough to make it. The people in charge here, had left her to rot in this room like an overripe vegetable. As far as they were concerned, this state of affairs could go on indefinitely. But that didn't satisfy Michi. If she truly was the only survivor from the *Thundercloud,* then it was her responsibility to warn about the invasion of New Edo and to see that word was passed to the proper authorities. Every moment she wasted in this room was another moment the enemy might be using to his advantage. She had to find a way to break out and make her presence known.

As she stood near the window in thought, the door slid open and a robot entered the room with her luncheon tray. Making a split-second decision, Michi raced for the door, slipping out just before it could close behind the robot. For a moment she felt the thrill of freedom, but it vanished completely when she realized she had not the faintest idea what to do next. Her action had been spontaneous—but unless she could follow it up, she would soon be recaptured by the army of robots and herded back to her room. They would then make sure she could not escape so easily again.

Arthur had mentioned a person living in this same building, a few floors up. It was not much to go on, but Michi had no other clues. She had to do something.

Her room was at one end of a long hall, with numerous other doors opening into the corridor. Michi ran barefoot down the hallway, looking for an elevator or a flight of stairs. As always, she held her belly loosely to make sure the stitches didn't pop open. Even as she ran, she could hear the door to her room opening again and the robot who'd brought her lunch emerging. She expected to hear alarms, but there was only silence. Perhaps the robots didn't need sound to communicate.

Within seconds, the doors to the hall were opening and a horde of robots was filing out after her. A group of them blocked her way in front, and one of them grabbed for her with its metal tentacles. She pushed the arms away and bent painfully to lift the machine off the ground. It was lighter than she had expected it to be, and she was able to hurl it a few meters forward into the middle of the pack, knocking over some other robots and clearing a path for herself.

She darted through the sudden opening and kept running. Ahead of her, in the middle of the corridor, was a stairway going both up and down. Without hesitation Michi started up. Behind her, the robots were at her heels.

Her stitches were throbbing with pain, and she was beginning to feel dizzy from her exertions. Already she was regretting her rash action in attempting this escape; if she'd been smart, she would have planned it all carefully in advance and waited until she was just a little stronger. But now she was committed to this course, and she would follow through on it or pass out trying.

Ahead of her, four more robots were coming down the stairs to head her off. Grimacing, she ran to a landing and positioned herself with her back to the wall, arms extended and ready to fight. As the first robot came racing toward her, she grabbed its outstretched arms and used its momentum to fling it around into the path of the machines coming up from below her. Her followers went down like tenpins.

The second robot coming down, seeing the fate of the first, approached with more caution. Still, as soon as it came within reach, Michi was able to pick it up also and fling it down the stairs, where it bounced roughly until coming to rest in an ignominious heap on the next landing.

The remaining two robots above her stood still in their positions, determined to obstruct her passively if there was no other way. Michi started up toward them, directly at the first one. As she neared it, she made a feint with her left shoulder as though to move around it that way. The robot took the feint and moved to block the new route; Michi dashed past it, puffing laboriously. She did not waste any time or energy with the last robot; she simply shoved it out of her way and kept on climbing.

There were more robots behind her all the time, and it seemed as though she'd been climbing stairs forever. The pain in her gut was now a fire, so strong that she dared not stop; she knew she'd collapse if she did so and could never start up again before her pursuers overtook her. Her foot missed a step, causing her to trip and bang her knee, but she got quickly to her feet and started upward again. Somewhere in all this maze, there had to be a real live person for her to confront.

She came to the top of the stairs after an eternity of pain. The corridor was quiet, but there was a difference here. There was the feel—and particularly the smell—of human habitation. At last she was on the right track. Looking both ways down the hall, she saw an open door to her right. Michi staggered down the corridor holding her arm to her side, her eyes focused intently on the bright rectangle of light framed by the open door. At last she made it to the doorway and stepped inside.

Even as exhausted as she was, she spotted him instantly amid the colorful furnishings. There was a man seated at a table. Though he had his back to the door, he seemed to sense her presence as she entered. He turned in his seat and started to rise, then froze in midmotion. He was tall with leathery skin, a shaggy mane of dark hair and a full, unkempt beard. He was wearing a simple white caftan trimmed in fur, with furry boots. His face was frozen with a mixture of emotions that Michi could not have read even had she been in perfect health.

Michi stood still for a moment, wavering dizzily on her feet. "At last," she said weakly, "a real live person. I have a report . . . some questions . . ."

She took a step forward and then collapsed onto the floor.

SEVEN

Confusion tinged with fear sped through Birk's mind as he saw the woman collapse across the room. How had she gotten up here when he'd left explicit orders not to let her out of her room? Had she somehow hurt herself, reaggravating her injuries from the crash? Had she perhaps done some irreparable harm to the delicate surgery the robots had performed? Would she die? And most important, was it has fault? Arthur had relayed her increasing complaints about being cooped up. Had the confinement, which he'd ordered for the best of motives, done more harm than good?

He shook off the paralysis that had momentarily gripped him, rose from his chair, and dashed across the room to the fallen woman's side. He knelt beside her and felt at her throat for a pulse; a distant part of his mind was telling him that this was the first time he'd actually touched the woman since she'd come, but it was a touch he could take no pleasure in. He was too concerned that his own stupidity might have endangered her life.

Even as he started to call for Arthur, the robot was racing into the room to help him. The woman's pulse seemed a bit uneven but definitely strong, for which Birk gave a silent sigh of relief. With Arthur's help, he lifted the body off the floor and carried her over to one of the chairs. Her eyelids were fluttering even as he set her down, and within another minute she was definitely starting to come around.

Thank God, Birk thought. *She was only weak, and she fainted. Let's hope it's nothing more serious than that.*

"Are you all right?" he asked aloud.

She started to nod, then winced with pain and grabbed at her side. "It hurts," she croaked.

"Of course it does," he said sternly. Now that his concern had abated, he felt angry that she'd risked her health that way. "You're not well enough to be out of bed and running around. It was a very stupid move."

"Probably," she agreed. "But I had to get out; I had to see someone."

Birk remembered back over the years to the moment he'd realized he was trapped on this planet forever, with no more human companionship. The feeling of being cut off from everything else had been overwhelming. He'd been on the brink of insanity for half a year before he finally forced himself out of the depression and made his own accommodation to reality. He could understand, after the fact, how Michi might have felt disoriented and deserted at her own forced isolation. He berated himself for thinking only of his own emotions and not of hers; but then, it had been so long since he'd ever had to consider anyone else's desires that he was out of the habit.

"I'm sorry I had to keep you alone like that," he said. "I thought at the time it would be for the best, to help you heal faster."

86

"Are you in charge of the hospital, then?"

"In a manner of speaking. Actually, I'm in charge of the whole planet."

The woman's eyes widened, and Birk tried to guess the thoughts running through her mind. Arthur had not yet told her they were the only two people on the planet, so she probably assumed there were others. Birk knew his appearance was not the common image of a world leader. She more than likely thought he was lying, and it was hard for him to suppress a smile.

Whatever her private thoughts were, though, she had to go on the assumption that he was telling the truth. Her body stiffened and she tried to rise from her chair. Birk and Arthur gently held her down, and the woman was too weak to struggle against them.

"Forgive me for not standing and saluting," she said. "My condition doesn't really permit it. May I ask your rank, since you're not wearing a uniform?"

"I'm a civilian, and no apologies are necessary. We're not strong on formality around here."

"I am Lieutenant Michi Nakamura, 456th Space Battalion assigned to New Edo. I have a report of the utmost urgency to be conveyed to High Command."

Birk struggled not to laugh. The woman was taking this matter very seriously, and she couldn't know yet how futile that report would be. It would not help his image in her eyes, though, if she thought he was making fun of her. "I've never heard of New Edo," he said simply. "Is it one of the newer colonies?"

Michi gave him a strange look. "The planet was first discovered eight years ago, and extensive colonization began more than five years ago. The planet's been built up to nearly ten million people."

"I see. I've been, ah, out of touch with things for a while."

"Five years?" She said it as though it were a lifetime.

Birk avoided the question by asking one of his own. "Arthur tells me you have a story about some sort of invasion. Is that what you want to report?"

Reminded of her mission, Michi forced her expression back into proper military bearing. "Yes, sir. We must get word to Earth immediately."

"Please give me the details." By letting her talk, even though there was nothing he could do to help her, he hoped to overcome some of the bad first impressions he may have inadvertently given her. She would think of him as sympathetic and helpful—and the more positive her opinion of him, the more he'd be able to help her over the trauma when he told her how hopeless the situation really was.

Michi sat back in her chair, trying to compose her thoughts and put the facts of her case into a proper, logical order. "It all happened so fast, I hardly know where to begin. All I can give are the few isolated facts I know, and a lot of subjective impressions. I'll do my best to make it as complete as possible." She looked around. "Shouldn't you be recording this?"

"Arthur has an eidetic memory. He'll serve as recorder."

Michi accepted that without question. Taking a deep breath and letting it out again, she began her tale.

"They attacked without warning. I'm not sure what direction they came from; I heard someone who was on watch then say they came out of the fifth octant, but that doesn't really mean anything—they could have circled the planet and come from any direction. They had a force of about fifty ships. A few, maybe five, were small scouts, and maybe twice that number were warships. I'm sorry I can't give more specific numbers, but everything was quite chaotic. The rest of their ships were troop carriers, bigger than anything I've ever seen in space—bigger even than the colony transports. We estimated that each of the carriers could hold thousands of their soldiers, plus all their attack equipment, and they had plenty of attack equipment.

"Since no one has ever had contact with other intelligent beings before—and especially hostile ones—they caught us completely off guard. They must have done some secret reconnaissance on us, because they knew just where to hit. The first thing their scoutships went after was our hyperbeam transmitter. We only had the one, since we were still a small colony. They knocked it out in less than two minutes, before we even had a chance to let High Command know there was any trouble. The rest of the Commonwealth will have no idea that anything happened; they'll just think we're having trouble with our transmitter.

"Then they came after our landing field. There were twelve ships permanently assigned to New Edo. One was in orbit in a mapping detail; the rest were aground. We don't know what happened to the one in space; there was never any word. Commandant Ibachi assumed it was blown up with all hands aboard. I know what happened to the ships standing out on the field because I was there and I saw it; all ten were blown to pieces before we could even have them manned and away."

"That's only eleven ships," Birk interrupted. "I thought you said there were twelve."

"Yes, sir, that's right. The *Thundercloud*—the ship that crashed here—was the twelfth. It wasn't on the field during the raid; it was in a hangar for repairs to the attitude jets. Maybe the enemy's intelligence wasn't that thorough, or maybe they just didn't bother counting once they started blowing things up. The world was pretty chaotic right then, and we weren't thinking that clearly ourselves. Commandant Ibachi did order repair work speeded up, but there were other problems that were just as bad.

"Once they thought they'd destroyed all our ships, the enemy carriers landed and soldiers came storming out like ants when you step on an anthill. There were thousands of them, landing in or near all our major settlements. They came out of their ships shooting, and nothing could stop them. The soldiers had no concern for their own personal safety, and they didn't know the meaning of retreat. If you shot the ones in front, the ones in back climbed over them and kept coming. It was unnerving, sir. We didn't have much time to organize, but we did put up some resistance in a few places. They just came in waves, pushing us back, and there were always more behind them."

"What did they look like?" Birk asked.

"Short, averaging about my own height, I guess. They had two arms and stood erect on two legs, but their bodies—what I could see of them—were all bright red. They were perfectly smooth and hairless. Double sets of eyes; two in front like ours and two in the sides where the ears should have been. There seemed to be slits in their faces; I didn't get a close look at them—that would have been suicide—but the guesses were that the slits might be for breathing, eating, or hearing." She gave a small, bitter laugh. "At any rate, they sure weren't the most beautiful things I'd ever seen.

"They had several types of weapons. One type fired beams of pure energy, like our own laser rifles, only they could fire a broad beam perhaps a meter across rather than a narrow pinpoint like ours. They had other weapons that seemed to give off sonic vibrations; we couldn't hear anything, but buildings collapsed and people keeled over. They had chemical explosives, too, which is what they used on our ships. I saw no evidence of nuclear weapons, but they were fighting more a tactical battle than a war, and they hardly needed nukes.

"It was a rout from beginning to end. I don't offer any excuses. They were prepared for the fight and we weren't; it's that simple. I was stationed near the landing field, so after the first attack I didn't see too much of the action. I helped guard the perimeter while the field personnel got the *Thundercloud* ready for takeoff. We knew the planet was lost, but we wanted to get away and warn High Command so no other worlds would be taken by surprise that way.

"The enemy troops were coming our way just as the *Thundercloud* was taken out of its hangar and readied for flight. We held them at the perimeter for a while and then fell back quickly. Commandant Ibachi squeezed as many of us into the ship as he could, and we took off at top speed. They sent two of their battle cruisers after us.

"One good thing, at least—their ships aren't much faster than ours. We had a short lead and we kept it most of the time. We ran for two days before they came within range, and we began shooting. We knocked out one of their ships, but the other hit us and caused some minor damage. Captain McCulloch noticed this dust cloud and decided to come in here. She hoped we could lose them in the dust and get ourselves more time."

Michi paused for breath. "We lost them, all right, but we found that the damage from the shot we took was more serious than we thought. Then the captain spotted this planet and decided to land for a while to repair the damage before continuing. I was in the hold with most of the other soldiers, but it was clear she couldn't keep control of the ship." Michi lowered her eyes. "You know the rest of the story."

Birk was afraid to speak for some time, afraid his relief would be too obvious in his voice. His major concern was that this ship had been seeking him—or, if not, that it would be missed by the military High Command and searched for. Now it turned out that neither alternative was the case; he was still safe from discovery.

"Yes, the crash was a bad one," he said at last. "We searched the wreckage thoroughly, but there were only six survivors—and of them, only you pulled through. A terrible tragedy that we couldn't save any more."

Michi nodded slowly, and Birk could see there were tears in her eyes. "Yes. I had some good friends aboard that ship."

"Was one of them a tall, blond woman?" The question was

past Birk's lips before he could stop it. His infernal curiosity was compelling him to find out more about the "second" Reva.

Michi thought hard for a moment. "No, I didn't know anyone like that. There were a lot of people aboard I *didn't* know, too. Why?"

"Not important. She was just one of the ones who almost made it. I wanted to know more about her."

"Sorry I can't help you." Michi gave him a hopeful look. "Can you get the news to Earth at once?"

Birk turned away from her and clenched his fists. He had the choice of either lying to her or telling the truth—and there was no easy way to do the latter. Lying, telling her he'd relay the message, would soothe her for now, but she'd find out soon enough it was impossible and she might hate him for betraying her. Better to get it all over with at once.

"There's no way I can do that," he said.

"What do you mean?" Her tone was instantly suspicious. "I thought you said you were in charge here. Who are you, anyway?"

"My name is Birk; the last name doesn't matter right now. And yes, I am indeed in charge of this whole planet. My powers, however, are very limited."

Michi shifted uncomfortably in her chair. Her suspicion and hostility were growing rapidly, and Birk's tiptoeing around the facts was doing nothing to quell them. *I'm going about this all wrong*, Birk thought. *This isn't the way I should be breaking it to her. But God, how can I find the right words?*

"I don't understand," Michi said slowly. She was in no position to threaten him and she was too well trained to snarl at someone she thought was a superior, but there was a clear tinge of anger to her words. "Perhaps you should explain the situation to me in more detail. Why can't we let Earth know about the attack?"

Birk prayed for divine inspiration. He was beginning to realize how hopeless this was, but he had to try. "This is a very unusual planet," he said. "As you know, it's right in the middle of a thick, obscuring dust cloud. Radiation has trouble getting through."

"I thought hyperbeams weren't affected by things like that."

Birk shrugged. "They probably aren't. It doesn't matter. There's no hyperbeam transmitter here, either."

"Then we could send out a ship. . . ."

Birk was shaking his head, still refusing to face her. "That's impossible too, I'm afraid. No ships."

Michi's voice was filled with disbelief. "There have to be ships. You must get supplies from somewhere."

"This world is rich in all sorts of things. There's no need for outside supplies."

"But if there are no hyperbeams and there are no supply ships, how do you communicate with Earth?"

"I don't."

The simplicity of the answer was beyond Michi's comprehension. "There must be ships," she repeated. "You and the others had to get here somehow."

"What others?"

Michi opened her mouth, then closed it again abruptly. Birk could read in her eyes the thoughts that flashed through her mind. She *hadn't* seen any other people since she'd been here—just Birk and the robots. "I . . . I just assumed . . ."

"I know. It would seem logical to me, too, under those circumstances. But the fact is that you and I are the only two human beings on the face of this planet."

There. It was out. He'd said it. The words hung in the air for a long time, almost tangibly, like a curtain drawn between them. Michi just sat there, stunned, and again Birk had some idea of the thought processes behind her silence. She was taking his words one by one, turning each over in her mind and examining it carefully for meanings other than the obvious ones. She could not accept the facts yet—no sane person could. She would try first to look for loopholes, some way of denying what he'd told her. She would not believe, not for quite some time.

He knew so well what she was thinking because he'd been there himself. Accepting the truth of this world's loneliness was a long and painful process.

Michi opened her mouth twice to speak, and twice closed it again without saying a word. On the third try she was more successful. "You must have gotten here somehow," she said weakly.

Birk nodded. "Yes. The same way you did. My ship crashed here. I was the only survivor."

She looked around, still in shock. "But then how . . . all of this. . . ."

"Built by the planet's original inhabitants, a very ingenious race I call the Makers. They died off two thousand years ago. The robots have kept things going since then."

92

Birk could feel the pain and confusion Michi was going through. His instincts told him to cross the room and put an arm around her shoulder, to hold her head against his chest and comfort her against the cruelty of truth. But the mere thought caused a stirring in his trousers. He dared not move too fast, dared not overplay his hand. He didn't trust his own reactions to a woman—and a reasonably attractive one, at that—after so long. He kept a rigid control and stayed coldly on the other side of the room.

"How . . . how long . . .?"

"Eleven years."

Michi shuddered and wrapped her arms tightly around herself. There were glistenings of tears again in her eyes, but Birk could see she was fighting them back. She was, after all, a lieutenant, and she had her duty to think about.

The officer in her eventually gained the upper hand. She straightened up in her seat and said, "There must be something we can do. From what I could see of the city from my window, these . . . Makers were sophisticated builders. They must have known about space travel. Maybe they'll have some ships stashed away somewhere."

Birk shook his head. "Not a one. I've already looked, long ago."

"Well, there's plenty of power and resources. We could build a hyperbeam transmitter and . . ."

"Do you know how to build one?"

Her face fell. "No."

"Neither do I. I know the basic principles—I'm an engineer and I studied it a little in school—but it's a long way from there to actually constructing one."

"There must be something we can . . ."

"Michi, listen. There is nothing either of us can do. I know it's unpleasant, but you're going to have to face the fact that, whatever happens between Earth and this new enemy, you and I are going to be trapped here on this world for the rest of our natural lives. There is no escape. Ever."

EIGHT

Michi looked up at him. There was no stopping the tears in her eyes now. "I . . . I . . ."

Go to her, one portion of his mind said. *Comfort her.* But he dared not move closer. His body was already reacting badly to her nearness and her vulnerable femininity. With less space between them, he couldn't be sure of controlling his actions. For the sake of his own sanity, and the future of their relationship, he had to stay distant and apart.

This is not going the way I'd hoped, he thought. *It's all falling to pieces, and I can't stop it.*

"I'm sorry if I was too blunt," he said. "I didn't mean to hurt you. But the sooner you accept the situation, the sooner you'll adjust to living here. It's not too bad, really. Quite comfortable, in fact, once you get used to it. And now that there's two of us . . ."

He had to bite his tongue to keep from completing the sentence. He must at all costs avoid giving her the impression that he considered her merely an available female body after so long a period of abstinence.

Michi hardly noticed, so deep was she within her own shock. She slumped in her chair and wrapped her arms tightly around herself as though to ward off an imaginary chill. "There must be some way," she whispered, so faintly that Birk could barely hear her. "Someone will find us."

Birk shook his head. "Who'll be looking? Who even knows we're here? I gave a lot of thought to that possibility my first few years here, but no one ever came. I had to resign myself to living here the rest of my life. The middle of a dust cloud is hardly the place people come to look for survivors of crashes they don't even know took place."

He took a step toward her, and again had to curb his impulses. "I know it's a deep shock; I went through it myself.

94

You, at least, will have things a little easier—you'll have both Arthur and me to help you and explain things to you. Imagine how it was for me—I couldn't even find out anything about this planet until I taught Arthur Worldspeak. You'll have the benefit of my experience and his knowledge. . . ."

"Why didn't the Makers have any ships?" Michi asked suddenly. "I could see some of the city from my window. They weren't a primitive people, and all the robots prove they had technological capacity. Why didn't they ever build spaceships?"

"You wouldn't have to ask if you ever saw the nighttime sky. Remember, this planet's star is in the middle of a thick dust cloud, and there are no other major worlds in the solar system. There may be some asteroids, but nothing big enough or bright enough to be seen with the naked eye. When the Makers looked up into the sky at night they saw no lights to challenge them. There was no starry heaven to set them dreaming—not even a moon to become romantic about. There's just the sun during the day and darkness at night. They thought they were alone in the Universe."

Michi was able, for a moment, to climb out of her own self-pity to feel something for the departed race. "How sad."

Birk nodded. "They had no real reason to study astronomy, although I imagine they learned about the workings of their sun when they grew more scientifically advanced. They certainly knew about nuclear energy. They developed missiles for warfare. But what would be the purpose of spaceships? There was absolutely nowhere for them to go except the sun—and no sane person would want to go there."

"But we can't just give up and accept this," Michi insisted. "We must keep trying. I can't live the rest of my life away from people."

She paused, staring idly at the wall. "I grew up in a suburb of Tokyo. I remember the crowds pushing and shoving on market day, and hearing the fans cheer at baseball games, and going to birthday parties for my friends. . . ."

She shook her head. "There must be some way off the world. I can't live without people around me."

"What about me?" Birk asked quietly.

"You're a person," Michi said. "You're not *people*."

Her words stung. They were a partial rejection of him, even though she might not have meant them as such. Birk was on edge anyway, and her irrational persistence despite the facts he'd shown her pushed his temper past the tolerance point. "We must accept this world as it is," he barked at her. "For

95

the sake of sanity, we can't go rushing off after every wisp of a dream. If you don't make your peace with reality, you go slowly crazy. I haven't stayed sane on this miserable rock for eleven years by frustrating myself with false hopes, and I won't let you do it, either. We need each other, Michi; the longer you're here, the more you'll realize that. I won't let you torture yourself by thinking there's some way out. I've thought of every possibility; nothing works."

"I have my duty to Earth. . . ."

"Earth no longer exists for us. Our duty is only for ourselves."

"I can't accept that."

Birk turned to Arthur, who'd been observing the entire conversation silently. "Arthur, take the lady back to her room. She's obviously too much in shock to think straight right now."

Arthur moved to comply, taking Michi's arm and gently helping her to her feet. The woman was still dazed by everything that had happened and offered no resistance.

Birk immediately regretted his outburt and, as Michi was leaving the room, he tried to soften his impact. "I won't try to isolate you anymore, I promise. Just rest up and try not to get too upset by everything that's happened. I'll be down to visit you at dinner, and we can talk some more. I can explain to you why escape is so impossible. Okay?"

Michi gave an almost imperceptible nod as she left the room with Arthur. Birk slumped into a chair, totally drained, and massaged his temples with his left hand. Nothing had gone right with this woman from the very beginning. He'd wanted to cradle her against the shock and the upset of learning the truth, and instead he'd only made the facts more brutal. He'd wanted her to like him, but had ended up yelling at her. This was not, he knew, the way to begin a promising relationship.

It had been so long since he'd had to deal with another person that he'd almost forgotten how. He was abrasive and distant at the same time, and in this crucial confrontation he could afford to be neither. He would have to learn better manners, and he'd have to do it before he alienated her completely.

Michi returned to her room with Arthur. She lay in her bed, her mind dazed by the impact of all she'd learned. Marooned here for rest of her life, cut off from friends and family forever, unable to warn the authorities of the invasion threat. To be stuck on this planet alone, without hope of redemption, without ever hearing another human voice except that of the strange man who called himself Birk. . . .

Her thoughts turned to him quite naturally. He was an anchor in the chaos, the one fact she could turn to in a sea of uncertainty. And yet, from what she'd seen he lacked basic stability himself. For all his ranting about having held on to his sanity, as she looked back on their encounter she could see a definite imbalance in his words and actions. He was cold and distant, as though wanting little to do with her, turning with unexpected violence to a hysterical fit. She reminded herself that he'd been here eleven years without other human company, and wondered how sane *she* would be after that long.

But still there were things that did not ring true. How could he possibly abandon hope of rescue? If she were ever to do that, she might as well slit her wrists. From all she'd read about people trapped in seemingly impossible predicaments, to give up hope was to die. Robinson Crusoe, she remembered from her literature classes, had never given up hoping for the sight of a sail. Hope—and a deep belief in his Puritan God—had been the spur that kept him going beyond the limits of pure survival. Hope had kept him human. Without it, he would have become an animal.

How could this man Birk live without hope? Didn't he have a family and friends he cared to see again? Something was desperately wrong there; Michi could feel that instinctively. She had no idea what it might be, but for her own sake she would have to find out. She did, however, know one thing: Birk could not force her to abandon her own hopes. Somehow they *would* get off this world; they *would* return to Earth; they *would* see civilization again. No one would be allowed to steal *her* dreams away.

Her flight from the robots, the climb up the stairs and then the emotional upset of learning her status had all contributed to a deep feeling of wooziness. She lay in bed for a while with her head spinning, and nothing made much sense for several hours. She did not sleep, exactly, but time drifted in and out of her grasp in awkward chunks until she was startled back into full awareness by the arrival of Arthur and Birk bringing her dinner.

Michi sat up in bed and ran a hand quickly through her hair to smooth it down. Despite her private doubts about

Birk's sanity, she managed to find a smile for him. "Hello again," she said. "Thank you for coming."

For some reason, her friendliness seemed to make him more uncomfortable. "I hope you're feeling better," he said, his voice so low it was almost a mumble.

"Yes, the rest helped a great deal. I must learn not to press my body beyond its limits. I'm still recovering from serious surgery. It's just that the situation seemed so critical at the time. . . ." Her voiced trailed off as she realized she was starting to tread on dangerous ground once again. She did not want to appear critical of his actions; that seemed to set off his temper.

Birk, though, just smiled at her remark. "You'll learn, after you've been here a while, that few things are so important. Time means little on this world; I—we have as much of it as we care to spend."

Michi mulled on that for a moment, then decided to change the subject. Looking down at the platter Arthur had set before her, she said, "The food has been delicious here, but I'm curious. What is all of this?"

She could see instantly that she'd said the right thing. Birk, after all, had lived here eleven years, becoming an expert on the planet; he was delighted at a chance to show off his knowledge. "Those little green balls are what I call sprouts, like Brussels sprouts; they come off a plant that's halfway between a tree and a vine. They're especially delicious when fried in animal fat. Those flat blue things are eaten raw; they're the soft seeds of a plant with a consistency like grapes, only not at all sweet. The meat is a filet from a small domesticated animal; the robots raise them in large pens out in the country. It's a very salty meat, but the chef kills some of the excessive flavor by cooking it in a sweet-and-sour sauce."

"You rely on the robots totally for food, then?"

"I could if I wanted. The agriculture and food processing on this planet were very highly automated before the Makers were wiped out, and the robots are geared to feeding far more than just one or two people. Actually, though, I prefer to do a little of the hunting myself. I go after some of the bigger game that the robots would seldom bother with unless I asked them specifically. There's enough variety, though, that you could have three meals a day and not repeat anything in a month—and that's just in the vicinity of this city. Other places have other indigenous foods, of course."

Michi tasted the food as Birk spoke, and found it quite delicious. She offered him some, but he told her he'd already eaten. She felt a bit self-conscious at first, eating while he watched, but he filled in the conversational gap with vignettes about the different foods he'd discovered since coming to this world, and mealtime passed swiftly. He was looking more at ease as she listened and accepted everything he said. Finally she pushed away her plate, saying she could eat no more, and one of the small helper robots took it away.

"That was good," Michi said, and meant it.

"All compliments go to Arthur and the robots under his command," Birk told her. "They're constantly looking for new ways to please me."

Michi turned to the big robot and thanked him for the superb meal. Arthur accepted her compliments with gracious humility, promising her even more wonders next time.

"I've been thinking," Michi said as she leaned back in her bed once again, "of ways to leave this planet." She was not looking specifically at Birk, yet she could feel him stiffen in his chair. Nonetheless, she pushed on. "We have unlimited robot resources and a sufficiently high technology. You said you know the theory of hyperbeam transmission. With some experimentation we could probably . . ."

"No, we couldn't," Birk interrupted. "The theory was known fifty years before teams of experts actually managed to build the first transmitter-receiver. It's a very complex and sensitive process. Even if we started today, I probably wouldn't live long enough to finish the job."

Michi was prepared to be shot down on her first attempt and had a stronger backup idea all ready. "You mentioned earlier that the Makers did build missiles for warfare. If they have that technology, we could adapt a missile to our purposes, make it into a spaceship."

Birk gave a nervous little laugh. "That's like saying we'll adapt an abacus into a GTZ-9000 computer. You obviously have no scientific background, or you couldn't even think such a thing. What was your specialty in the army?"

"R-and-S." When Birk looked at her blankly, Michi elaborated, "Reconnaissance and Survival."

Birk nodded. "I see. Nothing to do with the operation or maintenance of a ship."

"I'm willing to learn," Michi said stubbornly.

Obviously trying to be patient, Birk gave a small sigh. "It's not a question of willingness. If we had five lifetimes between us, it wouldn't be long enough to learn all we need to build a ship from scratch. All right, so I'm an engineer. My specialty is drive systems. I could build a hyperprop engine in my sleep—or at least I could at one time; I'm a bit rusty after eleven years. But let's assume, for the sake of argument, that we can have the robots build a missile big enough to hold us and that I put the proper engine in it. I know a little spherical trigonometry, and the robots could give us a computer to help with the calculations. I might be able to astrogate our way home. I still know nothing about guidance and control systems, and nothing about building the sophisticated sensors we'd need to chart our position. And, most important, the Makers' missiles were never manned. They have absolutely no technology for life support in space. Do you know how to design an efficient air-filtration system, or a waste-disposal system, or a thermionic heat-flow system?"

Michi shook her head.

"Neither do I," Birk said. "I'm just educated enough to know how much I *don't* know, and that is a considerable amount. I could build a ship that could take off and travel through p-space and maybe even reach some planet in the Commonwealth, but I have no way of keeping us alive in the process. And that, if I'm not mistaken, is part of the whole idea."

Michi was silent for several minutes. Not being an engineer herself, she had not considered the complexity of the problem; Birk obviously had, and she would have to bow to his expertise. There *was* more to building a spaceship than she'd realized. But she still was not prepared to abandon all her hopes and settle in on this world. The fact that Birk was a propulsion engineer was better luck than she might have hoped for.

Birk was sitting across from her bed, looking smugly triumphant, as though he had shot down her arguments once and for all. After some thought, Michi made another suggestion. "Perhaps we could send out a robot ship, one that doesn't *need* life-support systems. It would be like the old message in a bottle. If we send out enough of them in all directions, one is bound to get through. We could warn High Command about the invasion of New Edo—if they don't already know by then—and at the same time let them know where we are."

Birk's expression had changed abruptly from one of smugness to one of boiling anger. "No! I will not waste my time on foolhardy ventures like that."

"Why not?" Michi strove to be reasonable even in the face of his fury. "You just told me we had plenty of time to waste. What's wrong with something that gives us a litte hope?"

"Hope?" Birk snorted derisively. "Maybe for you Earth is hope. For me, it's the exact opposite. Earth is a cesspool of degradation. I want nothing more to do with it."

Michi could only gasp at this unexpected reaction. "I thought you'd want to be rescued after all this time."

"What do you know about me? Nothing. A few more people for company, yes, that would be delightful. But not Earth. Not ever again. I won't go back there, and I don't want them coming here."

Dumbfounded, Michi could only stare at him. How could he possibly feel this way? How could he not want to be rescued from this lonely world, no matter how charming and comfortable it might be? Who but a madman would willingly cut himself off so thoroughly from his own species? "Why?" was all she could think to ask aloud. "Why are you turning your back on humanity?"

"Humanity turned its back on me a long time ago. I helped give them the stars, and what did they give me in return? Hatred and humiliation, pain and ridicule." He shook his head violently. "I won't go back to that; I won't. Not even with a ship and a fully trained crew. Never. They don't deserve what I can give them."

"And what about me?" Birk's anger was contagious; Michi was beginning to feel it herself. "I have friends and family out there. I have my commission, my military duty. I can't cut myself off from that if there's any chance at all of getting back. Do you expect me to give up all that? For what? For you?"

"They're not worth it. They turn on you, betray you. . . ."

"I can't accept that. I don't know what happened to you, but there's nothing that bad for me. You're telling me I have to give up everything I've ever known and loved, just to stay here with you."

"Yes. It's not so bad."

"It's hell. It's disgusting. I think you're sick, I really do. You live here like a vegetable, surviving from day to day and not going anywhere. That's no way to be. If you ask me, you died a long time ago and your body just kept going out of habit. This planet is your grave, perhaps, but it won't be mine. I'll get off of here somehow."

"It'll have to be without my help. I won't lift a finger to contact Earth."

"Then it'll be without your help. But I will do it."

Birk laughed bitterly. "I'd like to see you try."

"Then watch me close. But don't choke on my dust."

Birk was across the room before he even thought, grabbing her shoulders and shaking her. "Now listen, you little . . ."

And then, like a bolt, it hit him what he was doing. Here was the only other person in the world, the only *woman* in the world, and he was threatening her with violence. He backed off suddenly and stared down at his hands as though they were alien creatures with minds of their own, and had betrayed him when he least expected it. Eyes filling with tears, he turned abruptly and ran from the room.

"Get out, you defeatist bastard!" she yelled after him—to little effect, for he'd already left the room. Michi found there were tears in her own eyes as well. Totally frustrated, she picked up a drinking glass and threw it at the wall next to the door. The tumbler bounced to the floor unbroken, its contents splashing on the smooth surface of the doorframe. Arthur walked over from the corner where he'd been silently observing the scene, picked up the glass, and left the room without a word. A few minutes later one of the smaller maintenance robots came in to wipe the stains off the wall.

Michi settled back on her bed, trembling both from rage and from the pain that rage engendered in her still healing body. She was marooned on a planet with a madman who would not help her get home. Never in all her life had she felt smaller and more alone than at this moment. Despite her brave words, she was totally at his mercy, and she knew it. She had alienated him, and now there was no one to turn to. She suddenly felt what Birk must have felt—isolated, cut off apart from all humanity. It was not a feeling for her. If she couldn't find a replacement for it, she knew she would go mad.

Her sobbing echoed across the entire floor as she cried herself, at long last, to sleep.

NINE

Birk fled the woman's room, rage masking the humiliation and insecurity that stabbed at his psyche. The noises in his throat were subhuman growls and half-words that never coalesced into coherent meaning. He was half blinded by tears as he lurched down the hall and up the stairs to his own level—and beyond. He went up to the roof, to the open air, to the delta that awaited him on top. The delta was the symbol of his freedom, his personal magic carpet to soar the open skies. Somehow, with the pain of his wounds searing at the edges of his mind, it was only natural that he would come here.

He climbed into his familiar seat and switched on the controls. The bubble came down and sealed itself around him. He knew that if he waited more than a minute or so, Arthur would be here too, requesting politely that he be allowed to go along. Spitefully, Birk twisted the controls and the delta flew off the roof with so much acceleration that he was pressed back hard into his padded seat.

The sun had just set, and the western sky was still tinged with red. Birk flew east, toward the darkness. At this particular time, he wanted only to be swallowed up by the night. He acted on instinct, without conscious thought. He didn't want to think, not just yet. The thoughts he'd have right now would be too painful to face.

The blackness of the sky blended with the blackness of the ground, creating one all-engulfing maw of night. Only the dim instrument lights reminded Birk that he was not alone in the Universe; only they told him he was flying a level course. As far as everything else went, nothing could touch him here.

That ungrateful bitch, he thought. The phrase repeated itself relentlessly for several minutes in his mind. He had saved her life. He had chosen her over that other person. She should be kissing his feet, delighted that he had thought her worthy of continued existence. Instead she snarled at him because he refused to return to the misery and degradation people like her had forced him into once before. He had given her life, and still she wanted more from him. She wanted him to sacrifice his own life for her precious duty. Well, that was too much to ask. She had no right to make demands on him. By everything fair and just, he was the one who should make demands on her.

There was a quieter part of him that said, *Give her time to adjust to the inevitable. This is as hard on her as it is on you.* But that part of him was small, and he didn't want to hear it. The angrier parts of him were quite capable of drowning it out.

How dare she come in here and give him orders? What right had she to tell him what they should or should not do to survive? He had lived here for eleven years, while she'd been here just two weeks; he knew more about survival on this world than she did. Any sensible person would have bowed to his superior knowledge and experience. Instead she issued ultimatums.

Just like the military, he thought grimly. All his previous experience with the military mind had proved how inflexible and self-righteous those people could be. They considered no one else's feelings but their own, and nothing else mattered but the performance of their duty. They didn't care how many people were hurt, as long as orders were obeyed and official policy carried out.

"You live here like a vegetable." Her words came back to sting him like a swarm of bees. How the hell could she make snap judgments like that? What could she possibly know about his life here? His exploration and cataloguing of this world could hardly be called vegetating. There were always challenging discoveries to be made. In eleven years he'd barely begun to sample the riches this world had to offer; a man could spend several lifetimes without seeing everything, no matter how fast and how hard he traveled. He hadn't chosen this existence of his own free will; it had been forced on him when his ship crashed. But he'd adapted to the necessities of his new life as best he could—and for that, she condemned him as a traitor to his species.

"I've been condemned as a traitor before," he said aloud to no one in particular. "With equally little justification."

It had been foolish, he could see now, to think that anything could come of this relationship. Michi Nakamura was part of the same military establishment that had treated him so cruelly a dozen years earlier. That type of person could not be dealt with on a rational basis; they had one-track minds, and nothing on the periphery mattered.

Better to have let her die, he thought. If she were dead, he could at least fantasize about how ideal the relationship might have been, as he could about the Reva duplicate. If she had died of her injuries, he would not have had to deal with the pain of having his hopes crushed like dried leaves on an autumn sidewalk. But she had survived—he had helped make sure of that—and now he had to put up with her insults, her demands, her ultimatums.

It's a big world, he thought resolutely. *If she doesn't like the way I do things, she can always go her separate way. We'll never have to see each other again.*

On the instrument console, a blue light flashed and a buzzer rang with gentle insistence. This was the first warning that the delta's fuel pack was running low and would soon need changing. Disturbed that such a purely mechanical interruption should break into his thoughts, Birk angrily punched the computer buttons to get a readout on his present position in relation to cities where fuel would be available. He was informed that the city Alpha-Epsilon was only a short distance to the northeast, so he altered course accordingly. The delta settled down on the rooftop of the building where Birk had once made his home, and he ordered several of the maintenance robots to bring him more fuel packs so he could continue his flight into the darkness.

When Michi awoke the next morning, her body was stiff from having slept in an awkward position. There was also a good deal of pain along her scar; the arguments of the day before had aggravated her wounds so badly that even sitting up was a major effort. Shortly after she was fully awake, the door slid open and Arthur glided into the room, carrying her breakfast on a tray. Despite the pain, Michi found that she was ravenously hungry, and cleaned off everything the robot had brought without even bothering to ask what it was.

"Where's Birk?" she asked when she'd finally finished, trying to keep her voice at a conversational level.

Arthur hesitated slightly. "He went out flying last night,"

105

he said at last. "Birk sometimes prefers to go on solitary expeditions. He says it helps him relieve pent-up emotions."

"He does a pretty good job of that in person, too," Michi said. She settled back in bed and let Arthur take the tray off her lap. As the robot started for the door, she suddenly spoke up again. "Arthur?"

"Yes, ma'am?"

"Why does Birk hate Earth so much?"

The robot hesitated longer than Michi had ever seen him do before. Clearly he was caught in a conflict of loyalties, between service to her and promises to his master. Michi marveled that a robot was even capable of weighing ethical responsibilities in such a complex situation.

Finally Arthur replied, "He was treated very badly by the government before he came here."

"Why was he treated badly? Was he a criminal?"

"Technically I believe that is correct, though he himself certainly feels he did nothing wrong."

"That's what they all say," Michi said sarcastically. "What's his full name, anyway?"

"Birk Aaland."

Michi was about to say she'd never heard of it, when facts began clicking into place in her mind. Birk Aaland. An engineer specializing in propulsion systems for spacecraft. Considered a criminal on Earth.

"But he's . . ." she started to say, then shut her mouth quickly again. She'd been going to say that Birk Aaland was dead, that the government said he'd died in a prison camp somewhere. But he obviously wasn't dead—he was here, marooned on this out-of-the-way planet. And for all the effect he had on the world, he might as well be dead.

She had not recognized the man, but she could hardly be expected to. She'd been only a teenager when the scandals had erupted and he'd been arrested in disgrace. It had been so long ago that she could not even remember any of the details. And, of course, the man's appearance had changed significantly during his time here alone; he was older, craggier, less neatly trimmed than those dimly remembered pictures of him she'd seen long ago. But she *did* know who he was.

He had claimed, last night, that he helped give men the stars—and she knew now that claim was perfectly justified. Birk Aaland had not invented the hyperprop engine; the theory had been known for more than thirty years before he came along, and working models—cumbersome, awkward contrivances—had been built. But it was Birk Aaland, the young genius, who at the age of only twenty-three patented the design that made the breakthrough in hyperprop possible. The Aaland engine transformed space exploration overnight. Before its development, the hyperprop engines were so bulky and so energy consuming that only small scoutships could roam the stars; the superefficient Aaland engine meant that ships with hundreds of people, and all the gear they needed for their survival, could be carried at a time.

Colonists were immediately dispatched to all the lovely planets the scouts had found. Transport ships could not be built fast enough to keep pace with the demand. The Commonwealth of Planets, as it was called, began slowly, but grew at an exponential rate—all of it due to the Aaland engine.

That much of it, at least, was history, taught in every school on every human world. But the details of Aaland's personal life were less clear to her. She remembered that Aaland had become quite wealthy from his invention, winning nearly every scientific award and honor it was possible to get. And then there had been the scandals, the fall into disgrace, the accusations of treason—but for the life of her, Michi could not recall any of the details, or even why it had happened.

If this man really was Birk Aaland—and she had no reason to doubt it—she was even luckier than she'd originally thought. Not only to have survived the crash of the *Thundercloud,* but to have survived with *him*—perhaps the one man in the Universe smart enough to overcome the obstacles and find a way of getting word back to civilization that they were stranded here.

But, of course, Aaland did not *want* to contact civilization. The scandals had hurt him badly, and he was content to live out his life quietly in this cosmic backwater.

Michi clenched her fists in frustration. If only she could remember more of what had happened, it might help her understand and better deal with the man who shared this planet.

"Arthur," she said aloud, "I do know who he is. He's the man who perfected the interstellar drive. But I was very young at the time of his troubles; I don't remember anything about it. Do you know what happened?"

"Yes," the robot answered slowly. "He told me about it in great detail. He was anxious, he said, to record his own testament, in case other humans someday found this world. Then his own story would be told."

"Can you fill me in on the details?"

"I could," said Arthur, "but I won't. The story was told to me in confidence, and I cannot betray that confidence."

"But you just said he wanted his side of the story told."

"That is after his death."

Michi sighed and shifted uncomfortably in her bed. "Arthur, you may have seen last night that Birk and I are in a very awkward emotional circumstance. We're stuck together on this world, and we must learn to survive together, even if our aims are different. To do that, we must understand each other. I'm willing to tell Birk anything he wants to know about me. I won't keep any secrets. But I must ask for the same courtesy in return. In order to understand his feelings and his thoughts, I must know what happened to him, what events shaped the way his mind works. I understand the need for privacy, but I think in this case the need for survival supercedes it. Please, Arthur. For his sake as well as my own, I must know what happened to him. If I don't know, I may inadvertently hurt him again. Neither of us wants that."

Arthur paused again. "I will think on the matter," he said at last, and vanished out the door. Michi lay back on the bed and closed her eyes, trying to will away both the pain and the frustration.

Half an hour later, Arthur returned. "I will tell you," he said, and Michi let out a long sigh of relief.

The robot moved closer to her bed, until he was standing right beside it. "I will play back for you the recordings I made of his speech. The recordings rambled a great deal; I have taken the liberty of editing them somewhat and of putting them roughly in chronological order, though that was not the way they were dictated. I think this will give you a better understanding of the way he thinks."

As Michi leaned forward, the next voice that came from Arthur's speaker belonged to Birk. The woman listened, fascinated, to the exile's tale of downfall and punishment.

TEN

The ancient Greeks had a word for it, Arthur [*Birk's voice said*]. They called it *hubris*, which has been translated as "o'erweening pride." It's what happens when a man gets too puffed up with his own sense of self-importance. He thinks he can do nothing wrong, and his actions challenge the gods themselves. Well, the gods usually weren't happy about such challenges, and they found all sorts of clever and humiliating ways to strike back. . . .

I suppose it was partly my fault, but I refuse to take all the blame. *I* wasn't the one who made Torres dictator, after all. I was just the guy who stood up at the wrong moment. I saw the crossfire, but I was stupid enough to think my armor was thick enough to stop all the bullets. I'll take the blame for the stupidity quick enough, but if Torres hadn't been there in the first place, none of the problems would have come about. . . .

I thought I had it made, Arthur. There I was, set for life. I had a beautiful, loving wife, a large house with a complete staff, and more money that I could ever use. The royalties from the patents on my engine alone brought in so much money each year that I never had to work a day in my life if I didn't want to. I didn't like being idle, though, so I did other things. I was in demand around the lecture circuit, and there were offers of teaching positions from universities all over the world. My opinion was always sought at scientific and engineering conferences; I was listed as a technical consultant on the boards of a dozen top companies. There were three publishers hounding me to write books on various subjects. I was even written about in celebrity gossip columns once in a while.

I had to say, without a trace of shame, that I loved every minute of it. I know it's a cliché to talk of fame as "heady wine" or some such metaphor, but sayings become clichés because there's truth in them. Perhaps if I'd been a performer, where millions of people knew my face, it might have been different; I know there are some stars who can't step outside their houses without a disguise, or they'll be mobbed to pieces by their fans. I wouldn't have liked that; there'd have been no privacy at all. But my type of fame was entirely different. I could be anonymous when I wanted to be, yet people still knew who I was and paid attention when I spoke. I could have anything I wanted. But what I liked best was the respect I commanded. There were people a lot older and, frankly, a lot smarter than I was who would nod their heads at anything I said, just because it came from me.

That much power went to my head. I tried to avoid the obvious pitfalls; I tried not to use my special position to hurt anyone else. I don't *think* I abused my power too badly. But all the respect I got led me to believe things were important just because I said them—and that's really what caused me most of the trouble. . . .

I suppose it's a pretty complex situation, how Torres came to power. You have to look at the whole picture, both on Earth and in the rest of the Commonwealth. I can look back on it with a certain amount of detached hindsight, but at the time everything was pretty chaotic.

There were many nations on Earth, each relatively autonomous—sort of like the city-states the Makers had, though each nation on Earth was composed of many cities. It had always been the dream of forward-looking people that one day the nations of the world would be ruled by a single world government. There were plenty of early attempts, always without success. But as we started going out into space and establishing colonies, the local boundaries on our own world began looking pretty puny. Then, too, there were all the multinational corporations, that is, financial companies with operations in many countries. They were rapidly becoming a law unto themselves because no single national government could control them. The various countries banded together more and more into treaties and international regulatory agencies just in self-defense, or else the multinationals would have pre-empted their power altogether.

Then, when colonies were established on worlds in other solar systems, something had to be done to control *them*. We called ourselves the Commonwealth of Planets and tried to make it all sound very beneficent and democratic, but the real truth was that Earth made all the policy and the colony

110

worlds were forced to live with it. But there had to be a central bureaucracy to run the Commonwealth, and the national governments again found themselves joining together under one blanket for a common purpose. . . .

I have a hard time talking about Torres with any degree of objectivity. I detest the man and everything he represents—or represented; for all I know, he may be dead by now. I'll try to be as unemotional as I can, but I make no guarantees.

His name was Fernando Torres. There was a lot more to it, as I recall; the Spaniards were always big on giving long strings of saints' names to children, but I don't remember what the rest of Torres's name was. I don't suppose it really matters. Anyway, he was a general, and one of the top officers of the Commonwealth. I suppose, like any opportunist, he saw the trends developing and grabbed at them to make them his own, before anyone else could. That requires a certain amount of shrewdness that I'll have to credit him with—the shrewdness of, say, Julius Caesar or Napoleon or Hitler. I suppose the damned historians will rank him with those men as one of the "great historical figures of all times." Well, I guess Caesar and Napoleon and Hitler got where they did by being ruthless, too, and I'm sure they were all hated in their time. Torres, I know, was never going to win any popularity contests.

Anyway, Torres probably saw the drift toward world government and decided that, since it was inevitable, he might as well help it along. He was most likely working at it for several years without anyone really knowing about it. He probably spent a lot of time working his supporters into the key international regulatory agencies. I know that by the time he finally made his move, he had everything sewn up tight. . . .

All dictators, I guess, need some excuse, some turmoil to seize power. Torres aimed specifically at the big conglomerates. A couple of the multinationals were putting the squeeze on the poorer, resource-producing countries. The wealthy have always been a favorite target, so Torres and his buddies in the regulatory agencies moved hard against the corporations. The corporations protested and tried some not very subtle economic blackmail. That gave Torres the excuse he was looking for. The first thing anyone knew, he had troops all over, he'd arrested all the major corporation executives, and he'd declared martial law until the chaos could get itself sorted out. Not once did he ever say he was setting up a world

111

government, but that's effectively what it was. The individual nations still had some autonomy within their own borders—as long as it didn't conflict with anything Torres wanted to do—but his government regulated all international commerce.

He kept saying his actions were only temporary, and I guess everyone wanted to believe him. He didn't invent any silly titles for himself, like Emperor of the World or President of Earth. He was simply General Torres—but he controlled the Commonwealth and his puppets controlled the regulatory agencies, which in turn controlled the countries. I suppose he hired an army of public relations people to keep him looking modest and unassuming; a lot of his real power was hidden behind others, and not many people realized at first how much of a threat he really was.

A lot of people disappeared during those first few months, but most of the public didn't care. It was only the fatcats, getting what they deserved, according to Torres's propaganda. A few of the bigger names were given showy trials to prove that Torres had done the correct thing by stepping in and taking over; most of the executives were just taken to prison camps and tortured or killed. I met a number of them myself, so I know. . . .

I'd never been much into politics. Like most scientists and engineers, I was more at home with numbers than with people—they're more exact and predictable. At first, I felt very ambivalent about Torres's takeover. On the one hand, I was listed as a board member of some of those corporations, and I was a little worried for my own safety—but I was never really in control, just a technical advisor, and I was pretty safe. I did know some of the people who were put on trial, though, and I thought at the time that their treatment was unjustly harsh. I knew they weren't the out-and-out monsters that Torres's propaganda machine said they were.

On the other hand, I'd always been an idealist. I'd always believed in concepts like the Brotherhood of Man, and that one centralized world government was the ultimate way to eliminate war and regional prejudices. I thought Torres's coup—that's what it really was, although he never called it that—I thought it would be a step in the right direction. I was willing to overlook a certain amount of mischief if it brought about a more stable world in the long run.

But more and more stories kept spreading about Torres's reign of terror. People started getting arrested who had

112

nothing to do with the corporations; they merely represented power threats to Torres in other directions. Mostly, I guess, they were political and religious leaders—anyone with a power base to organize resistance to Torres's regime. When the news media began carrying too many stories about brutality toward political prisoners, Torres cracked down on them. It's impossible, these days, to control *all* the news, but he did a fairly thorough job. No government in the history of the world, however, has ever been able to stop rumors.

A group of my fellow scientists got worried. They knew that political repression historically led to scientific repression as well, and they wanted to stop that. They formed a committee for scientific freedom—I don't even remember the exact name, anymore—and they asked me to join. I wasn't sure, and I refused the first time. I had things pretty easy then and, after all, no one had violated any of *my* rights yet. But they kept telling me all the horror stories about what had happened to other people, and some of them were verified. Eventually I got mad, too, and I joined their committee to speak out against the government atrocities.

I was still big on the lecture circuit, and I was able to travel all over the world telling people what I thought. After the first momentary scare about being listed on various boards of directors, I didn't give a thought to being arrested for what I said. After all, my years of fame had proved to me that I was an important person. They wouldn't dare arrest anyone of my stature because it would create such an uproar that everyone would rally to my defense and overthrow the government. That sounds awfully egotistical, looking back on it, but it's pretty much the way I felt at the time. You have to remember, I'd been idolized as a genius for a decade by now, and I'd started believing my own press releases, as it were.

At any rate, I wasn't arrested—not then, at least—and looking back on it I guess that's the most surprising thing of all. I know I was saying some pretty hard things about Torres and his crew. Maybe I really *was* too important for them to tamper with; I suspect, though, that they probably thought I wasn't dangerous enough. No one ever listens to scientists, anyway. I did find that the number of speaking invitations dropped off alarmingly after a while, but there were no other attempts to silence me.

Up until that point I was a tolerable pest, more trouble to get rid of than to let alone. If I had stayed at that level, I might have weathered the storm. But conditions seemed to get worse. More and more stories were coming out about Torres's prison camps and torture chambers. There were some incursions onto college campuses—not into the sciences, as my colleagues and I feared, but against the students. For some reason, students are always in the forefront of revolutions; I guess it's because they have nothing better to do, no responsibilities and nothing to lose. Anyway, troops began marching onto campuses around the world, which only made the students angrier and more defiant. They weren't *Torres's* troops, just the local peacekeeping forces, but everyone knew who was behind the crackdown. The more we saw of what was going on, the more scared we on the scientific committee became. Something drastic had to be done to show our concern.

This is where my own *hubris* came in. I felt I was untouchable. My years of fame had built up my ego, and the lack of challenge to my anti-Torres speeches had reinforced it. My colleagues pointed out that I had one weapon I could use against the government that could hurt it badly, and I was foolish enough to try.

I finally came out in the press and told the government that I was withholding the right for them to use my patent on any more engines. In essence, I was calling a halt to the entire colonization and exploration program. Legally I had every right to do so—my lawyers assured me of that, although they warned me it was a foolish and dangerous move. I didn't listen to them. I was convinced—hell, I still am—that what I did was morally correct. Torres was a dictator of the worst order; it was my duty to do everything I could to cripple him and put an end to his rule.

But that was the move that put me beyond the pale. Torres, remember, was the titular head of the Commonwealth; his original power base was the space colonization program. Instead of just being a loudmouthed scientist, I was now a threat to him personally. Torres wasn't a man who tolerated threats well.

I'm not even sure my statement ever became public knowledge; I was arrested early the next morning. The police came at about four-thirty, without warrants, and just dragged me off without explanation, without even giving me time to get dressed. They deliberately picked awkward times like that; they know a person is confused anyway if you wake him out of a sound sleep, so he can't offer as much resistance as he normally would. The fact that I was naked would serve to humiliate me more. They were good at that—coming up with ways to humiliate the prisoners, I mean. A man who's humiliated enough breaks more easily, and that was the point of this whole exercise. They were out to break our spirits and our resistance. . . .

I was held for close to two months without any word about what was to happen to me. For the first full day I was left naked in a cell with about fifty other prisoners. They told me they were out of prison uniforms my size. Even then I didn't really believe them. It was cold, too, despite all the people crowded together. I'm lucky I'm not generally susceptible to diseases, or I'd have caught pneumonia that first night. . . .

Day after day went by without a word of news from the outside world. I think that was really the worst thing of all, being kept in ignorance of what was happening. For all I knew, they could be deciding to take me out tomorrow and shoot me. Or they could have decided to just let me rot down there and not tell anyone where I was. Perhaps they were waging a smear campaign in the press to discredit what I'd been saying all these months; I'd seen what they could do to other people's reputations, and it was vicious.

But worst of all, I kept wondering what was happening to Reva. I loved her, Arthur, I really did. I was never unfaithful to her, not once in seven years of marriage. There were plenty of temptations, too, let me tell you. I was on the road a lot, traveling to meetings and giving lectures. She usually preferred to stay home. It got so lonely at times without her, and there were so many willing, available women, like after the lectures and the broadcast appearances. It would have been so easy, and she would never have known. But I didn't, not once, because I loved her.

But during those two months, I had not a single word either from her or about her. I didn't know whether they had arrested her, too—they were perfectly capable of that, even though she'd never done anything. She and I had talked about it, of course, and she agreed with the stand I took, but she'd never done anything openly; we both agreed it would be safer that way. That wouldn't have stopped Torres, though; he was no respecter of innocence.

I had to sit there in my cell—my cells, actually, because they kept moving me from cell to cell at random every few days—I had to sit there not knowing what was happening to Reva. I didn't know whether she was dead or alive. They could have confiscated all our property and tossed her out on the street. I found myself wondering how many of our friends would be brave enough to take her in if that happened, knowing that she was marked as the wife of a political troublemaker. She could be in some prison herself, being beaten, tortured, or raped by sadistic guards. I had no way of knowing, and it ate away at me for two months.

The first news they brought me was that Reva had filed for, and been granted, a divorce. Of all the things they could have told me, that was the one I was least prepared for. I was ready to hear that she was dead, or in prison, or impoverished and begging on the streets, but never that she was divorcing me. I went around stunned for several days. The thought occurred to me that they were lying, that it was only another trick to break my willpower. I clung to that hope, even though I had nothing to base it on but my own feelings for Reva. . . .

My trial came three days after I heard about the divorce. I was still in a daze from that news; the trial came almost as an anticlimax. They didn't give me any warning or any time to prepare. They just woke me up one morning and took me from my cell without telling me where I was going. I was more scared then than I've ever been in my life—I was sure they were going to shoot me, without any further ado. But they took me off and gave me a new suit of clothes, a shave and a haircut, and I guessed they wouldn't go to that much trouble just for an execution. So by the time they hustled me into the courtroom, I had some inkling of what was going on.

The trial lasted three days. They gave me a lawyer—a man I'd never seen before in my life—but his job was mostly to make formal motions that were denied. Reva was there in the courtroom. I tried to talk to her, but they wouldn't let me near her, and she refused to make eye contact with me. Maybe she was ashamed of her part in all of this. I don't know. I fervently hope so. I hope she was forced to do what she did. God, if I ever learned she meant it, I'd really go crazy. . . .

I never really learned what the charges were against me. I don't even think the prosecutor knew. His job was just to smear me as thoroughly as possible. They started by calling me a traitor and quoting from some of my speeches. That was fair enough, although they took a lot of remarks out of context. I stood by those words when I said them and I still do. But then they started tearing down my professional reputation. They said I didn't really invent my engine design, that I stole it from other people. They got friends of mine—

former friends—to testify that the ideas weren't original with me, that I merely lifted them out of previously published works and presented them as my own. I could barely believe what I was hearing. Some of these were respected colleagues who knew damn well what I did. Sure, every invention relies to some extent on things that have gone before; they could cite plenty of works before mine that incorporated parts of what I designed. But they knew that those earlier works were all incomplete, that they wouldn't have gone anywhere without my putting everything together. It probably sounded pretty damning to the general public, though. . . .

Some of those men were the same colleagues who had come to me at the beginning and persuaded me to speak out. That's what galled the most, to hear those hypocrites bleating their perjuries to save their own necks. I wouldn't have been there if it hadn't been for them, but they weren't content with that; they wanted to drive the nails even deeper into my coffin. . . .

When they'd finished tearing apart my reputation as a citizen and as a scientist, they then went to work on me as a human being. They put Reva on the stand, and she told all sorts of lies about me. I practically wept right there in the courtroom to hear what she was saying. She said that I'd often bragged about stealing the engine invention from the proper people, that I was cruel and beat her several times a week, that I was an alcoholic and a sexual deviant. She refused to look at me the whole time she was on the witness stand. Poor girl, so ashamed of what she was doing; I can't really blame her, I suppose; God only knows what tortures they put her through to make her say those things. I would never have done that to her, I loved her too much, but different people have different breaking points. Anyway, she denounced me as a traitor, as a thief, and as a warped human being. Then she left the courtroom, before my lawyer even had a chance to cross-examine her—not that he did very much cross-examination anyway. I never saw her again. . . .

I tried to speak up once in my own defense, on the first day of the trial. That night, when I returned to my cell, my guards beat me unconscious about the body, but nothing that would show in public. I learned my lesson—I wasn't supposed to interrupt and spoil the show they'd planned. . . .

The judge—did I mention that they didn't even bother with a jury?—the judge deliberated a full half hour before returning with the verdict. I don't know why he took so long; maybe he had to go to the bathroom. He found me guilty, and somehow I wasn't surprised. Even in an unrigged trial, given the evidence as presented, it would be hard to draw any other conclusion. He sentenced me to thirty years at hard labor. That surprised me a little because there were a lot of death sentences being given at that time. Maybe the state thought I might be of use to them sometime in the future and wanted to keep me around, just in case. As if I would ever lift a finger to do anything for them again. . . .

I spent the next year or so being shunted around from one prison to another. I don't know whether they wanted to keep me off balance or whether they genuinely didn't know what they wanted to do with me. Each prison I went to seemed worse than the one before. The crowding was certainly bad; civil disobedience had become so strong that Torres was arresting people faster than he could process them. There were constantly rumors that there would be mass lineups and executions any day, and that we were all as good as dead no matter what our sentences were. Somehow it never came to that, at least not as long as I was in the prison system. I can't vouch for anything after I left, of course. . . .

God, should I talk about the tortures? I've been doing my damnedest to forget them, and I know I never will. I don't like even bringing the subject up. Still, I suppose for the sake of completeness I should say something. People have to know how General Torres treated the guests of his rehabilitation system.

I lost track of the number of times I was beaten. Once a week at least, sometimes more. Sometimes a guard would come into my cell while another one looked on; sometimes they took me to a special room where they could do a more thorough job without being cheered on by the other prisoners. Sometimes groups of guards got together in some sort of game, like soccer with prisoners as the balls. Sometimes it was military officers who came to "interrogate" me, although they seldom asked any questions and I didn't know anything even if they did ask. There just always seem to be people who enjoy beating up someone more helpless than themselves. If you ever want to see the dark side of human nature, just become a political prisoner. You're fair game, then, for all the sadists in the world.

Then there were the special tortures, the ones I'm sure my guards sat up late at night thinking about. I was chained down naked for two days on the floor of a rat-infested cell while dozens of those disgusting creatures crawled all over me. My body was covered with rat bites by the time I was let out. I was once left in a darkened cell for days while they fed me emetics and laxatives to make sure I'd wallow in my own filth. One time they told me they were going to castrate me. They wheeled me into an operating room and put me under. I woke up back in my cell and panicked for a second until I checked; they'd left my testicles and just given me a vasectomy. I didn't know whether to laugh or cry; I think I did both at the same time. . . .

There were electroshocks and other casual cruelties. I'm only glad I wasn't one of the "prettier" ones. Several of them committed suicide after being gang-raped repeatedly. . . .

I was sentenced to hard labor, and there was plenty of that. Not that they had anything worthwhile for us to do; at the rate Torres was filling his prisons, there were far too many prisoners for any amount of meaningful work. We were given strenuous exercise sessions every morning before we even started work. Most of what we did consisted of digging graves in the hard ground—there was a constant need for graves—or building long, high brick walls in one part of the prison yard while tearing down walls in other parts. It was trivial, but we had to do it, sometimes as much as sixteen hours a day. There wasn't much water, and I think the food must have been computer-calculated for the minimum amount needed for survival and nutrition. They said it was some kind of soy paste on hard bread, and it was tasteless as wall plaster.

I was lucky. I was still young, just thirty-five, and in reasonably good physical condition. I would end each day exhausted, barely able to stuff the food in my mouth before falling asleep. But a lot of the others weren't so lucky. Political prisoners fall into two classes: the young student radicals, who disrupt society with their exuberance, and the older, more experienced people who are dangerous because of the knowledge and power they accumulated over the years. You seldom see anyone in between.

The older men couldn't stand the strain. Hardly a week went by that five or six of them didn't drop on the spot during a work period. I remember one guy in particular. He must have been in his fifties. He was working right next to me, and it was raining. We worked in all kinds of weather; the guards thought it was very funny to watch us slipping and sliding. Anyway, the guy next to me, I forget his name, couldn't take any more and collapsed on the ground, face down in the mud.

I moved to try to pick him up, but a guard pulled out his shocker and forced me away. The prisoner just lay still in the mud while the rain poured down on him. I don't know whether he was dead when he fell, but he certainly couldn't have lived long with his face buried in mud. I kept looking over my shoulder at him while I worked, until finally the guards realized what a distraction the body was and had two other prisoners haul it away. . . .

We didn't get too much news from outside—only what the newer prisoners could tell us. But just from the rate prisoners kept coming in, I could tell that Torres was becoming more and more dictatorial. Conditions were getting so crowded that we got prisoners stuffed ten to a cell, and the cells were only built to hold two or three. We knew things couldn't keep going on this way, or there'd be an explosion. We were sure Torres was going to start ordering mass executions any day—and we were so far gone that none of us was even sure whether it might not actually be a blessing. . . .

When the crowding reached a critical level, Torres came up with a solution. Since he was in charge of the Commonwealth, and since the colonies were always in need of manpower, he'd ship us off there. It wasn't quite the same as when Australia was founded; from what I understand in that case, prisoners were offered their freedom if they would settle permanently in the new land. Nobody was offering us any freedom; we would just be a cheap labor source wherever it was needed. And it would take us out of the overcrowded prison system on Earth, leaving room for all the poor victims to come after us. We would still be prisoners, but far enough out of Torres's hair so that we wouldn't bother him anymore.

A couple hundred of us were loaded aboard a ship and we set out for somewhere. They never told us our destination, and obviously we never arrived to find out. The ship had been a colony transport, hastily rigged out to carry prisoners instead of ordinary colonists. As a result, the security system aboard was not adequate to contain us all. I suppose the people in charge were counting on the fact that none of us knew the first thing about running a spaceship. They figured that it would be suicide for us to mutiny, since it would only mean our own deaths in space as well as the guards'. What they failed to take into consideration was they were dealing with two hundred or so very desperate men—men who'd been to the point of death a dozen times over, men who'd been degraded and beaten and humiliated so harshly that nothing

120

could be worse than more of the same. We weren't precisely rational, none of us—and I include myself in that. We'd given up all thought of the future; we lived only in the now.

It was a trivial thing that set it off—someone complaining about the food. Everybody complained about the food, every day; it was hardly something new or unique. A guard told the man to shut up, and the man threw the bowl in his face. That touched off the entire riot. We became a mob, and I was as animalistic as any of them. All I could think about was the treatment I'd had for the past year. There was nothing in me but hate, a boiling red sea of it. If anything remotely resembling a guard were to appear in my path, I would have torn it to pieces with my bare hands or been shot to death trying. I have no idea whether I actually did or not; I was in a killer state for an hour or better, and I honestly can't remember a thing I did during that time. I suppose I'm better off that way.

When the riot was over, the ship was a mess. Every guard, every member of the ship's crew was dead. So were more than half the prisoners. Not all of our own casualties were the guards' doing, either; there were a lot of smoldering hatreds and rivalries among the prisoners that tore loose when everything else did. All told, there were seventy-six of us left alive in that ship—and some of those were pretty badly injured. I was lucky; I'd come out with just a few scratches. There were others who'd had arms or legs burned off by guards, or their eyes torn out by other prisoners. The dead, of course, looked even more grisly than the survivors. Most of us were pretty sick when we came to our senses and had a good look around us.

We rested for a while, and then our predicament began to sink in. Not a one of had ever even been aboard a ship in flight before. None of us knew how to run one, or steer it in a direction we wanted to go. We didn't even *know* where we wanted to go. We were free for the moment—but what good would it do us?

I was the only one, it turned out, with any technical background at all. I knew all about the engines, of course, and I could guess at the workings of the rest of the controls. The ship's computer was intact, and it helped me through a crash course in astrogation. I became the new captain more by default than by any innate powers of leadership. The rest of the prisoners accepted my authority in matters relating to the ship, although there were some of them who were jealous of my power. We worked together because we had to, not because we liked each other.

121

One of the first orders of business was to clear away the debris. We spent a whole day hauling dead bodies to the airlock and chucking them outside. We had neither the time nor the energy for funerals; we had to be callous and look on it as mere waste disposal. We did it as fast as we could, but even so the whole ship stank of death for the rest of the voyage—a remarkably appropriate odor, all things considered. . . .

The riot had left the insides of the ship badly damaged. The mob had battered down solid steel doors, supposedly locked airtight, to get at guards and crewmen who'd tried to hide. The control room had been one of the major battle sites, but fortunately the controls themselves weren't too badly damaged. I spent about three days assessing the damage and trying to repair any broken systems with the inadequate tools stored aboard the ship. Even if the ship had been in perfect shape, though, I still think I would have botched the landing. It simply took a skill I didn't have. . . .

So there we were, free of our bondage at last. We were still prisoners, though, inside that damned ship—and condemned to death if we couldn't do something to save ourselves. We had only a limited amount of food, water and air; when they ran out, we'd all die. I was learning, slowly, to pilot the ship through space—that part was relatively simple. I could have managed to take us to one of the colonies—all the coordinates were listed in the astrogational computer—and we could have radioed to the control center to send up someone to land the ship for us. But then we'd be right back in Torres's clutches—and worse, we were all mutineers. The traditional punishments, I presumed, still applied. After a most speedy trial—if there was any trial at all, that is—we'd be taken out and shot. That wasn't exactly what we had in mind.

As we talked it out among ourselves, it soon became clear that we could never land on any world that had been settled by the Commonwealth. We would have to find an unsettled world, preferably one that was even unexplored. And we would have to find it within the next couple of weeks, before our supplies ran out. We wouldn't be able to land anywhere and replenish our stock; I knew well enough, even then, that landing the ship would be something I dared attempt only once.

I set a course as far from the nearest Commonwealth planet as I could and still stay within our fuel limitations. We ran across three star systems along our route, and we stopped to examine each. We had no equipment for long-distance sensing; I had to estimate by intuition what each world was like—and some of my decisions weren't popular with my fellows.

The first system was easy to discard. I made a rough calculation of the star's energy output and, from that, computed the band of habitability within which a planet might have comfortable enough temperatures for us to survive. There were two planets within that band, but both were small and practically airless, somewhere between Mars and Mercury in livability. Nobody wanted to stay there.

The second system we visited had two eligible planets. On the one closer to the star, I couldn't spot any signs of water; it looked like one vast desert. There may have been rivers flowing there, but I couldn't take the ship near enough for a good look without risking getting trapped in a close orbit and forced to land. The second planet just seemed too big; from the calculations I made with the help of the computer, the surface gravity would be about two gees. People can stand that for a while, but even if the atmosphere was breathable—and I had no way of analyzing it; there wasn't even so much as a spectroscope aboard—I didn't think we could last more than a year under such strenuous conditions.

I heard a lot of grumbling when I decided to pass that system by, too, and try something else. We were nearing the point of no return, and everyone was edgy. There was a big argument, but I won out and we went on.

The third system we tried was almost irresistible. The planet was the right size and had large oceans. There was an atmosphere, although I couldn't tell whether there was any oxygen; we'd have to risk that. My only worry was that it was too close to its sun, a blue-white giant. I was worried about too much radiation. I told the others so. I told them I'd seen people dying of radiation poisoning, and that it wasn't a pleasant sight. A lot of them didn't believe me, or else didn't care; they were willing to take the risk just to be free of that damned ship. The confinement and the helplessness was getting on all our nerves; it was too reminiscent of our prison experience. We had a lot of strong arguments, and some of them damn near came to blows.

I remained convinced, though, that we wouldn't be able to live very well down there, and I had the last word. They threatened to kill me a couple of times, but they knew that I was the only one who had a chance to land the ship, which I refused to do on that world. In the end, they had to go along with my decision, but I made a lot of enemies doing it. I began to get a little scared of *ever* landing the ship; the instant I did so I'd be expendable, and there were plenty of people who'd already sworn to kill me. It may have been one of the factors that botched my landing attempt when I did make it.

Our supplies were running very low, now, and we'd passed the point of no return. We couldn't reach any of the Commonwealth planets before our air gave out. We were more desperate, and tempers grew testier. Fights broke out, and there were several stabbings over purely trivial things. It was beginning to look as if we'd kill ourselves off and save Torres the trouble.

I knew the sort of place I was looking for. I remembered what I'd heard about the mutinous crew of the H.M.S. *Bounty,* and how they managed to escape. They found an island that was not on any of the official British charts of the time because of some navigational error. They figured that even if Captain Bligh survived being set adrift and sent the British fleet searching for them, the odds against their being discovered were high enough to protect them.

That was what I wanted—someplace off the charts where no one would think to look for us. That was another reason why I wasn't happy with those first three systems—they were right out in the open. At the rate the Commonwealth was expanding, scoutships would have found us within a couple of years, and the nightmare would begin all over again.

That, really, was what prompted me to fly into this dust cloud. Our astrogational computer had it marked as an unknown hazard. Normally, I would have tried flying around it, but then I realized other people would do that, too. If there was something inside there, it might be a safe place for us to settle. Admittedly, I was taking an enormous risk; if the cloud was nothing but dust and gas, I'd have used up most of our remaining fuel and air on a wild-goose chase. I didn't bother consulting the rest of the prisoners on the matter; I just went ahead and did it. I figured I was close enough to death anyway that one more gamble could scarcely matter.

For once, though, my gamble paid off. Near the center of the cloud we found this nice yellow star that looked enough like the Sun to be its twin. We could only find one planet circling it, but it looked perfect in every respect. Again, there was no way to check the composition of the atmosphere beforehand; we'd have to land and take the risk. It wasn't too bad a risk in this case; explorations had shown before that planets of the right size and within the temperate zone of their solar system, and with large bodies of water, usually had atmospheres with enough oxygen for human survival. Compared to all our other risks, that one was minimal.

I tried to bring the ship down near a seacoast, figuring that would give us the most versatile environment for survival. But the landing went bad right from the start. I was nervous to begin with, and that didn't help; I knew it was going to be a delicate process, and I knew I didn't have the training. The ship was not in perfect condition after the riot, either; I'd fixed what I could, but I knew the controls were sluggish and slow to respond. If I really tried to make a list of all the factors contributing to the crash I could probably find a dozen things or so, at least. None of them really seems important right now, though. All that matters is that we did crash. . . .

I'm going to feel awkward about this part. I'm actually talking to you, Arthur, but I know you're recording this as my record for posterity. I'll talk about you in the third person, but I'll feel awfully funny doing it. . . .

I don't remember what happened after the crash, and for a good deal of time I was unconscious or so deep in pain that I couldn't think straight. I learned later that the robots from the nearby city raced immediately to the crash site and tried to rescue us. There were several people alive then and the robots did what they could to save us, but it was an uphill fight. They weren't used to human physiology; the Makers, while externally similar, had an entirely different arrangement of their internal organs. One by one, my fellow survivors died—but with each death, the robots learned a little more about the way human beings are constructed. One of the best things about these robots is that they're quick learners; they're all tied in with a radio link to a central computer system, and they never forget a thing once they've learned it.

As it turned out, I was the last one left—and by that time they knew enough to help me. I lived—obviously—or I wouldn't be dictating this story, would I? I recovered. Arthur tells me it was nearly a month before I regained consciousness, but I did recover. The robots have been taking care of me ever since.

The most helpful one, of course, has been Arthur. I don't know what I'd have done without him. I understand he's a very advanced and, when he was built, a very expensive model. There aren't many like him around. He's capable of independent thought and action, and he took over my case—sort of a boss robot. He's unique, too, in that not all his memory is automatically channeled into the central computer. That makes him an individual.

At first we had to get by on sign language and gestures, which was a frustrating way to behave. I had no idea where I was or what was happening to me. I started teaching Arthur Worldspeak mostly out of self-defense. It was six months or more, though, before he was fluent enough to carry on a civilized conversation. . . .

I visited the crash site as soon as I was able to get around. Other than disposing of the bodies—I told the robots how humans bury their dead—the ship had been left as it was; the robots didn't want to disturb anything that might be important.

The ship had been twisted beyond all recognition. You'd have to have a good imagination to picture that battered hulk as a spaceship. I spent several days scavenging through the wreckage, picking out a few oddments here and there that weren't too badly damaged and that I thought might have some use to me. There wasn't much, though. I've got a whole world's resources to draw on, after all. I don't need *that* many things to remind me of Earth.

After I'd taken what I wanted, I had the robots bury the ship under several tons of dirt. The whole area's been relandscaped; it'll take a pretty sharp-eyed geologist to spot that one hill as anything but natural. That's the whole idea. If they come looking for me, I'm going to make it as hard as possible. . . .

ELEVEN

Michi listened to the story in total silence. She was aware that Arthur was watching her closely all the time the recording played; the robot didn't have an active role in the narration and could devote his full attention to her. Michi supposed Arthur would be looking for any signs from her that might reveal antipathy toward Birk; at the same time, he would also be looking for signs of sympathy, something to show that the story touched her and moved her to a clearer understanding of the man who'd been stranded here alone for eleven years.

He gave in and played that recording for me awfully easily, she thought. *I wonder whether he's capable of having ulterior motives.*

Michi was moved by Birk's story, but she tried not to let any of the emotion show. She didn't like other people knowing what she thought until *she* told them; it was not considered good military form to be obvious.

The story was probably true in its general outlines, although some of the details had obviously been colored by Birk's unhappy experiences. It jibed with many of the facts she herself knew about the Torres regime, although the extremes of cruelty were a little hard to swallow. If nothing else, the story explained perfectly well why Birk Aaland was so vehemently opposed to returning to the Commonwealth.

What can I do? Michi wondered. *What can I say to him? How can I reach him after he's suffered so badly? It's a wonder, after all he's been through, that he's even as sane as he is.*

Arthur ended the recording and continued looking at her. When she did not speak immediately, he said, in his own voice, "There is, of course, much more to the recording than I have played for you—many personal revelations that it would

127

not be appropriate for you to hear. I have edited the story together in its simplest, most basic form. Does this help you understand Birk any better?"

Michi nodded slowly. "Yes, very much so. Thank you for letting me hear it. I hadn't realized it was possible for one man to suffer so much. I'd like to talk to him again, to see if I can smooth over our differences. Would that be possible?"

"He has been out of touch for quite some time. He is probably in the delta. . . ."

"The what?"

"The delta, a triangular flying craft. He uses it for rapid transport around the planet. He flew off in it last night and has not returned since. There is a radio in the delta."

"Then you can call him."

"Yes, but that's not wise. I've learned that when he has one of these moods, it's best not to disturb him. He'll come out of it on his own and get back in touch with me. He'll be calmer, then, more in a mood to talk."

"Will you please let me know when he contacts you? And please tell him I'd like to talk to him again. I'd like to overcome our problems."

"I'll do what I can," Arthur said. "But I can't guarantee he'll want to talk to you."

Michi shrugged. "We're trapped here together; he'll have to talk to me again sometime."

Arthur didn't reply; he just turned slightly and glided out of the room. Michi was left alone with her thoughts once more. Settling back on her bed, she pondered the whole incredible story of Birk's experiences, and wondered just exactly what she *would* say when next she spoke with him.

Birk stayed out of contact with Beta-Nu for more than a day and a half, traveling three quarters of the way around the world. He had no particular destination in mind; anywhere was fine with him, just as long as it was away from Michi. After a while he calmed down and looked at himself more closely—and was frankly dismayed by what he saw. He'd thought he'd buried those feelings and emotions long ago, way down where they'd never bother him again. He'd thought he could discuss with Michi in a rational, emotionless manner the reasons why they couldn't return to Earth; instead, he'd found past fears and hatreds rising as though they'd never been away. There was something about this woman that rekindled the old pains—and that made her dangerous.

Partly, he supposed, it was sexual. His hopes had been so high that she would want to be his companion and helpmate, with the emphasis on "mate." He hadn't even admitted to himself how much he wanted her—and for her to reject everything he believed in, for her to call him a defeatist with a sick and disgusting lifestyle ... those were blows not merely to his pride but to his very manhood.

The most damning thing about her, though, was her military outlook. He could understand the rejection on its own terms—she obviously hadn't had time to become fully adjusted to the situation and resigned to spending the rest of her life here—but what really rankled him was the way she so casually dismissed his entire philosophy as defeatist—without knowing any of the circumstances, without knowing anything about him, without even caring how he felt.

But then, that was typical of the military mind. Those people liked simple, straightforward answers to every problem. Their concept of duty was unconcerned with morals or ethics. If Michi Nakamura's duty was to report to High Command about the invasion, then she would find some way to do that or die trying—and if it happened to ruin Birk's life, why, that was just too bad, wasn't it?

It had been the military who largely supported Torres and enabled him to do as much as he did. He appealed to their sense of discipline; he would make order out of chaos for them and make the world a safer place for the army. That was really all that ever motivated them; the arts and sciences were only useful insofar as they promoted military aims. With Torres and the army running the show, human culture was headed for certain destruction. Birk had only to look around him on this world to see the proof of that.

Still, his hopes for Michi had been so high that they had a long way to fall before being dashed. It took him hours to sort out his feelings and decide to abandon her. He had lived without a woman for the past dozen years; he had not been totally happy, but he had survived. Michi had been too thoroughly indoctrinated with the military viewpoint to ever be happy here with the way he lived. She would never see him as a lover; he was merely a tool to help her return to the Commonwealth. The thought of raping her came briefly to mind, but he discarded it. In her present condition, such an act of violence could very well kill her; and when she was more fully recovered, she would be able to fight him off. Then, too, he'd never had to resort to force before to get a woman; no matter how desperate he felt, his pride would not let him start now.

He had learned, over the long, lonely years, that there was one sure cure for disappointment. If you didn't want something, you couldn't be hurt when you didn't get it. If you didn't try, you couldn't lose. If you don't think about it, you don't have to deal with it—a simple and effective formula for living. That was how he'd survived his ordeal so far. By separating himself as much as possible from all emotions and desires, he could live from day to day without the suicidal depressions that had marked his early years here.

That formula had been upset ever since Michi's ship crashed here. Suddenly he'd been forced to think of things he'd avoided for years. He'd been forced to cope with emotions he'd deliberately suppressed all this time. He'd allowed himself a glimmer of hope that conditions might be better than they were—and that was the worst tragedy of all.

He could not blame Michi; she was only acting according to her nature, which was different from his. *He* was to blame for having violated his own unwritten laws of survival. Hope was the demon, the tempter; it pointed his eyes at the sky and let him ignore the pitfalls on the ground. Hope was a twin-sided coin with its cousin, Despair.

It took him more than a full day, but he realized that, no matter how painful it was, he had to reaffirm his old values. He and Hope were incompatible; there was no hope for him, ever. He had to cut himself off from it if he were to survive. And, since Michi set such great store by Hope, that meant he had to cut himself off from her, too. Being around her would be too painful; she was the constant reminder of a universe that was closed to him. He would have to abandon all thought of her and return to the life of peace and tranquility he'd known before she came.

After all, he reasoned, *we've got a whole planet to ourselves. We could each wander for the rest of our lives and never see one another again.*

With the decision made and settled firmly in his mind, he turned on the delta's radio and put through a call to Arthur back in Beta-Nu. He knew the robot would be waiting for some word, and sure enough Arthur acknowledged instantly.

"I won't be returning to Beta-Nu," Birk said. "It's rather obvious that Lieutenant Nakamura and I don't get along

130

very well; we'd only make each other miserable if we stayed together. I'll move on and continue my explorations elsewhere."

"Will that be fair to her, sir?" Arthur asked politely.

Birk closed his eyes, restraining the impulse to say he didn't care whether it was fair or not. She didn't care whether what she wanted was fair to *him*. "I don't propose leaving her alone and helpless. You will, of course, tell all the robots to look after her while she's recovering. And see if you can find another model like yourself and program it for Worldspeak. You can instruct it to be as helpful to her as you've been to me. Then we can leave the lieutenant's destiny in her own hands. She'll be free to do whatever she chooses with her life—and she'll have a hell of a lot better headstart at it than I did when I first came here."

Birk paused and reflected back on what he'd said. "I'd say that's eminently fair, wouldn't you?"

"Probably so, sir. By the way, the lieutenant asked to speak to you when you called in."

Birk set his jaw. "Uh, no, Arthur, I don't think so. I really don't think we have that much to say to one another."

"She's been quite insistent on it. I believe she genuinely wants to settle the differences between you."

Hope was stirring once more in the back of Birk's mind, and he ruthlessly crushed it. The problem was that he wanted her entirely too much, and that made it painful to have any dealings with her. *Stick to your resolution,* he told himself sternly. *Ignore her.* "That's impossible, I'm afraid," he said.

Arthur, like the perfect servant that he was, did not push the argument any further. "What should I tell her, then, sir?" was all he asked.

"Tell her the truth, that I just don't want to speak to her again. Tell her that she and I are two separate individuals with different needs and desires, and that I can't see any hope of reconciling them in the near future. Tell her . . . tell her I'm sorry I snarled at her, but that I have very personal reasons of my own for not wanting to go back to Earth, reasons that have nothing to do with her."

"Very good, sir."

"How long will it take you to get her all set up with a robot of her own, so that she won't need us anymore?"

"No more than two days I should think, sir. I don't know whether there are any robots of my type in Beta-Nu. If there aren't, I'll trace one down and have it flown in here.

131

The programming is simply a matter of giving the new robot access to some of my memory storage."

"Fine. Start work on that immediately. Then gather a retinue and meet me at the Firefalls. I feel like getting away from cities for a while and camping out in the middle of nature. The change will probably do me some good."

"As you wish, sir."

Birk broke off the connection and turned the delta toward a nearby city. He would need food and supplies for his impending camp-out, and he might as well pick them up now. Arthur would bring a more complete selection when he came, but that wouldn't be for several days, and Birk needed something to exist on in the meantime.

He had just landed the delta and was beginning to get out when the radio spoke to him again. "Sir?"

"Yes, Arthur?"

"I'm sorry to disturb you, but Lieutenant Nakamura is *most* insistent on speaking to you now. She demanded that I call you."

"I already said no, Arthur."

"Birk, please, listen to me." It was Michi now; Birk had been reaching to switch off the radio before she could speak, but her voice suddenly paralyzed him. "I know we have our differences, but I really think we can work them out."

Birk's mouth was dry. "You don't even know the half of it," he said coldly. "There's nothing to discuss."

"Yes there is. Arthur . . . Arthur played the tapes for me, the ones you made describing what had happened to you. Not everything, not the really personal things, but enough to let me know what you've been through."

The news came like a physical blow. "He had no right to do that," Birk said.

"Perhaps not, but I begged him. And he did it for your sake more than for mine. He knew that I couldn't begin to coexist with you rationally until I knew your background."

Birk felt his anger welling up again, directed partly at her and partly at Arthur for disobeying his instructions. "And now that you know," he said, ice hanging from each syllable, "I suppose you'll consider it your 'duty' to arrest me in the name of the Commonwealth."

Michi paused, possibly holding in her own temper at that unwarranted taunt. "Fernando Torres was assassinated five years ago, Birk. There was a countercoup. His people are no longer running things. They're out, completely out."

Birk was silent, pondering the news. It surprised him, and he didn't know why he should feel surprised. Assassinations and countercoups were standard operating procedures under dictatorships like Torres's. Nothing could last forever; even while Birk had been in prison, Torres's unpopularity had been well known. Dissatisfaction was growing. Perhaps what he *should* have been most surprised about was that Torres managed to hold on as long as he did.

"I suppose you're going to tell me," he said after a while, "that the dictatorship has been ended, and that the nations of Earth have all gone back to their own respective governments."

Michi hesitated again. "No," she answered slowly. "Earth is still ruled by a junta—the entire Commonwealth, for that matter. It would be unrealistic to allow things to return to the previous chaotic state. We need unity if our race is to face the Universe successfully."

Birk grunted. That had been one of Torres's favorite slogans.

Either Michi did not hear Birk's wordless comment or she was ignoring it, for she continued right on. "Many of Torres's policies have been discredited. Not everything; we don't hate him, not as much as you obviously do. He did some very necessary things, and now we're trying to correct some of the mistakes he made along the way."

Birk bristled a little at the thought that he might be considered merely a "mistake." It sounded to him as though the successors were carrying on the same game and trying to sweep Torres's worst cruelties under the rug. "What about political prisoners?" he asked. "What about the thousands of innocent people Torres jailed and tortured? What is this new government of yours doing about them?"

"There was an amnesty of some sort. I can't honestly remember all the details—I was just twenty years old. I was starting a serious affair with another cadet, I was about to graduate from the Academy and worried about final exams, and it didn't even concern me, so I never paid much attention to it. I know it wasn't a general amnesty—there were still some people considered too dangerous to set free. But they did let a lot of people go. As far as I can remember, the only condition was that they had to swear allegiance to the new government."

"What about me? Am I one of those people 'too dangerous to set free'?"

"I don't know what their standards are . . ."

"In other words, you're asking me to go back just on the off

133

chance they may forgive me if I promise to be a good boy and obey their every whim."

Michi's voice sounded tired, as though she'd been climbing a steep hill. "What did you want, Birk? Did you want me to reach into my pocket and pull out a scroll that says, 'Please come home, all is forgiven, love, Earth'? Did you want it signed and notarized? Or perhaps you would have been happier if I'd brought Torres's head along with me. I don't know how the government will react to you. I doubt whether *they* even know. They think you've been dead a decade or more. They probably have better things to do than sit around wondering whether to pardon a dead man."

She paused. "One thing that may interest you. We've gone back to calling it the 'Aaland engine' rather than the 'cross-field hyperprop.' Maybe that will give you some indication of the government's willingness to forgive."

There was a little glow of warmth returning to Birk's stomach. Maybe—just maybe—Earth had come to its senses after all. Maybe they were willing to acknowledge at least some of their past injustices. If they could put his name back on his invention after the thorough job of vilification Torres had done to him, then perhaps they might . . .

No! He ruthlessly suppressed that onrushing train of thought. It smacked of Hope, an emotion he had just forsworn as counterproductive to his very survival and sanity. Hope brought pain, and anger, and disappointment. Hope was the enemy and insofar as Michi Nakamura represented that Hope, she, too, was an enemy.

Birk deliberately let the clouds of his hatred build again within his soul, to scourge him of the demon Hope and wash away all traces. "You're lying," he snarled into the radio. "You have no proof for anything you say."

"If I were lying," Michi said, "I would have made much more convincing lies than that. I could have said they made your birthday into a world holiday to commemorate all of Torres's injustices. I'd have promised you parades and honors and celebrations. But I thought the best way to convince you was to be open and honest. I don't know all the answers, and I'd be lying if I said I did."

"How do I know you're telling the truth about anything? Torres could still be alive, still tossing millions of people into prison. Maybe there wasn't any coup. Maybe they didn't put my name back on the engines. Maybe you're making this whole story up just to trick me into helping you get back to Earth."

There was a long silence from the radio. "I don't know what I could say that would convince you."

"That's just it. You can't. I know this world. It's safe for me. I can live a good life here. There's no telling what might happen if I go back. Why should I give up a sure thing for your uncertain promises? Why in the world should I listen to a word you have to say?"

When there was no immediate answer, Birk switched off the radio in disgust and walked away from the delta in search of some robots to help him prepare for his camp-out.

TWELVE

Michi tried calling him back several times during the next three days, but Birk made a point of not answering. He didn't even respond to Arthur's calls, fearing that the woman might try to reach him through the robot as she'd done before. Ignoring the robot was also a form of revenge for what Birk considered a massive betrayal on Arthur's part. *He never should have played those tapes for her,* he thought. *Those were private and personal. He had no right to share them.* What irked him the most was that Michi had been allowed a glimpse into his soul, while he had no corresponding insight into her own motivations.

He refused to let the fire of his rage burn out, deliberately stoking it with the anger he felt at the robot's betrayal. Hope was a tough beast to kill; even the small glimmering Michi had handed him with her news of conditions on Earth needed a strong weapon to destroy it. Anger would be his sword, and rage would be his fortress.

As he'd told Arthur, he gathered together a small band of robots and set up a camp near the Firefalls. He always used to enjoy camping out on this planet, with just the flickering of a campfire at night to chase away the darkness. He told himself he'd been living in the cities too long, and that this excursion into nature would give welcome relief to his troubled spirit. But it was not so. He was just as overstrung here as he'd been back in Beta-Nu—perhaps even more so. The tranquil surroundings took just enough edge off his hostility that faint rays of Hope were able to shine through, ruining his sleep with undefinable dreams. To make matters worse, his mind was increasingly bombarded by erotic images of Michi Nakamura, and no amount of willpower could stop the fantasies his brain persisted in creating.

Without question, the woman's arrival was a major disturbance in his orderly existence, like a rock dropped into a placid pond. There were ripples spreading out from the center of the disturbance and bouncing back against themselves as they rebounded from the shore. It would take quite a while for the effects of the splash to die out completely—if, indeed, they ever would.

On the third day, Arthur arrived at the camp with a more complete store of provisions and a comfortable tent. To Birk's great annoyance, Michi followed Arthur down in a delta of her own. With her was a robot similar to Arthur in construction—a robot, Birk learned later, that Michi had named Kagami.

"Why did you bring her along?" Birk demanded of Arthur as soon as the robot emerged from the craft.

"I didn't bring her, sir," Arthur replied calmly. "I provided her with a robot similar to myself, as you requested. They chose to follow me. There was nothing I could do to stop them, short of destroying their delta—which I didn't think you would approve of."

"Right now, I'm not so sure about that." Birk stalked angrily over to the second craft, where Michi was just stepping out. "Why did you come here?" he yelled.

Michi had made remarkable progress in the past few days. She was dressed in a simple blouse, skirt, and boots, with a wide sash tied around her midsection to bind her wound. She looked healthier and stronger than Birk had expected possible, and she did not shrink from his verbal attack. She held her ground and looked him straight in the face. "I wanted to see you again. We still have some things to talk about."

Birk shook his head. "There's nothing to talk about. Not as far as I'm concerned. So you can get back in your delta and go somewhere else."

"I don't take orders from you."

"Why not? Because I don't have the proper insignia on my shoulders?"

Her reaction was instinctive: she reached out and slapped him. The slap was not hard because she was standing a bit too far away and tried at the last moment to stop the blow altogether. But neither of them had expected her to do that, and for an instant they both stood there stunned.

Finally Birk took a step backward. He made no move to apologize for his remark, but his tone was more level as he said, "It's obvious we weren't fated to get along. Why prolong our mutual antagonism? Two people should be able to share an entire planet without too much discomfort. Just leave me alone and I'll leave you alone."

Michi shook her head. "I can't accept that. On the radio the other day you as much as called me a liar, and I won't live with that charge hanging over me. I was raised with a strict code of honor, and you've challenged me. I have to prove myself."

"How can you? There's no way you can possibly prove you're telling the truth."

"You could return to Earth with me and see for yourself."

"Sure, and I could chop off my head to prove there's no life after death. Some theories are too risky to test."

"Then you could get to know me," Michi insisted. "Spend some time with me; find out who I am and what I'm like. Once you know me, you'll know I can be trusted. I know what hells you've been through; I wouldn't lie to you about this. But you can't trust me if you force me to remain a stranger."

Birk felt it again, that damnable spark of hope rising within his chest. He looked at the petite young woman and felt the flow of desire once more. From her face, he could see she hadn't meant to imply anything sexual by her offer, but his body was choosing—independent of his will—to interpret her remarks quite differently. He wanted, needed, her companionship—the warmth and closeness of her delicate, feminine body. Her very proximity now was melting the resolve he'd worked so hard to achieve. Maybe if she got to know him better as well, she might . . .

But trust led to Hope, and he could afford neither. He reminded himself of the pain she'd already brought him, and of the inexhaustible well of it she could tap if he allowed her inside his defenses. The conflict in his feelings was tying his tongue in knots and he stood transfixed and silent.

She was studying his face closely, reading him for any sign

137

of weakness. "I need you, Birk, I'll admit that. I can't accomplish anything constructive without you—I don't have your specialized knowledge. I think we'd make a good team. Together we could . . . My Lord, what's that?"

In spite of himself, in spite of the tension of the moment, Birk had to smile. Michi had caught sight of the Firefalls for the first time, and her look of awe at the startling phenomenon was an expression of pure beauty.

Birk was camped in a small clearing surrounded by hilly forest. Several hundred meters to the northeast, a cliff face towered high and sheer, more than a kilometer above their heads. A waterfall cascaded over this cliff and down into a river that wandered through the forest. This waterfall was impressive enough under ordinary circumstances—a sheet of white roaring over the stony face of the cliff, making it necessary to raise one's voice just to be heard. Michi had probably noticed the falls when she arrived, without having the time to admire their true beauty.

But now the entire nature of the falls had changed abruptly. The water was suddenly sparkling with light, a glowing rainbow glittering like liquid flame in the late afternoon sunshine.

"That's the Firefalls," Birk explained, his voice more gentle. There was a degree of pride and superiority in his tone. "One of the more spectacular natural wonders this world has to offer."

"But . . . but how does it do that?"

"Near the top of the falls there's a fissure that goes down to a large reservoir of oil so that there's a continual trickle of oil infusing the water. The cliff face itself is mostly crystalline quartz, reflecting sunlight onto the slightly oily water. When the sun reaches a certain angle in late afternoon, its light bounces off the crystals and the oil film to provide that effect. Depending on the season, it can glitter like that for up to half an hour a day."

Michi could not take her eyes off the spectacle. "It's breathtaking."

"Yes, it's one of my favorite sights. You see, this world isn't such a bad place to live."

His remark brought the woman's attention back to the point. Turning to face him again, she resumed their argument. "I never said it was. Please don't put words in my mouth. For all I know, this could be the nicest planet in the Universe. But my duty at the moment lies elsewhere."

138

"Duty." Birk snorted and turned away.

"Yes. Some people do have a commitment to something other than their own skins. You thought you had a duty at one time too, didn't you? You had a duty to speak out against what you saw as oppression."

"And look at all it got me."

"Does that make all duty bad?"

Birk did not answer, but his body stiffened. After a moment, Michi softened her tone as she continued, "Please, Birk, all I'm asking is a chance to prove myself to you. What's so horrible about that?"

How can I tell her? he wondered. *How can I explain that she represents everything I've exorcised from my life in order to stay alive?* He was willing to concede that she didn't mean to hurt him, but she *was* hurting him by her very presence. Maybe when she'd been here as long as he had, she'd understand how much pain misplaced hope could bring, but until then there was no way to communicate the depths of despair she could plunge him into.

"You simply cannot understand," he said and then, before she could reply, he walked rapidly into the woods away from the camp. Talking with her always brought him discomfort; he had to escape before the pressures built beyond the safety point.

Michi followed a few steps after him, reaching the edge of the clearing before stopping. She watched him disappear into the forest, then hesitated and did not follow him farther. He soon lost sight of her as he tramped angrily through the brush.

Birk did not return to camp until he saw Michi's delta rise above the trees and head back toward Beta-Nu.

He had originally planned to camp beside the Firefalls for a few weeks, but after Michi's visit the place did not seem the same. The mood of tranquility had been spoiled; her presence haunted the clearing and the woods like a sorrowful ghost. After a night of total sleeplessness, Birk ordered Arthur and the robots to break camp and move elsewhere. At random he chose a lonely stretch of beach as his next place of refuge.

Without a moon, the seas of this world had no respectable tides. The shore was placid and calm, more like the edge of a lake than of a major ocean. It was a little late in the season to be visiting this particular beach, as a brisk wind blew in off the ocean and chilled Birk down to his bones; but he put up with the discomfort to achieve the serenity that had fled his life in the past weeks.

He had four hours of solitude before that peace was shattered by the arrival of a delta. Michi had found him once more.

There was no place to hide this time; the countryside was level for kilometers around, with open grassland struggling to within a few dozen meters of the pebbly shore. Birk had been sitting on a large rock gazing over the expanse of ocean when he spotted the craft descending. He rose with disgust and, at a pace little short of a run, began walking away from the landing site paralleling the ocean. Behind him, the delta landed and Michi climbed out. With her shorter legs, she had to run to catch up with him.

He did nothing to make it easier for her, maintaining his harsh pace. She finally reached him, though, and walked beside him in silence for several minutes. When it became obvious he was not going to speak, she took the initiative. "You can't hide from me forever, you know," she said.

Birk only smiled, thinking about Alpha-Xi, his ultimate refuge. Even she wouldn't be able to follow him there if he made the decision to hide away permanently.

When he failed to answer, she continued doggedly, "I'm not some monster trying to kill you. I just don't think it's fair for you to make the decision unilaterally to strand us both here forever. Don't you think I should have some say in the matter?"

Birk stopped and turned abruptly to face her. "I tried to tell you before, but you wouldn't listen. *Neither* of us has any say in the matter. There isn't any way for us to get off this planet. That's one of the harsh facts of life here. When you adjust to that, maybe we can talk some more." He started walking along the shore again.

The woman again had to hurry to catch up. "I have to try, don't you see? I can't live without hope."

And I can't live with it, Birk thought, but said nothing aloud.

"Even if we ourselves can't leave," Michi went on, "you have enough technical knowledge to build robot-controlled rockets. Kagami tells me the automated factories here could produce thousands of them if you gave them the basic design. We could send them out in all directions with an SOS. Someone would be bound to find them and rescue us."

"And then what happens? Do I get sent back to prison? You

140

admitted you can't promise I won't be jailed the second I set foot on Earth."

"You're in prison now," Michi said firmly. "This is worse than solitary confinement. You can move from cell to cell, but that's the limit of your freedom. You don't have any guards, but you torture yourself quite well without them. There aren't any walls, but you've built enough barriers around your soul to hold you in. If you think you're free here, you're only fooling yourself."

"I like it here," Birk said. "It's quiet. It's peaceful. It suits me." But his words sounded hollow, even to him.

Michi switched to another tack. "Wonderful. You're fine and cozy in your little backwater. But what about the rest of the human race? They need to be warned about the invasion threat. Can you just sit by and let perhaps millions of innocent people die, all because you want to stay comfortable?"

"Where were all those millions of people when *I* needed help? They were perfectly willing to stay in their comfortable niches and not lift a finger for me. Okay, now I'll return the compliment. When you stand up for other people, you only become a target yourself. I did that once, but I won't be fooled again."

"I'm sorry," Michi said, so quietly it was almost a whisper.

"What?"

"I said, I'm sorry. I guess I misunderstood your character. The story you recorded for Arthur led me to think you were a sensitive man who cared about something other than himself. But you don't, do you? Not anymore. Now there's just Birk Aaland and whatever keeps him going."

"You make it sound so simple, don't you? Simple answers for simple minds. If I'm not all white, then it stands to reason I'm all black. That's typical of your kind; everything has to be sorted out by stereotype and catalogued into its neat little pigeonhole."

"You keep referring to my 'type.' I'd love to know what my 'type' is—if you even know what you're talking about."

"Sure I do. It's the military mentality. You follow your orders; you do your precious duty. People lose their individuality; they become simply units to be pushed around on your chessboard. Anything that doesn't lie along the straight path between you and your duty is an obstacle to be overcome any way you can. I've seen enough of the military to know that. Right now, I'm your obstacle, and you'll keep pushing at me until you wear me down and convince me to go along with

141

you. You can't let me exist independent of you because it spoils the order and symmetry of your universe."

Michi stopped and Birk kept striding forward. He expected her to come running after him again, but after a few moments, when she didn't come, he turned around to see what had happened.

Michi had sat down crosslegged on the pebbly ground and bowed her head. Birk couldn't see her eyes, but he could tell from the way her body was shaking that she was crying.

This was something he had not expected, and for a minute he stood frozen, not sure what to do. If she had yelled back at him or walked away indignantly or slapped him again, he would have known how to behave, and he would have felt justified in his original vehement outburst. But tears were something he didn't know how to handle.

Slowly, as though in a trance, he walked back up the beach to stand beside her. He didn't say a word, but she couldn't help but be aware of his presence. She made no effort to stop the flow of tears; eventually, though, she did look up straight into his eyes.

"Is that what I am?" she asked. "Just a uniform that walks and talks and makes impossible demands of you? Are you denying me even the simplest shred of humanity? I happen to be a real, live person, Birk. I'm twenty-five years old. I have a mother, a father, two brothers, and two sisters. I had birthday parties when I grew up, with chocolate cakes; I always insisted on chocolate cakes. I went to school and I made some friends. I got into a fight once over a pencil box. I took dancing lessons, and had a mad crush on my geometry teacher. I started going out with boys when I was sixteen and had my first affair when I was twenty. I have a pet dog and a talking kavalla bird, and my favorite color is red.

"I didn't join the army to become a robot. I come from a military family, but I joined personally because I think our future lies in the stars. By serving an extended hitch, I get a choice of colony positions when I get out. I wanted to build a family on some world that's not as tired as Earth.

"But none of that matters, does it? I'm just Lieutenant Nakamura, cog in the impersonal military machine you see as your enemy. I have no feelings except to fulfill my mission and maybe get a medal and a promotion. Least of all, I have no feelings for other people. They're just dust to grind under my feet as I march in formation. Isn't that right?"

"I . . ."

"And you have the nerve to accuse me of stereotyping you! Tell me, is it easier to hate me if you pretend I'm not real?"

Birk was dazed, not knowing how to respond to this unexpected barrage. And yet some response was expected of him; he had to say something to fill the painful silence following Michi's speech. "I . . . I don't hate you. I just hate what you're trying to do."

Michi wiped the tears from her cheeks with the back of her right hand. "I'm just trying to be myself, so it amounts to the same thing, doesn't it?"

"If you would only learn to accept things here. . . ."

The woman was now in control of herself again, sniffling back the last traces of her upset. "I can't. This planet is death—you can feel it all around you. What I want to do would bring you back to the world of the living, pry you out of your nice, shiny coffin. That's why you're fighting. Being dead is much more comfortable. I remind you too much of life, so you have to drive me away."

Birk closed his eyes and shook his head slowly from side to side. "You don't understand at all. You have no idea what eleven years alone here can do. You can only beat your head against a stone wall for so long. You have to make compromises with reality or it'll end up crushing you. You break or you bend. I nearly broke—several times—but I learned to bend to the conditions here. Otherwise, the oppression is so massive. . . ." His voice and his attention drifted off.

"You're right," Michi answered, more softly. "I have no idea what eleven years here can do to a person's mind. And frankly, I'd rather not learn. That's why I want to get out of here, before I'm forced to change, before I . . ."

She stopped abruptly. She'd been about to say, "Before I become as warped as you," but she realized how damaging that would be to her cause. It would only give Birk an excuse to lapse into one of his angry outbursts again and avoid the central issue entirely. Her own display of emotion had softened him up; now that she had gotten him this far, she didn't want to slip back.

So instead, she said, "Birk, I need you. I can't put it more simply than that. You're still serving your sentence, in exile rather than in a prison, but what about me? Forget about Earth for the time being. Forget about dictatorships and injustice and military bureaucracies. What about me as a thinking, breathing human being? Aren't I a person, too? Aren't I entitled to some consideration? Can't you, just

143

once, think of the welfare of someone other than Birk Aaland?"

She took a step forward, reached out and took his hand before he could pull away. "Please, Birk. I'm a proud woman, and begging is hard for me, but I'm begging now. Help me. I think you'll find you're helping yourself at the same time."

From the moment she touched his hand, Birk stood frozen. The feel of her skin against his, even in so innocuous a context, caused an unconscious stirring deep within him. Masculine needs and desires were rumbling awake after a long hibernation through the winter of loneliness, and they made Birk distinctly uncomfortable. He had survived by keeping them, like Hope, dormant in his soul. But nothing had been the same since Michi's ship crashed, and these feelings foreboded even more significant changes in his orderly life.

He wavered in his resolve. A long-buried part of himself was struggling to resurface, but it had to make its way through more than a decade of both deliberate and unconscious interment. In the end, the years of dampening proved too strong a force, and the renascent soul slipped back into its pit of darkness.

She was doing it to him again, he realized. She was trying to bring him pain disguised in the cloak of pity and hope. Eleven years of denying his needs had set him more strongly in his ways. Temptation must be resisted, or the penalty—when it came, as he knew it would—would be enormous.

He pulled his hand away and stepped back two paces. He glowered at the woman who looked back at him, puzzled. "No," he said. "You think you can trick me into going back. I can't. I won't; not ever. I won't be hurt again. Even if you are telling the truth, I have no place back there. Earth and I have gone our separate ways, divorced just like me and Reva. I'm fine here if you'll just leave me alone."

His whole body was trembling now with a mixture of emotions so confused he could not have labeled them. "Leave me alone! Leave me alone!" He sank to his knees, not even noticing the pain as the pebbly ground cut at his skin. He bowed his head and squeezed his eyes tightly shut to hold in the tears. At the same time, he held his hands to his ears to shut out any further arguments this seductress might use to sway him from his purpose.

He wasn't sure how long he knelt there on the beach. His eyes were dry, but the corners stung as though wanting to

144

cry. He opened them slowly and looked around. Michi was gone. The only trace of her was the receding shape of her delta flying back to Beta-Nu. Birk stared into the glare of the sky until the delta had completely vanished from view. Then, slowly, he rose to his feet once more and trekked back to Arthur waiting at the camp.

Michi's mind was in no less a turmoil than Birk's. Despite her best arguments, despite her patience with the man—patience that had seriously cracked only once—despite all the powers of reason she could muster, he still refused to help her. Admittedly he was afraid, and she could understand the basis of his fear; but refusing to let her even try to convince him of his safety was something she didn't know how to fight.

"He looks rational enough on the surface," she mused aloud as she paced through the tower that had been Birk's residence, and which was now hers alone. "But eleven years here has affected his mind. He's not quite sane. That's the only explanation for his hysterical overreactions. And how do I deal with a lunatic?"

She stopped her pacing and looked at Kagami, who stood obediently silent in one corner of the room. "The trouble is, I'm walking uphill against the wind, and it's damned tiring. He's got inertia in his favor. He doesn't have to do anything to defeat me, but I have to make him actively cooperate if I want to get what I want. A stalemate's as good as a loss. He must know that. He figures he has time on his side, that he can wear me down to a walking corpse, as soulless as he is." She gave a humorless laugh. "He's probably right. Eleven years . . ."

She fell silent for a moment, then turned to her robot. "What makes him tick, Kagami? How can I reach him?"

"Arthur only gave me a limited amount of programming," the robot said. "I know your language, your customs, and your bodily needs. He gave me no information about the man Birk Aaland, nor is that portion of Arthur's memory stored in the central computer. I have no insight into Birk's mind."

The word "insight" caused Michi to think of her maternal grandfather. The old man had been the last in her family to follow Buddhism and the old ways. He died when she was twelve, but she could still remember vividly how he used to meditate crosslegged on the ground out by their pond, searching for what he called insight. He had talked to her often, speaking in those strange parables and paradoxes the Buddhists loved so much. She wondered what Grandfather would make of the strange man she had to deal with, and whether Birk would have tried even that old man's seemingly endless patience.

As the day wore on into night and Kagami brought her the evening meal, Michi found she could not get her grandfather's image out of her mind. She tried harder to remember the things he'd said. "When a tree bends in the wind," he'd told her, "does the wind triumph because it humbled the tree, or does the tree triumph because it survived the wind's attempt to uproot it?"

The ten-year-old Michi had thought for a moment and replied, "They each won, because they each got what they thought they wanted."

"Then if both can triumph, is not triumph itself a product of the mind? And if that is so, is triumph not illusory?" And, having thus concluded, he refused to speak further on the topic.

Michi pondered her grandfather's words as she lay sleepless in bed for several hours that night, and his conclusion was first in her thoughts when she awoke the next morning.

"Kagami," she said when the robot came to bring her breakfast, "put in a call to Arthur and ask him to relay a message to Birk for me. I don't think he'll refuse to listen, it's just a two-word message: 'You win.'"

THIRTEEN

"What kind of trick is this?" Birk's voice was hostile and suspicious when he called back ten minutes later.

Michi was right in the middle of her breakfast. She put down her fork and quickly finished the bite of food in her mouth as she turned to face Kagami's radio speaker. "No trick, Birk. I mean it."

"But *what* do you mean?"

"Please, let's stop these word games. You know what I mean, or you wouldn't have called back."

Birk was silent for a minute. He quite obviously did not believe her and was weighing each word and inflection for hidden betrayal. Finally, "What caused this sudden turnabout? Yesterday you were so absolutely against staying here. You called it a prison, a coffin. You didn't want to desert all those millions of innocent people of Earth. Now you want me to think you've changed overnight, abandoned everything you believed in. I find that a little hard to swallow."

Michi did not even try to hide the weariness in her voice. "I'm tired. It's as simple as that. I've come back from the point of death, but I'm still healing. Everything I do is a pain, everything wears me down. My system is fighting just to keep me alive; I can't fight you, too. I need rest and peace and tranquility, and I'll never get them as long as we keep sniping at each other."

More silence from the other end as Birk considered her words. Michi let him have all the time he needed. "And there won't be any more talk about building ships to send out messages? No more wild ideas about contacting the Commonwealth?"

She sighed. "No, I haven't got the strength. It's a struggle you had to win, because I needed your active cooperation and you didn't need mine. As you said yesterday, you can only keep banging your head against a stone wall for so long. I have to bend before I break." She paused. "Maybe if I weren't still so weak, if I had my full strength, I could have held out longer against you, even persuaded you. But not in my condition now. I simply can't."

"And what happens six months from now, when you are back to your full strength? Do we start fighting all over again?"

Michi shrugged, even though Birk could not see the gesture. "I don't know. I haven't thought that far ahead. I don't *want* to think that far ahead. Maybe by then you'll have convinced me that this planet is the paradise you claim it is. Maybe I'll see for myself how hopeless escape is. By that time, anyway, I doubt the Commonwealth will need my warning; there'll probably be a full-scale war going on."

Birk was silent again at the other end. "It's got to be some kind of a trick," he mused, half to himself.

"Fine. It's a trick. Believe what you want—you would, anyway—but I just thought you'd like to know how I felt."

Michi gestured, and Kagami broke the connection. Let *Birk* stew for a while.

Birk called back just a few minutes later, before Michi had finished her breakfast. "How do I know you're not lying?"

"If that's all you called about, forget it. I told you, I'm tired of playing that game. No one says you have to trust me. Like you said, you can go your way and I can go mine, and we never have to see each other again if that's the way you want it. I just thought your masculine vanity might like to know you beat me." She once again instructed Kagami to sever the connection, and continued eating her breakfast.

When Birk called the third time she was tempted not to answer it, but then decided not to press her luck too far. "What is it now?" she asked when communication was re-established. "Have you found a new way to impugn my integrity?"

"I . . . I think we should talk some more."

"About what? You've already made your point that I'm a petty, deceitful automaton serving only the whims of my military masters, and that you want nothing more to do with me. What else is there to say?"

"You're determined to make it hard for me, aren't you?"

Damned right I am, Michi thought, but said nothing aloud.

"All right, I didn't mean all those things I said. I . . . I'm sorry if I hurt your feelings. But you hurt mine, too, and I was just striking back. You know why I can't go back to Earth, and you had no right to insist once I said no. The fight was as much your fault as mine."

Michi kept her silence.

"So—did you want to talk?"

"I thought that's what we were doing."

"I mean in person, face-to-face."

"The last time I did that, you insulted me and told me to leave you alone." She found it enjoyable making *him* sweat for a change.

"Things are different now. Since you've changed your mind, there's no reason we can't work together. Why don't you come back here and I'll . . ."

"No," she said emphatically. "You come back here. There's more to explore in the city, and that's my specialty after all. As long as I'm stuck here, I might as well learn something about my new home." She had Kagami break off, and refused to answer any further calls.

*   *   *

148

Birk caught up to her several hours later while she was roaming at random through Beta-Nu. She had tried to push all thoughts of Earth and duty from her mind, and certainly there were enough wonders here to occupy her attentions. She'd seen little enough of this planet since she arrived—just the tower and what she could see from its windows, plus her two long, exhausting trips to argue with Birk at the Firefalls and the beach.

There were plenty of details to capture her eye: the bustle of the small gray maintenance robots, tidying the streets and repairing the city; the towering buildings with their bright, cheerful colors; the patterned mosaics of the broad walkways; the strange diamond pattern of the street plan. She walked through Beta-Nu gawking like an unabashed tourist. She'd seen big cities before—she grew up near Tokyo, and bigger than that it was impossible to get—so the sheer size of this one did not awe her. At first she found it difficult to put her finger on what made this place so incredible; it took more than an hour before the explanation came to her.

It was the silence. There was no traffic—nor had there ever been—since all vehicles traveled through underground tubeways here. There were no people. There were no radios, no loudspeakers, no street vendors hawking their wares. There was no one here besides herself. The maintenance robots made little noise, just the faint movement of their feet along the sidewalk—a sound multiplied thousands of times, but still barely audible. There were birds and insects making their minute clicks and cries, lending just enough familiarity to make the scene that much eerier. But there were none of the busy sounds of life that Michi associated with cities. Beta-Nu was as dead as a graveyard, with skyscrapers as headstones.

Michi shivered. She did not belong here. No individual person did. A city was a place for the masses, and even she and Birk together would echo hollowly through these canyons of emptiness. She knew she could never withstand a decade of this solitude.

After a while she saw Birk's delta fly overhead to land on top of the tower where they lived, and half an hour later she could hear him walking toward her through the deserted streets. She would actually be relieved to have his company, but she could hardly afford to let him know that yet. She carefully composed her expression of disregard.

Birk came to within a couple meters of her and stopped.

149

"Hello," he said awkwardly when she failed to acknowledge him.

She looked up, as though noticing him for the first time. "Hello. I see you made it."

"You said you wanted to learn about this planet, so I came to help. What did you want to know?"

There were millions of things, but Michi took the most obvious one first. "What happened here? Where did the people—the Makers—go? Why were their cities left so intact?"

In a sense, she was cheating—she already knew the answers to those questions. They were the first things she had asked Kagami after her personal robot had been activated. But she was dealing with Birk now, and that called for special handling. She had already seen how much more at ease he was when talking about this world and its many facets; if anything could break down the tension between them, it would be asking him to explain the mysteries around them.

Sure enough, she could see Birk's posture change in a matter of seconds. He had been tense, braced for any possible confrontation, but now he began to relax. He even smiled as he said, "Yes, I'd been waiting for you to ask that. It's the natural question. The answer's pretty simple, too, in a horrifying sort of way." He thought for a moment, and his smile broadened. "Come on," he said, nodding in one direction to indicate the way they should go.

"Where are you taking me?"

"Instead of just telling you about it, it might be instructive to let you see part of the reason for yourself."

He did not enlighten her further, and she had little choice but to follow him. This was his territory and his game, and she had tacitly agreed to play by his rules for the time being.

Neither of them spoke as Birk led Michi down into one of the underground tubeways and they walked through the dimly lit vehicle tunnels beneath the streets to their destination. They surfaced again before a large, squared-off building with thick stone walls. Without hesitation, Birk walked up to the massive bronze doors, which swung open automatically to admit him and Michi.

Michi was prepared for the musty smell of a long-disused room, but the maintenance robots had been effective here, too; the interior of the building was spotlessly free of dust. The pair walked down a long, lighted corridor with offices on either side until they came to a series of larger rooms. Shelves lined the walls and were arranged in long rows for the length of the rooms. The shelves were covered mostly with boxes, though a few special nooks cradled unusual-looking pieces of machinery. Michi began to wonder at the point Birk was making.

"What is this place?" she asked.

Birk merely smiled and continued on his way through the maze of storerooms. More and more boxes, thousands upon thousands, were crammed in here, and the building seemed to go on forever. The crates were of different shapes and sizes, and some were so big that Michi could have stood erect and walked around inside them. She was beginning to feel a little annoyed as she tagged after Birk through room after identical room.

Finally they came to a bigger chamber, a vast auditorium like a spaceship hangar. Crowded around the floor were vehicles that, while built to an alien design, Michi could not help but identify: tanks.

"This," Birk said with pompous finality, "is Beta-Nu's major arsenal. There are, Arthur tells me, six others scattered about the city, although I've only visited three of them myself. The others aren't quite this big, maybe only three-quarters this size. And you haven't seen all of this one yet; there are subsurface levels as well, where some of the really big pieces are stored."

In spite of herself, Michi was impressed. She'd been in weapons storehouses before, but never in anything nearly this size—nor this well stocked. And Birk said there were six more in this city, almost as large.

"Was Beta-Nu a military capital?" she asked.

"Hardly. Beta-Nu was one of the smaller cities of little strategic importance. It was known primarily as an artist's haven, not as some powerhouse of military might."

"But all those weapons . . ." Michi's mind boggled at the size of the army that would need so much equipment.

"You have to look at their basic situation," Birk began to lecture. "Here they are, stuck in a solar system without any other planets, without even a moon. The only object in their sky is the sun during the daytime; nights are completely black. This didn't bother them too much at first. They evolved as day creatures and eventually discovered fire, lanterns, and candles to help them at night. Their civilization rose steadily, much as ours did. The only difference seems to be that they had very few large empires; for the most part, their people remained in autonomous city-states scattered over the

151

globe. The concept of a nation never was born; tribalism was the ruling allegiance.

"Their technology grew better and better, able to sustain more and more people—again, just as ours did. Finally they had a world packed with people, bursting at the seams, depleting its resources, polluting its environment—just like we had in the . . . what, the twenty-first century? I think that was about when . . . oh, it doesn't matter. The point is, we had somewhere else to go—up and out. We could look at the sky and see other planets, other stars. No matter how bad things became on Earth, there were always those few who managed to leave and go elsewhere—first to the Moon, then the space colonies, then Mars and the asteroids, and finally other solar systems.

"The Makers didn't have that option. The sky held nothing for them, literally. For all they knew, they were the only world in the Universe. They couldn't even conceive of living beyond their atmosphere. Even if one of their geniuses had thought of space colonies, the materials to build just one would have bankrupted them. We were able to mine the Moon and the asteroids; they would have had to cannibalize their own planet. No one city-state could have afforded such a venture, and no league of city-states could have held together long enough because of old hatreds and mutual mistrust. For better or worse, they were stuck on this one world.

"So there they were—with accelerating technology, growing population, and diminishing resources. If you remember your history, there was a man named Malthus who theorized about such conditions. He saw several possible options. . . ."

"War," Michi muttered under her breath.

Birk nodded. "War, plague, and famine were the big three, and of those only war is remotely controllable. There'd always been wars, of course; the city-states squabbled with their neighbors over all sorts of things. But as the situation grew more desperate, the wars grew more fierce. The only way the Makers could keep their culture stable and provide enough food and comforts for their people was to kill off excess population during the wars."

"But Beta-Nu looks untouched," Michi said. "If the Makers completely annihilated themselves through war, there should be nothing here but rubble. Was this city one of the lucky ones to be spared, or did the robots rebuild the whole place afterward?"

"No to both questions. When they realized what was happening on their world, the leaders of the various cities held a conference and actually laid down the rules for war. It was all very civilized, in a gruesome sort of way. They agreed that the wanton killing had to be continued, but that there should be some order to it. Cities were supposed to be sanctuaries, safe from enemy attack. All the battles were to take place out in the countryside, army against army with no civilians involved. The whole process, in theory, became as abstract and formalized as chess—which is only a war surrogate itself. The Makers thought they'd set up a steady-state system that would last forever. And if they'd kept to it, it very well might have. With so many cities involved in the free-for-all, alliances seldom lasted very long, and no one side could ever gain a clear-cut victory and obliterate another."

"From the way you said that, though, I suppose they didn't keep to the agreement."

"Of course not. How can anyone keep war within civilized limits? In order to get people to fight well, you have to inflame their emotions, get them really mad at the enemy. When people are in that state, they don't think rationally, they don't always obey the rules. The military mind thinks first in terms of victory; morals are at best a secondary consideration.

"There were always small violations on either side of a conflict, usually ignored by both parties. There were still plenty of legal ways to humble your enemy without bombing his city—like cutting off his trade routes or burning all his crops and starving him into submission. But with each war, hatred grew a little more strong and people were more determined to punish their enemies. A few cities actually were destroyed despite the rules—I've been to the ruins. Usually that was a crime so heinous that the victor's neighbors banded together against it and destroyed *it* as well. But it started happening more and more frequently.

"Then one of the city-states came up with the bright idea of trying biological warfare. That was explicitly against the rules, but this city had been beaten many times by a number of different enemies. Its people were bitter and resentful. The leaders had their scientists design a bacterium that would be fast breeding, hardy, and extremely lethal. From what I'm told, victims died within a day or two of contracting the disease, and it was so specific that it only affected people, none of the lower animals.

"They tried the disease on their enemies, and it was a

153

spectacular success. Within a couple of weeks, three whole cities were decimated. The disease's inventors had stored up a large supply of vaccine for themselves, so they sat back and triumphantly watched the results of their work.

"But their scientists did the job entirely too well. They had developed the bacteria with a rapid reproductive rate, but in this case that also meant a high mutation rate. Within a month, the bacteria had mutated into a strain that was immune to the vaccine—and then the plague really rolled into high gear.

"The developers didn't want to admit they'd violated the rules so badly, and by the time the rest of the world caught on, the disease was totally out of hand. It moved faster than it could be quarantined, and it mutated faster than any new vaccine could be developed. Pretty soon there were six or seven different strains of the same disease all over the world. Even those people who might have natural immunity to several of the types couldn't fight them all off. The Black Plague in Europe during the Middle Ages killed off, I think, roughly half the population and that was considered pretty horrible—and it was a piker compared to this one.

"Within a year it was all over. Ninety-five percent of the population was dead within three months. The rest lingered on awhile, but nothing much came of them. The cities were already fully automated, and the robots could support them in grand comfort, but their will was gone. Arthur couldn't tell me for certain, but I'm willing to bet most of the survivors killed themselves rather than live with the shock of all the devastation around them. It must have been a dreadful ordeal, and I'm not sure *I'd* want to live after watching everyone around me die that way. At any rate, one year after the plague began, the robots couldn't find a trace of any of the Makers left on this world.

"The robots have been runnings things ever since. They keep the cities clean and free of dust, weeds, and vermin because that was what they were ordered to do. They keep the buildings, themselves, and the solar-power stations in good repair; they farm the land and breed livestock—at least enough to raise food for me—and they even mine and process the fuel to keep their nuclear plants going. For most of them, I guess, that's reason enough for existence. They do their jobs and think of nothing else. All the corpses were burned or buried two thousand years ago—and when the Makers died,

154

so did the disease. Either that or it has no effect on humans because I've seen no trace of it during my stay here."

Birk paused and looked straight at Michi. "Do you see now why I'm so bitter about the military? It's not just the fact that I was unjustly imprisoned, although God knows that's reason enough. But this is a dead world, and it was the military that killed it. Billions of good people, with as much right to live as you or I—an entire species doomed to extinction because their military power got out of hand. It's a cosmic tragedy, and I hate to think of it happening again."

Michi could see tears in Birk's eyes. She realized, for the first time, that the man was closer to the long-dead inhabitants of this world than he was to the still-living ones of his own.

FOURTEEN

Although Birk's comments about the military were an indirect slur against her, Michi held her tongue admirably and did not answer his charges at once. Instead, she chose to ask technical questions about the Makers' weapons and their effects, then asked Birk to demonstrate some of them. He looked for a moment as though he might comment on her interest in weaponry, but he, too, seemed bent on showing restraint. Both people knew how crucial this new relationship of theirs was, and neither wanted to jeopardize it with rash remarks.

Before Birk demonstrated the weapons, Arthur brought them a late lunch on a small mechanized cart. The two people ate sitting outside the arsenal on the patterned walkway, with Birk once again lecturing cheerfully on the origins of the food they were served. Both stayed strictly on neutral topics, and survived the meal with no fresh stab wounds on either side.

Arthur departed after lunch, leaving the pair alone once

more. Birk began looking uncomfortable in her presence, so Michi reminded him of his promise to demonstrate the Makers' arms for her. Taking an assortment of weapons, Birk led Michi to Beta-Nu's largest park and spent the rest of the afternoon demolishing trees, bushes, rocks, and statues. He went about the demonstration with such boyish enthusiasm that it seemed to belie his hatred of military mentality.

For her part, Michi was vastly impressed. They may not have had space flight, but the Makers were decades, if not centuries, ahead of humans in their weapons technology. She only saw the handweapons that afternoon, none of the really big pieces, but it was enough to convince her that this world was a military treasure trove. The arms here were far superior, not only to those of Earth, but to what she'd seen the invaders of New Edo using as well. With a war between the two races inevitable, the weapons stashed here on this planet could easily spell the difference between victory and defeat. But how could she convince Birk of that?

They returned to the tower for dinner, where Arthur and Kagami had combined to prepare yet another sumptuous meal. Birk prattled on about native plants and animals, but Michi's mind was still on what she'd seen that day in the arsenal and in the park. Finally, during a pause in the conversation, she decided to broach what she knew would be a dangerous topic.

"You'll probably accuse me of being brainwashed," she began tentatively, "but I think you're wrong about the military being responsible for what happened to this world."

"Oh?" There was an expression of amused superiority curling Birk's lip. "The people died because of a military invention. The plague was inspired by hatred born of more than a century of continual warfare. Cause and effect seem pretty strong to me."

"In most cases, the military doesn't set the policy; it just carries it out. The government and the people decide on their objectives—those are civilian prerogatives."

"The government rarely asks the people. And what about military dictatorships like Torres's? The military was the government, and none of the people could stop it."

"I'll admit the lines get blurred there," Michi nodded. "But running a government is a full-time job; nobody can do that and be a general too. Torres may have come from the military and held a military rank, but when he took over the government he had to hand those duties to other people."

156

"That's hairsplitting. The military mentality was still stamped on his brain. He still thought everything could be handled by force if he applied it right."

Michi pushed her chair back from the table but made no attempt to stand. "I'm tired of always taking the blame for civilian cowardice. People always give the job to the military because that's the easiest solution. Go fight it out, they tell us, and we do because that's our job. But we aren't responsible for the failure of their imagination. If the government was willing to work, if the government was willing to make the sacrifices instead of the military, there wouldn't be any wars."

"Isn't that statement a little extreme?"

"No more than yours was. Twenty years after every war, historians are always pointing out how simply it could have been avoided—if the politicians were willing to compromise, if the leaders of the opposing sides were willing to put aside their pride and make sacrifices for the common good. Instead, we—the soldiers—become the sacrifices, and they put wreaths on our graves once a year when they eulogize us for having died for their cause. It's the people who *don't* fight who demand the sacrifices, and the people who *do* fight that pay them."

"What about the Makers? They didn't have a choice."

"Oh shove it! Of course they did, there's always a choice. They didn't have to decide on perpetual war to keep things in line. There were other ways. The leaders of all the city-states could have set a severe policy of birth control and rigid breeding laws. They could have cut back their standard of living, made do with less so that everybody could at least have *something*. They could have passed stiff laws against waste and encouraged conservation. They might not have been as comfortable, but they would have survived.

"But they didn't do that, because they knew it would be unpopular. That way, *everybody* would have had to sacrifice. Instead of having everyone sacrifice a little, they found a system where a smaller percentage sacrificed a lot and the rest sacrificed nothing. The majority of the people remained contented in their comfortable lifestyles, and the soldiers were marched off once again to the slaughter."

Birk was thoughtful a moment. "You told me you joined the army of your own free will."

Taking a deep breath after her diatribe, Michi nodded her head in agreement. "Yes. But personal benefits aside, there

157

are some of us who believe in what we're doing, who are willing to die for our causes if that becomes necessary. But what I'm saying is, don't blame the soldiers for the war—blame the diplomats and the politicians who lacked the guts to make peace."

Birk looked as though he wanted to continue the discussion, but Michi held up a hand as she rose from her seat. "I know we can probably go on like this all night," she said, "but I'm tired. I'm still a long way from full recovery, and I've had a busy day. I'm exhausted. We'll have plenty of time together to argue. At least now we seem able to do it in a civilized manner. I'm going to bed. Good night, Birk." She started out the door to return to her own room.

Birk rose, too, as he watched her leave. "Michi, I . . ."

"Yes?" She turned to look at him. "What is it?"

There was a kaleidoscope of expressions playing across Birk's face. His fists clenched and unclenched in frustration and small, inarticulate sounds escaped his mouth as he looked at her. Finally he looked down at his feet and said, "Never mind. It was nothing. You're right; you do need your rest. Go on to bed, and I'll see you in the morning."

Michi gave him a warm smile and left the room.

At breakfast the next morning, Michi said, "If you don't mind, I'd like to go back to my ship today."

"What for?" All the old suspicions had instantly returned to Birk's face.

"I won't try rebuilding it if that's what you're worried about. I thought we were past all that."

"Sorry." Her minor flare-up had made him sheepish. "But I just don't see the point. . . ."

"Some of those people on there were my friends. Can't I at least say my farewells to them in person?"

"Oh, certainly. It's just been so long since I mourned for anyone that I forgot about the rituals."

You're lying, Michi thought. *You mourn for yourself every day.* But she kept her words sweet and simple as she discussed the arrangements for the day's journey.

Birk and Michi flew to the crash site together in one delta, leaving their robots behind in Beta-Nu. Unlike his first journey to the spot, Birk had the craft fly at a leisurely pace; there was no hurry anymore.

They flew for the first few minutes in silence. Then Michi

158

said suddenly, "Tell me, what would you have done if the ship had landed safely instead of crashing?"

Birk let out a long sigh. "That's something I've often wondered myself, both before and after the fact. I honestly don't know. I suppose I'd have kept you under observation for a while without showing myself to you. The Makers had little devices I call spy-bees, flying cameras no larger than an insect. I could have watched everything you did and decided on that basis whether you were any threat to me or not."

"We wouldn't have been interested in threatening anyone. Our only thoughts were to fix our ship and take off again as soon as we could warn Earth of the invasion."

"But you would still be a threat, don't you see? Even if you didn't bother to look for me, you would know that the planet was here. That would be reported to Earth. Eventually, after the war is over, someone would have come here to explore. I wouldn't have wanted that. Probably I would have stopped you from taking off again."

"How?" The sudden image filled Michi's mind of all the Makers' weapons at Birk's disposal. "Would you have used that arsenal against us? Would you have murdered us with those weapons, your own people, just to keep your secret safe?"

She regretted her words immediately; they had put him on the defensive. "I wouldn't have murdered anybody. I wouldn't have to use those weapons to disable your ship."

"I don't understand."

Birk hesitated, as though debating whether to trust her, and finally decided in her favor. "I mean, I don't have to blow a ship apart to keep it from taking off. I've found a simpler way."

"Oh?" Michi's eyebrows arched, and she made no attempt to hide her interest. "Was it something the Makers had?"

"No, I invented it myself. I do know something about hyperprop engines, after all. The first three or four years I was here I was particularly worried about being found. I thought someone would certainly send out a hunting party to get the escaped prisoners back, so I planned the whole thing out in detail. I didn't want to hurt anyone, but I didn't want anybody going back to Earth and telling people this place was here, either.

"What I came up with was a hyperprop jammer. You have to realize that the hyperprop engine works because of a careful interweaving of electromagnetic and gravitational fields. My original invention wasn't so much for the engine itself—that had been around for years—but for a fine tuner, if you will, that made it much easier to specify the fields you wanted. If the fields aren't tuned properly, dire things can happen.

"My jammer works on an interference principle, like static jamming a radio broadcast. It generates a counterfield that confuses the tuner of a hyperprop engine so it doesn't work properly."

"So the ship would just sit there."

"Essentially, yes. If the engines are really powerful, the jammer might cause some of their circuitry to fuse. But I figured it was a nonlethal way to make sure no one left if I didn't want them to."

"Have you tested this jammer? Are you sure it works?"

"What could I test it on? As I've told you several times, there aren't any hyperprop engines on this planet, and the technology to make one is far too great an investment for the use I'd get out of it. It would take a year to build a hyperprop engine just to break it, and that seemed pointless."

"Then how do you know . . .?"

"I spent three years thinking it through from every angle. The theory is sound. I built the jammer and turned it on, and I was able to measure the field it generated. Everything behaved the way I expected it to. I've never actually used it against a hyperprop engine, but I'm pretty sure it would work."

Michi's mind was racing. To the best of her knowledge, no one in the Commonwealth had ever thought of such a thing. Its military implications were staggering—particularly when Earth faced the possibility of a space war against this alien race. This jammer, combined with the weapons from the Makers' arsenals, could spell the difference in the whole war effort. That made it all the more imperative that she convince Birk to help her return home.

She kept her thoughts to herself, however. She knew full well that now was not the time to mention such things.

The wreck of the *Thundercloud* was coming up on the horizon, and Michi turned her full attention to that. As they approached and she could see the full extent of the damage, she was horrified by the devastation—and more than a little amazed that even one person had survived. The ship was a total loss, smashed and twisted almost beyond recognition. The hot metal had torn large patches out of the surrounding hillside, leaving an ugly brown scar on the face of the land.

160

How had she survived that? She tried to remember where she was when the crash occurred, but her mind was a total blank. All she could recall were the screams of her fellows, the knowledge that they were plummeting to certain death, and that their mission to escape from New Edo had ended in failure. There was nothing coherent beyond that until she woke up in the bed in Beta-Nu and the second part of her waking nightmare began.

Birk landed the delta beside the wreck and the two people emerged slowly. The first thing to hit them was the horrible smell of three-week-old corpses left to rot in the open air. Michi walked as though in a trance, right up to a spot where the ship's hull had twisted apart. "Be careful where you go," Birk warned. "Pieces of the hull are loose. I wouldn't want you killed now by a falling piece of metal."

His words brought her partially out of her reverie. "I wouldn't have thought the ship would break apart that easily."

"It's not all from the crash. The rescue robots had to cut into the hull and pull it apart to find the bodies. I had them put it back together as best they could afterward, in case another ship came looking for you. But it might be dangerous to try getting inside."

Michi heeded the warning and moved around the perimeter of the wreck, looking for a better opening to peer through. Her thoughts were filled with the memories of friends who'd been aboard with her—dead now and forgotten under an unnamed sun.

She came to a gaping hole in the ship's wall, and through it she could see the jumble of bloated bodies inside. The stench of death was so strong here she had to turn away in disgust. Michi took a few steps and gagged, but managed to avoid throwing up.

She climbed higher on the hill so she could take in the entire spectacle at one glance. She looked at the tortured metal and the shattered lives, and thought of what a waste the whole affair had been. What cruel joke had the Universe been playing, allowing them to escape the invasion only to end their lives anonymously on this desolate hillside? Why had they even been born if all their efforts were to come to this?

She realized suddenly that there were tears in her eyes, and that she had been crying for some time. Behind her, she could sense Birk standing nervously, uncertain what to do, but wanting to do something. Giving him his cue, Michi turned to face him and let her grief rule her actions. She crossed the gulf between them, threw her arms around him, and wept uncontrollably against his broad chest.

For almost a minute Birk stood rigid as a statue, as though afraid to let even a trace of his feelings leak out. Michi's own emotions did not abate, however, as she continued to sob against him, and eventually Birk's floodgates broke. Michi suddenly found herself awash in emotions the man had been holding in for a dozen years.

Both of them were sobbing now, clinging to one another for mutual support and comfort. Birk's arms were around her, clawing at her back and squeezing her so tightly that she nearly cried out with pain. In this moment, as at no other time in their relationship, they were united by a bond of common misery.

As Michi's tears subsided, she looked up to see that Birk had also stopped crying. The look on his face was ferocious now, a boiling sea of lust that reached out to engulf her as well. Their caresses became less comforting, more sensual, and their mouths sought one another for a passionate kiss. Birk's embrace became even tighter, and Michi thought he might break her in two with the force of it. Her eyes filled with tears from the pain to her still-healing body, but Birk was beyond noticing.

He began clumsily trying to yank her clothes off her, but the fabric was well made and did not rip easily. Almost in self-defense, to avoid being smothered in her own garments, Michi helped by wriggling out of them as he pulled. Birk was beyond all reason now, consumed with pent-up sexual desires. She did not protest as he tossed her roughly to the ground and struggled out of his own clothing. Her emotions were almost as keyed as his as he joined her on the grass, and their union was an event of mutual passion.

He made love to her six times in the space of two hours, with the unrelenting fervor of an adolescent in first sexual blush. He had so much stored energy that he probably would have continued for several more hours had not Michi rolled away from him. Her vaginal lining was chafed, and the pain from her wounds had increased steadily from the first moment of his embrace. She was not well enough to sustain such prolonged activity. "I think we'd better go back now," she said, trying to keep her voice steady.

Those were the first words either had spoken in all this

time, and they jolted Birk out of his trance. "What? Why?" Then, with more than a trace of worry in his voice, he continued, "Did I do something wrong? Was I too rough? I thought—that is, I didn't mean to force myself on you, but . . ."

Michi shook her head. "It's not you, it's me. I'm still healing, remember. It hurts."

That brought Birk tripping all over himself in apology. Michi interrupted him and said, "I'll survive it; don't worry. I was as caught up in it as you were, and I don't regret a second of it—but please, let's get back to the city where I can rest a little more comfortably."

Birk offered to carry her back to the delta, and the thought appealed to her even though she could have made it on her own. They slipped back into their bedraggled clothing and returned to their craft. The delta lifted gently off the ground as Birk flew very slowly back to Beta-Nu.

With the episode firmly behind them, their behavior reverted to its previous formality. The flight to Beta-Nu took nearly twice as long as the trip out, as Birk seemed to want to drag out the moment, but it passed quietly; both were afraid to speak, embarrassed now by the intensity of the passion and the feelings they had displayed. They scrupulously avoided eye contact, trying to pretend that everything was as it had been when they left the city that morning.

Overlying the pain, Michi could feel the flush of triumph. She'd known that she'd have to seduce Birk sooner or later; sex was obviously a major weapon to use on a man who'd lived alone for eleven years. She was not used to the role of vamp and had feared she'd be too obvious in her ploy; but everything had worked out perfectly—and she had to admit that the experience had turned out to be far more enjoyable than she'd dared hope. She'd been prepared to sacrifice her virtue for the cause, but the end result was nothing like that at all.

Birk had let down the barriers to her, trusted her with his innermost feelings for the first time. She had to make him dependent on her, make him trust her even more, before again broaching the subject of returning to Earth. By letting him think he'd won, she was paving the ground for her own victory. She'd been tempted, back there on the grass, to suggest returning while he was in his impassioned state, but had stifled the impulse. At this intermediate stage of their relationship he was at his most volatile, and the slightest twitch could send him over the edge in any direction. Now, more than ever, she had to move cautiously.

The delta landed on the roof of the tower and Michi insisted on getting out without assistance. Arthur and Kagami both came to meet them as they emerged from the craft. There was nothing in the mannerisms of either robot to indicate emotion, but Michi felt a definite sense of foreboding as Arthur spoke. "I'm glad you returned from the journey when you did, sir," he said to Birk, almost ignoring Michi entirely. "I was on the verge of calling you."

"Why? What's the matter?"

"Another ship has arrived. It landed just two minutes ago beside the wreckage."

Both humans suddenly tensed, though their emotions were quite dissimilar. "What did it look like?" Michi asked when she dared speak.

"I've dispatched a dozen spy-bees to the site. They should be arriving at any moment. Their pictures will be relayed onto a screen I've set up downstairs, since I thought you would be interested. If you'll follow me . . ."

Although Arthur moved rapidly, his pace seemed agonizingly slow to the humans who trailed behind him. Michi and Birk were both impatient to catch a glimpse of this latest change in their situation—and the minds of both were racing as they considered the possibilities this new event could bring.

The large trivision receiver in Birk's bedroom merely showed the terrain the spy-bees were currently overflying. They had not as yet reached their destination, and there was no sign of the new spaceship. Michi sat down in a chair to ease the pain in her body, but Birk was too nervous to sit. He paced the room restlessly, but his eyes never wandered far from the image on the screen. Michi noticed that he was constantly licking his lips.

"How do you get one picture from a dozen cameras?" Michi asked to fill the time. "Do you photograph primarily from one of the bees?"

"Each bee transmits a separate image," Arthur explained. "Since they're currently flying in a tight swarm, the computer receiving the images can correlate them and give a composite picture that you see before you. At any time, if you wish, the formation can be split up and we can display twelve separate images."

"This will be fine for now," Michi said, and turned her full attention back to the screen.

Seconds dragged by like hours and the screen remained frustratingly free of interesting details. Silence descended on the room; Michi and Birk were both too nervous to talk, and the two robots respected the humans' silence. Finally the terrain pictured began looking familiar, and Michi found herself leaning forward on the edge of her seat.

The new ship came into view quite suddenly. It was big, far larger than the *Thundercloud* it had landed beside. It seemed an odd shape for a spaceship, a squashed spheroid resting on four stilty legs like a giant half-limbed spider.

Michi could not stifle her gasp. "It's them."

Birk looked at her. "Who?"

She took her gaze off the receiver and looked straight in his eyes. "The aliens, the ones who invaded New Edo. They finally tracked the *Thundercloud* down here." There was a touch of irony in her voice as she added. "We're not alone any more, Birk. Whether you like it or not, the war has come to you."

ACT 3

FIFTEEN

Ship's-leader Rafalyi's career had been filled with controversy, and he was not above using it blatantly to further his ambitions. The controversy had started at his very birth, with accusations around the Gene Hall that he was really of half-caste descent. His mother firmly denied the rumors of her association with a high-ranking member of Ideation, and his father had proudly registered the birth as recognized and legitimate, so no direct action could be taken by the Pure Caste Council. But the rumors and the suspicions persisted, and his career had always been more closely scrutinized than most.

Whether the suspicions were true or not, Rafalyi had no way of knowing. But it was a fact that he was blessed—or perhaps cursed—with a quality of imagination generally absent from other members of the Echelon Caste. This was not considered an admirable asset. He was a leader of soldiers, not a Tactician, and too much curiosity was a drawback.

Rafalyi's questing mind had gotten him into trouble on numerous occasions. While his peers rigidly followed orders and completed their assignments, Rafalyi frequently led his troops along a parallel path that promised to be more interesting. He'd been reprimanded repeatedly for exceeding his authority, though he was always able to find ambiguities in his orders that let him evade punishment.

It was also true that his record of success was higher than that of his peers, which was the sole mitigating factor in many Review Board inquiries. Rafalyi himself was of the opinion that, if he hadn't taken the initiative so frequently, his questioned parentage would have assured him a permanent low rank; as it was, his career moved only fitfully ahead. But it did move ahead.

He was proud to be a part of the first raid on the alien

colony, but disappointed when his ship—possibly because of his reputation for eccentricity—was ordered to remain in space as reserve to guard against unexpected situations. Rafalyi was actually happy when the one ship managed to escape; it meant action, a chance for him to do something. Along with another ship, commanded by a senile Ninth Ranker named Pannelusx, he took off in pursuit.

The chase lasted more than two days at maximum speed before they drew within range of the fugitive craft. It was a frustrating time for Rafalyi, for he was not in complete charge of his own destiny. Had he been on his own, he would have diverted some of the weapons power to his engines in an effort to overtake the fleeing ship sooner, before it had a chance to reach a safe port. He was certain such an unortho-dox approach would garner yet another victory for his record.

But he was not in command. Pannelusx, for all his senility, outranked Rafalyi and kept him under tight rein. Rafalyi was not even total master aboard his own ship, for he'd been saddled with a Seventh Rank Tactician named Balsifour-Ai. Rafalyi was expert at creatively interpreting orders from his superiors, but he could do nothing while Balsifour-Ai was there with him constantly.

He did not even mention his idea for diverting weapons power to the engines; he knew precisely what the Tactician would say: "If we did that, we wouldn't have anything left to fight with when we caught them."

Rafalyi would have counterargued that Weapons Reserves had enough power to engage the enemy ship in combat, slowing it sufficiently for Pannelusx's ship to catch up for the kill. But that wouldn't have mattered. Even a Tactician, a member of the Ideation Caste revered for its intellectual capacity, could often fall victim to petrifaction of the brain.

When they finally did catch up to the alien vessel, Pannelusx's senility was even more in evidence. Disdaining evasive tactics, the Ninth Ranker's ship flew straight at the alien, obviously thinking to destroy it in one all-out attack before it could fight back. The alien vessel, however, had a little more fight in it than Pannelusx had supposed and blew the pursuing battle cruiser apart with a volley of well-placed shots.

Rafalyi was more successful by being less foolhardy. While the alien ship was occupied with Pannelusx, his own man-aged to place a disabling shot while sustaining only superficial damage itself. The alien ship took off again, with Rafalyi now in sole pursuit.

He would have caught it, he was sure, had it not been for the nebula. The alien commander, seeing a chance to shake pursuit, dove into the cloud and vanished from Rafalyi's long-range scanners. Rafalyi's impulse was to dive into the cloud after the fugitive, but that impulse was checked by Balsifour-Ai.

"We will remain outside the cloud," the Tactician ordered, "keeping it always between ourself and the planet the ship came from. The alien commander will have only two choices: either to return the way it came or else emerge in our direction."

"There is a third option," Rafalyi insisted, not the least bit hesitant to challenge an Ideation Caste member. "They may find a planet in there on which they can make repairs, and wait until it's safe to come out again."

"It will never be safe," the Tactician assured him, offended that someone of Echelon Caste would speak to him in those tones. He'd been warned of Rafalyi's eccentricity and was prepared to be stern. "We have our orders to ensure that no word of our raid reaches other planets in these aliens' realm, and we obey our orders. We are of a temperament to stay here and wait for them to emerge. From what we know of these creatures, they are much less patient. We can wait them out. We shall extend our scanners to maximum range so that nothing coming out of the cloud can get by us, and we shall wait."

And so they waited.

And waited.

And waited some more, until Rafalyi was certain no ship would ever come out of that cloud.

He discussed the situation briefly with Klondanar-Nakonal, his Ship's-second-leader. "We can wait here forever, until we all die from lack of air, and that ship is not going to come out."

"Then we shall die in our duty and earn our places in Paradise," Klondanar-Nakonal said placidly.

Rafalyi gave his aide an icy stare. "You are a true member of our caste," he said. "I'm sure you'll rise to high rank." He did not like his subordinate and had reason to believe the dislike was mutual. If Klondanar-Nakonal noticed the sarcasm in his superior's voice, however, he did not choose to comment on it.

They waited some more. The Tactician showed no signs of wavering in his purpose, and Rafalyi was having increasing difficulty concealing his contempt.

But Rafalyi's patience was rewarded after a fashion. After sixteen ship-days of waiting, Balsifour-Ai called the ship's-leader to his cabin and explained that he was approaching the onset of his fourth Metastasis. "I will soon retire into dormancy, and that will leave you in command," he said slowly.

With great effort, Rafalyi hid his delight at the news.

"However," the Tactician continued, "that will not give you free license. Going into the cloud after the aliens would be a serious mistake. Once inside the nebula, our long-range scanners would be useless, and the enemy could slip outside and away before we knew what had happened. Therefore, before I enter Metastasis I shall leave recorded orders—which you will acknowledge!—that you must not abandon this watch post outside the cloud. Is that clear?"

Rafalyi said it was, even as he began thinking of ways to circumvent it.

He barely waited until the Tactician was fully into Metastasis—and beyond interfering—before he began issuing orders of his own. He had sworn to maintain a watch at this position, and he would do so, but he had made no guarantees of how that watch would be conducted. He ordered two of his soldiers to take Balsifour-Ai's Metastasis capsule with them into one of the scoutships so that it remained floating free in space at this position outside the cloud.

"I don't think this is what Tactician Balsifour-Ai had in mind," Ship's-second-leader Klondanar-Nakonal commented. His displeasure was written all over his face.

Rafalyi didn't care what his subordinate thought of his actions. "Do you challenge the orders of someone a full rank above you?"

Klondanar-Nakonal covered his front eyes. "No, sir," he said more humbly.

"I didn't think you would," Rafalyi said. "You're too much a product of your training. At any rate, the scoutship has orders to watch for the enemy ship, fulfilling the Tactician's orders. That leaves us free to go in and actually *find* the ship."

Rafalyi's craft moved slowly forward into the cloud. While he may have been venturesome, he was not eager to die needlessly; there was always the possibility of an ambush,

171

however slight that possibility was. His own personal assessment of the aliens was similar to Balsifour-Ai's: They were not patient enough to have waited this long before trying to make their move. That left two alternatives: Either his weapons had done them more damage than he originally thought—in which case they were now dead or dying—or else they had found some place of refuge within the nebula itself. Either way, waiting outside accomplished nothing. Rafalyi was someone who had to know the facts.

He moved cautiously through the cloud but detected no signs of anything until a star was spotted close to the center. With a feeling that bordered on premonition, Rafalyi ordered a closer inspection of the star, and thus discovered the single planet orbiting it. A habitable planet. No ships orbited the world, so Rafalyi considered it most likely the fugitive vessel had landed there.

His original hypotheses thus strengthened, he ordered his ship in for a closer look. To his great dismay, his reconnaissance scan showed many cities dotting the face of the planet, and that set him thinking. Did the aliens have a secret base here, one that Intelligence had not known about? If so, then his mission was already lost, for the fleeing ship would have contacted others and word about the raid would have spread. The key element of surprise would be lost forever.

Or could there be another race living here, one totally apart from either side in the current conflict? That thought excited him as he thought of the honors to be bestowed on the discoverer of such a race. In either event, he would have to take the initiative now; merely to report back these findings would mean that another ship, a specialist from Intelligence, would be sent to investigate further, and all the glory would go to someone else. Rafalyi was willing to take the risk to keep the honors for himself. It would be dangerous, but it should not be fatally so. After all, he had a full battle cruiser and more than five hundred battle-trained soldiers at his disposal. What could go wrong?

He stayed in orbit for two ship-days, monitoring radio frequencies and photographing the landscape that drifted past beneath him. In all that time, there came no challenges to his right to orbit this world—and while there was some trace of radio activity, it was negligible compared to what he expected to find.

Eventually a member of his reconnaissance team found what they were looking for: the remains of a ship suspiciously similar to the one they'd been chasing, crashed into a hill well outside the nearest city. Not much more could be determined from this altitude; if he wanted to learn anything else, he would have to land.

He might not have done so had there been more radio activity. But, prompted by an apparent lack of native communication, Rafalyi ordered his ship down. He did, however, keep all hands at battle stations, ready to defend the ship at a moment's notice should they be descending into a trap.

The landing went without incident, and soon his ship was sitting beside the shell of its adversary. Rafalyi dispatched a squad to investigate the wreck, and the report quickly came back that the other ship had crashed upon landing. The bodies of its occupants were in an advanced state of decomposition, and there were so many of them that it was unlikely any others escaped the crash.

Any other member of his caste would have considered his mission now accomplished. The original orders had been to stop the fugitives from communicating with their command about the raid, and these fugitives were certainly beyond any further communication. Technically, it was now his duty to pick up the soldiers he had left outside the nebula in the scoutship and return to base to make a full report. If Ideation wanted further knowledge about this hitherto unknown planet, they would order Intelligence to proceed through appropriate channels. There was no further reason for Rafalyi to remain here.

But Rafalyi was far from typical and did not consider the matter closed. After all, while there were apparently no survivors of the crash, it was still possible for the ship to have communicated with the inhabitants of this world before its crash. Word about the raid could still be spreading, and preparations being made to launch a counteroffensive. While it was not within Rafalyi's specific orders, he was sure it was his duty at least to check out the possibility.

One of those intriguing cities was located not too far away, just a short flight in a scoutship. He could send a small squad of soldiers to investigate and discover what type of beings lived here. Depending on what they found, he would plan his further strategy from there.

SIXTEEN

Birk didn't answer Michi's taunts about the war having come to him. His eyes were glued to the receiver as he watched the enormous ship that squatted on the ground beside the wreck of the *Thundercloud*. Even as he and Michi looked on, a hatch opened in the side of the craft and a boarding ramp was lowered. A dozen or so alien figures trooped down the ramp and began examining the wreckage of the human ship.

As though reading Birk's mind, Arthur sent some of the spy-bees in for a closer look at what was happening. The picture on the screen broke into a series of images, each now the transmission from a single bee. The aliens were as Michi had described in her initial report—short, smooth, and hairless, with bright red skins, having two arms and walking erect on two legs. They also had two pairs of eyes on their oddly shaped heads, one pair in front and a set where the ears should have been. They had no discernible noses, but there was a broad slit in the center of their faces that seemed to be a general-purpose orifice. The slits opened and closed at varied intervals; the spy-bees were not equipped to transmit sound, but Birk could imagine that the creatures were talking back and forth to one another as they combed the wreckage.

The aliens were thorough and single-minded. They let nothing distract them as they examined the crash site, methodically counting bodies and making damage estimates. Birk watched them, a sinking feeling in his stomach. He began silently cursing himself as all sorts of a fool for not having buried the wreckage as he'd done for his own craft. If he hadn't left it just sitting there on the landscape, there would have been no evidence of the *Thundercloud* to draw down the pursuing vessel.

"What do we do now?"

Michi's voice behind him almost made him jump. In the

174

tension of the moment, he'd forgotten her presence. He closed his eyes and tried to think. She would be one more complication in an already confusing situation.

"I don't know," he replied. "Let's see what happens. Maybe we won't have to do anything. Maybe they'll be satisfied with the wreckage and take off again. Maybe they'll leave us alone."

"And maybe they won't," Michi said quietly.

"We'll wait and see," Birk growled. He was not used to this pace. After eleven years of quiet, things were suddenly happening much too quickly. In the space of three weeks there had been the first crash, the agony over whether anyone would survive, the horrible fighting with Michi, the reconciliation, the incredible episode of this afternoon—and now this. His brain was trying to switch into high gear, but as yet there were no results.

Perhaps Michi sensed the desperation behind his snappish answer, because she did not press him further. The two of them continued to watch as the aliens spent three hours sifting through the wreckage for signs of life. At last the creatures had gone over every centimeter of the demolished ship without discovering anything to excite them. They gathered together again as a unit at the foot of the ramp, then marched upward back into the ship. The ramp pulled up behind them and the hatch closed once more.

Now came the most suspenseful moments. What would the aliens do next? Were they satisfied that their enemies had been destroyed? Would they return to their home base? Or would they decide to explore this new planet now that they were here? Birk was transfixed by the motionless image of the alien ship, the agony of indecision wearing away at his nerves.

After half an hour, a broader hatch opened near the top of the ship. A smaller vessel emerged and flew off in the direction of Beta-Nu. Birk banged a fist against the wall in frustration. Everything would have been so much simpler if only they'd gone away when they were done. Now he was again forced to make decisions.

"We can't afford to wait any longer," Michi said. "We have to start thinking of what we're going to do."

Her words only served to fuel the anger he felt. "I know!" he snapped at her. "Just give me a minute to think."

"I'll give you all the time you want," Michi retorted. "But

175

they might not be so considerate." She nodded toward the image of the scoutship on the receiver screen.

"Up to the roof, then," Birk decided. "We can get in the delta and fly out of here before they see us."

Michi shook her head. "No good. I don't know what kind of equipment they have, but I'll bet they'd spot a flying craft in a second. A delta wouldn't stand a chance against their armed scoutships."

"The Makers had fighter planes, too."

"Oh? Were you planning to fight?"

"No," Birk said. "But if they spotted us and started shooting, we could . . ."

"Listen to me," Michi interrupted in a commanding tone Birk had never heard from her before. "This game has shifted to my ballpark, and I know the rules. Reconnaissance and Survival was my specialty, and I may be able to deal with *their* recon teams. It's obvious they're not very expert at it. . . ."

"Why not?" Birk asked. "I mean, how can you tell?"

Michi began ticking off the reasons on her fingers. "First, that's one of their battle cruisers; its mission is usually to fight, and its crew probably doesn't have much experience exploring new planets. Second, they're being entirely too open about what they're doing. They made no attempt to conceal their landing by coming down at night, and their scoutship is flying brazenly into a city that they know nothing about. That screams of either ignorance or arrogance."

"Maybe it means they're so well armed they don't need to worry about opposition," Birk suggested.

Michi ignored his comment. "And third, it's late afternoon. It'll be dark soon. You just don't send an exploratory mission out this late in the day; they'll barely have a chance to see anything before it's time to turn around and go back to the ship—a complete waste of manpower. And it can't be because they want to see the city at night when they can't be observed themselves because we've already established that they don't mind being seen." She shook her head. "I'd say we've got an overeager commander who's rushing in over his head."

"But the scoutship will be here any minute. How do we keep from being spotted?"

"By staying exactly where we are and not panicking." Michi tried to project a confident, reassuring tone to soothe Birk's jangled nerves—and he had to admit her calm was infectious. "As I said, these are amateurs. They have no idea

176

what they're really looking for. They're like the bear who went over the mountain, just to see what he could see. What do you really think they can find in the hour and a half or so before sunset?"

Birk did not reply, so after a few seconds Michi answered her own question. "They'll see a city. They'll see motion in the city. That in itself might be enough to frighten them off. If not, if they come closer, they'll see that the motion is produced by a million maintenance robots, gliding about the streets on their various jobs. What they won't see is a single sign of life, *because we aren't going to stick our fucking heads out of this tower*.

"All right. They'll see a lot of robots running around. They'll be curious. They'll follow the robots for a while to see what they do. They'll see a city that's dead and lifeless except for the machines that go around dusting and repairing. This is a big city. This tower may be the tallest building, but it's only one of many. There's nothing here to attract their particular attention."

"Our two deltas are parked on the roof," Birk pointed out.

"But they're not moving. They're just sitting there. For all the aliens know, they may be pieces of abstract sculpture. I repeat, the odds are billions to one against the scouts even noticing this building.

"So, after an hour and a half of looking at the funny little robots and the pretty buildings, the sun will go down and they can't look at the city anymore. They'll have to go back to their ship and explain to their commander. Maybe he'll be satisfied that their mission is accomplished and order the ship home. Maybe he'll decide to take the ship to one of the other cities to see whether they're all like this. Or maybe he'll be curious enough to explore this city in more detail tomorrow. But—assuming he's relatively sane—he wouldn't just decide to bomb the city haphazardly in the dark.

"All of which," she summed up, "means that there's no need for panic. We'll have at least until dawn tomorrow to look at the problem rationally and develop a policy for coping with the situation."

Some of the spy-bees had followed the scoutship on its journey to Beta-Nu, and the image on the receiver showed the alien craft approaching the city's periphery. "I'd suggest," Michi whispered, "that we don't talk too much. I doubt they'd have sound detectors *that* sensitive, but why take the chance? We'll just sit here and outwait them."

177

As she commanded, they waited, watching the action on the screen. The scoutship was taking its time, making a leisurely circuit of the city limits and slowly spiraling inward toward the center. Michi was looking confident that her prediction would hold; at that speed, the ship wouldn't even come near the tower before sundown.

Then, as the scoutship was flying over the northern quadrant of the city, the spy-bee relayed a picture below it of bombed-out devastation and rubble. Michi, who'd only been half paying attention, suddenly sat upright. "What's that?" she asked.

Birk felt embarrassed. "I, uh, while you were healing and when several other possible survivors died, I was feeling very frustrated. To relieve the tension, I took one of the tanks from the arsenal and shelled a useless part of the city. The maintenance robots haven't managed to clear all the rubble away yet, I guess."

"Wonderful," Michi muttered. "In the middle of this perfectly average city, with everything going on as normal, we have a few square blocks that have been thoroughly demolished by weapons fire within the past three weeks. The aliens now have a signpost saying that something here is not what it seems."

"That was not a consideration at the time."

Michi's tone softened. "No. No, of course not. But it will alter the situation somewhat. No need to panic, we should still have until morning—but not much beyond that. The alien captain now knows that something here is capable of being vicious. He may consider that a challenge." She lapsed into silence once more to consider the possibilities. Birk kept his eyes guiltily on the screen until at sunset, as Michi had predicted, the scoutship turned around and headed back to its base.

Birk and Michi were unusually quiet as Arthur served them dinner, both lost in thought as they contemplated what needed to be done. Birk would occasionally look up at Michi, to search her face for some clue to her thoughts, but she always avoided looking at him. His own brain was bemired, and following a train of thought felt like swimming a river of mud.

Halfway through the meal he realized he was eating only out of habit, not because he had any appetite. Abruptly he pushed his plate away and stood up. "If the aliens want this planet," he said, "they can have it."

The suddenness of his declaration took Michi by surprise. "What? What do you mean?"

"This is a big place. We've got a whole world to hide in. We can go away and they'll never find us."

For a moment, Michi could only stare at him openmouthed. "Just like that? I don't believe it. What made you decide that?"

Her hostility made him nervous. Spreading his hands, he said, "What other choices do we have?"

"Thank you for asking. They are the enemy, Birk. They kill human beings for no apparent reason. They give no quarter. The best defense is a good offense. We have to take some action against them while we still have the element of surprise on our side."

"What can we do—two people against that huge ship and all its soldiers?"

"We're not just two people. We've got armies of robots at our disposal, and all those weapons in the armories. If you look at it that way, we outnumber them."

Birk shook his head. "I'm no fighter."

"That is becoming increasingly, painfully obvious."

Her bitter tone made him wary. Her voice was sounding the way it had before yesterday, before she'd reconciled herself to living here. "Listen, all the Makers' weapons won't do us the slightest bit of good. All they have to do is take off in their ship and orbit above us, bombing the city to smithereens from space. The Makers had no defenses against that."

"There's that ... what did you call it, that hyperprop jammer you said you built. We could use that to keep them from taking off."

"It only has a range of two hundred meters or so. We couldn't get it close enough to their ship without them spotting us. Besides, the jammer is absolutely harmless unless they turn on their hyperprops—and that's even assuming they use hyperprop engines that work on the same principles ours do. For all we know, they may have something else entirely."

Michi also rose from the table. She stood with her hands on her hips, staring at Birk. "I don't believe it. This planet is your home, the only one you've got, and you're willing to give it up without a fight! You'd let these invaders take away everything you've got rather than try to defend what's yours." She shook her head. "I just can't understand that kind of mentality. Maybe it's barbaric of me, but I have to draw the

179

line somewhere and tell the world it can go so far but no farther—that is, if I want to have any self-respect at all."

Birk was sweating, trying desperately to restore the feeling of cooperation that had been building between them the past two days. "Look," he said, "they're not at war with me; they're at war with the Commonwealth. They don't even know I exist. If we're careful, they'll *never* know we exist. We can go off by ourselves. I have a place all prepared. We can seal ourselves in and they'll never find us, even if they were particularly looking for us. It's a beautiful place. You'll love . . ."

Michi was trembling with unconcealed rage. "No! I won't have it! I'm not a rabbit, running from hole to hole in a never-ending search for false security. Somewhere, sometime, there has to be an end to running. Even for you, Birk. There has to be an end."

"Sure. As I said, they'll never find this place. It's underground. . . ."

Michi gave a harsh laugh. "So. You've been dead for eleven years, and you finally decide it's time to bury yourself. What about all the weapons?"

Her change of subject threw his thoughts off track. "Huh?"

"The arsenals, the stockpiles of arms in every city on this planet. What about them?"

Birk shrugged. "What about them?"

"We'd have to abandon them. The aliens would get them instead of . . ." She broke off abruptly and let the end of her sentence dangle awkwardly in the air.

A sudden insight flashed through Birk's mind. "What? Instead of what? Go on, finish what you were saying. *Instead of what?* Or should I say, instead of whom?"

Michi glared at him. "We could win the war with those weapons, Birk."

" 'We' ? You mean you and me?"

"I mean the Commonwealth. Those armories could mean the difference between . . ."

"You bitch!" Birk took two steps to close the distance between them and delivered a vicious backhand slap across Michi's face. The blow was so sudden and hard that the woman staggered against the dinner table, clutching at it for support. Birk took another step and hit her again. His hand was stinging from the force of the blow, but nothing registered on his consciousness past the red curtain of fury in front of his eyes.

Michi looked up at him, unprepared for the tempest of hatred billowing through the room. "Listen, I . . ."

Birk hit her a third time, this time so hard that she went sprawling backward across the table, causing it to collapse on the floor with a loud crash. His rage went beyond words; there was nothing he could say to express the boundlessness of his animosity. His fists clenched of their own accord, and his only thought was how pleasant it would be to smash her to a bloody pulp.

It was obvious, now, how she had betrayed him. She had never given up her thoughts of leaving, she had only pretended to acquiesce to trick him, to lull him into a false state of euphoria. She had wanted to soften him up, make him more pliable to her demands. It was a well-laid campaign, obviously devised by someone versed in military strategy. Hit the enemy where he's weakest, drive him to his knees.

She had found where he was weakest. Loneliness was his flaw; desire for companionship—physical and spiritual—was his Achilles heel. She had attacked his vulnerabilities, and he had buckled just as she thought he would. That entire scene of mourning for her dead comrades was probably just an act, a chance to seduce him without letting him know he was being seduced. She probably had not felt a single sincere emotion in all the time he'd known her. She was just a cold-blooded little bitch, willing to do anything to get what she wanted, willing even to betray the man who offered to share his entire world with her. She had *used* him, shamelessly, and he was so angry at himself for falling for her deceit that he was ready to kill her for it.

He advanced on her with death in his eyes and heart. She cowered before him, stunned by his attack and weak from her wounds and the day's activity. Birk reached down and grabbed a leg from the shattered dinner table to act as a club. He raised the weapon over his head . . .

There was a light tap on his shoulder, and he spun abruptly to face a possible new menace. But it was only Arthur. "Sir," the robot said, "I've got the delta ready. We can leave any time you say."

Birk stared uncomprehendingly, blinking as the distraction totally confused him.

When the man did not respond at once, Arthur repeated his statement. "The delta is ready. We're set to go any time."

"Go?" Birk asked, his mind struggling to make sense of the offer.

"Yes, sir. We can go to Alpha-Xi. The invaders won't find us there. You'll be perfectly safe."

The club was still raised in his hand as he blinked at the robot. "Alpha-Xi," he echoed quietly.

"Yes, sir. I thought that was what you wanted when you mentioned hiding from these aliens. I took the liberty of getting everything prepared. That *was* what you had in mind, wasn't it, sir?"

Birk slowly lowered his arm. "Yes, but—" But. There was something he'd left unfinished, something he'd meant to do, but his mind was not working clearly and he couldn't think of what it was.

"We'd best go quickly, sir, before the aliens suspect someone's here. If we leave right now, I doubt they could track our delta in the dark."

Birk's right hand was hurting, and when he looked at it he could see he'd been gripping the table leg so tightly that all his fingers were white. He loosened his hold and felt a tingling as blood surged back in. Twisting slightly, he looked behind him to see Michi sitting on the floor in the middle of the shattered table, shivering and clutching her sides. Her eyes were cast downward and away; she would not even look near him.

In disgust, he threw his club at the ground beside her; it hit the floor and bounced away, while the woman flinched. "Come on, Arthur," he growled, "let's get out of here while there's still time."

Sitting in the darkened passenger bubble of the delta while Arthur skillfully piloted it away from the city, Birk's mind had a chance to recover its balance. His ego was still quaking from the immensity of Michi's betrayal, and his hatred of her and all that she represented continued unabated; but he was at least able to realize that she was not to blame for his stupidity. He had, once again, violated his own rules for survival—and once again, he had paid the penalty. He'd let himself be blinded by Hope, despite the fact that he knew this woman was of the military and not to be trusted, despite the fact that he knew she wanted only one thing and would resort to any trick to obtain it. Despite these things, his own weaknesses had betrayed him. Michi merely exploited the vulnerability she found; it was he who was really at fault for exposing the weakness in the first place.

Staring out into the darkness as they flew, an image formed in Birk's mind—the image of that window in the art gallery, of the two figures standing in darkness. Once again those faceless faces took on familiar shapes. Once more the person lying on the ground, helpless and pleading, was himself; the figure standing arrogant and heedless in the foreground was Michi. She was oblivious to his cries for help, oblivious of his need for her, oblivious to all but her own selfish desires.

Well, her cleverness had backfired this time. He smiled warmly at the thought. She had finally managed to chase him away for good, chased him to a place she would never find. Only he and Arthur knew about Alpha-Xi. It would be their little paradise for the rest of Birk's life. There would be no more worry about intrusion by Michi, by Earth, by the aliens, or by anyone else. No more worries about anything.

And if Michi wanted to play soldier, she was free to do so. It would probably make her feel very heroic to go up against these aliens single-handed. She could conduct her private little war any way she wished, but she would do it without him.

SEVENTEEN

Rafalyi was not happy with the progress he was making on his exploration of the alien city.

The initial overflight had greatly intrigued him with its view of a city devoid of living beings, yet still functioning perfectly. There were robots everywhere keeping the processes of life in operation, but no sign of the inhabitants. Rafalyi wondered whether it was possible for the robots to turn against their creators, kill them all, and continue on as though nothing had happened. He sent his scoutship to make forays over other nearby cities, but the findings were still the same: municipalities deserted except for the machines that kept them running.

The image that haunted him the most, though, was the

183

bombed-out section of the nearby city. None of the other cities had been touched by the same devastation that had leveled several blocks of the nearby one. He kept a watch on the area over the next two days, and realized that the destruction must be of recent origin; the robots were continually at work cleaning up the debris, and if the bombing had occurred more than a few months ago there would be no signs of it left by now.

Something was definitely amiss in that city—and since it was the city closest to the crash of the enemy ship, the coincidence made it worth investigating. Despite all evidence to the contrary, there might indeed have been survivors of the crash, and it was certainly his duty to explore that possibility.

Sending scoutships out to make aerial scans was not an efficient way to conduct such an investigation, so, on the third day, he moved his entire vessel to the outskirts of the city and began sending troops in on foot. He tried a few at first, and when they met no opposition from the robots he dispatched more in waves. They fanned out looking for signs of life, but found none.

Or at least, none that were reported back. Rafalyi might have been more willing to believe the reports had it not been for the accidents that began befalling his soldiers almost from the instant their search started in earnest. That first day, two of them were found dead of crushed skulls, buried beneath large chunks of masonry that had apparently come loose and fallen upon them. Rafalyi would not have given that much thought—the lives of soldiers were as meaningless to him as pebbles on a beach—but on the second day of the exploration more accidents occurred. In one spot, an apparently solid stretch of pavement collapsed, sending an entire squad of warriors tumbling several meters into a hole. Three died of broken necks, and others were incapacitated with cracked bones; they had to be shot, since it was not worth the effort to treat them medically. That same day, elsewhere in the city, ten soldiers died while walking across an open patch of ground that turned out to be electrified.

Rafalyi remembered his teacher's advice: Once may be an accident, twice may be coincidence, but three times is enemy action.

There were several possibilities to consider. There may have been one or more survivors of the crash, now hiding here in the city; such survivors would do all they could to

184

hinder Rafalyi's efforts. Or the city might not be as dead as it looked, with the original inhabitants still around—though as yet undiscovered—to take offense at his open trespass. Or perhaps the robots themselves were causing the trouble, pretending to ignore the invaders while secretly working to kill them. It was an interesting puzzle, and one that his cunning mind delighted in. He ordered that henceforth his troops were to explore only in teams of three or more and were to fire at anything remotely suspicious.

On the third day came an interesting development. A large building not far from the ship was found to contain enormous stockpiles of armaments. This one arsenal housed more offensive weaponry than five ships the size of his own. As Rafalyi listened to the squad leader's report he could barely contain his excitement. This discovery could add new dimensions to his career.

In the middle of this fascinating report, the transmission went dead and the whole city shook with the force of a monumental explosion. Even the ship itself rocked from the shockwave of the blast—and when the shaking had stopped, Rafalyi found he could not regain contact with the squad leader at the arsenal.

Subsequent exploration revealed that the entire building had been boobytrapped to blow up if investigated too closely—and when that much offensive power was released, it was no casual occurrence. Buildings were leveled for four blocks around the former armory, and the blast had claimed the lives of nearly one hundred of Rafalyi's soldiers.

There could be no doubts about enemy action this time. Rafalyi was tempted to level the city in retribution, but disdained that as being the easy way out. The enemy would not destroy *all* its weapons; there had to be more of them stashed somewhere. These were weapons designed along totally new principles, that much had been clear from the initial report; Rafalyi could not simply destroy this city and hope to find more weapons elsewhere. He wanted to bring those arms back with him, to prove that this excursion had been a worthwhile effort.

He began making plans for an all-out effort against the saboteurs. He would have his troops go from house to house, if necessary, but they would flush out any enemy who dared to oppose them. Then he could return home in triumph, conqueror of a new world.

*   *   *

Michi spent most of her first night alone in shock. Birk's attack had come too suddenly for her to defend herself, and with such violence that, despite her training, she could only cower before him in fear and pain. Her body—still recuperating from her surgery and still recovering from the afternoon's exertions—had failed her, and now her spirit failed her. Birk's hatred poured over her in waves, paralyzing her soul. Birk had become a maniac, riding a tide of vehemence that could only lead to her death.

Only Arthur's clever intervention had saved her by deflecting Birk from his intended path. She could not bring herself to look at the man who towered over her as he hurled his club to the floor and stomped out of the room. Mostly it was out of fear, but there were tinges of guilt around the edges. He was right—she *had* been meaning to betray him; she *had* hoped to win enough of his trust to convince him of the rightness of her plan. But now, through her own foolishness, that hope was gone forever.

The room became deathly still after he was gone; the calm that followed his storm was almost more than she could bear. As much to fill the silence as to relieve her own feelings, she began to cry. Slowly, at first, with soft, delicate tears—but once started, she could not stop until her whole body was wracked by a series of convulsions. There was no one to help or console her; Kagami was not yet enough of a person to cope with her mistress's changing moods the way Arthur could cope with Birk's. Michi just lay on the floor and cried until no more tears would come, and then slipped peacefully into a deep and dreamless sleep.

She awoke suddenly, and in darkness. She cried out, traces of fear still haunting the edges of her mind, and was answered instantly by Kagami. "Why is it so dark?" Michi asked the robot.

"I turned the lights out when I saw you were asleep. I thought you had no need of them."

"I do now. Please turn them on again."

Instantly the lights were on, and Michi had to gasp at the pain to her unaccustomed eyes. As she blinked back more tears she looked around the room, and was surprised to see that Kagami had completely cleaned up the mess from the broken table and the spilled food. There was no evidence that a fight had ever occurred here—and aside from the fact that she was lying in the middle of the floor, Michi might almost have been willing to dismiss the entire incident as some hideous nightmare.

But this was worse than nightmare—it was reality, the harshest she'd ever had to face. She knew now she was alone, totally alone—the deepest, most overwhelming solitude a person could experience. It was not merely being by herself, she'd experienced that many times. It was much more than that. There was a gulf separating her from the rest of life, a knowledge that no matter how much she needed someone, there'd be no one to help her. Birk was certainly beyond calling, and Arthur would be forced to mirror his master's feelings. Kagami was just a clever machine, hardly a boon companion. Michi had no one now, and the loneliness pressed in upon her. She felt like screaming against the inner darkness to let the sound of her voice reassure her soul that something existed in this world.

No wonder Birk went mad, she thought, trying to anchor herself in reality. *Eleven years of this. I don't think I could stand it.*

She shivered again at the concept, and pulled herself away from it by focusing on the more immediate problem: the alien invaders. She had no idea what they would do next or whether they would even stay on this planet once they'd seen the wreck of the *Thundercloud.* But she had to assume the worst and make contingency plans; if nothing else, it would keep the hysteria away for a while.

Looked at in purely military terms, her situation was quite simple. She was an officer stranded behind enemy lines. As such, she had two primary duties: to return to her own side as quickly as possible, and to cause as much damage to the enemy as she could in the meantime. The first objective was totally beyond her reach, so she would have to concentrate on the second.

Theoretically she was quite well off. She had at her disposal all the weapons of a city geared for warfare. The arsenals of Beta-Nu could arm several legions. But she didn't know how to make it work for her. She'd had only one afternoon to see these unfamiliar weapons demonstrated—hardly time to acquaint her with their finer points. Kagami might be able to give her basic instruction, but that was a far cry from expertise. If Birk were helping her, perhaps they could mount an effective campaign against these aliens; Birk knew the technology backward and forward by this time.

But Birk wasn't here; he'd gone into hiding in his underground paradise and was unlikely to be lured out by anything she could say or do. She would have to write him off as a lost cause and do the best she could on her own.

Considering how badly she was outnumbered, a frontal assault was out of the question. Even if she equipped a robot army to make the charge, she'd seen the weapons the aliens had at their disposal, and they were formidable. She would have to settle for underdog tactics, guerrilla warfare, and hope to harass the enemy sufficiently to produce results.

After daybreak she kept tabs on the alien ship by using the spy-bees. The enemy captain seemed content, for the moment, to keep his main ship where it was and send out scouts to investigate other cities in the area. Perhaps he would only make a preliminary report and leave, bringing back more trained help at a later date. Nevertheless, Michi began making her plans and setting traps, just in case the enemy did come to Beta-Nu.

She held her breath when the spy-bees showed the ship taking off once more, but she soon saw that it was only going to land on the outskirts of Beta-Nu, in a better position to explore the city more thoroughly. Swarms of the aliens poured out of the ship, eager to find whatever they could within the city. Hiding from such an army would be difficult; she would have to keep on the move at all times, with little chance for rest. She spent ten minutes in a meditation state, calming her shaky nerves and rallying her energies for the ordeal ahead, then moved out to begin her campaign.

She moved cautiously at first, perhaps too cautiously. She'd only been in one real conflict in her life, the battle against the aliens on New Edo. There'd been no time then to think about what she was doing; she'd had to react on impulse. This was different, a planned and deliberate attack on other beings, and it left her feeling much like a virgin on her wedding night—eager, while simultaneously frightened by the possibilities before her.

The aliens were content, the first day, to confine their investigations to street-level sites, which gave Michi the freedom to prowl the upper floors and roofs. She had to be careful about sneaking up behind these creatures, continually reminding herself that they had *two* sets of eyes and, therefore, a much wider field of vision. She did manage to kill two of them by dropping pieces of masonry on them, thereby making it look like an accident each time; she had no illusions that she could fool the alien commander about her presence here for very long, but every bit of misdirection was a help. Still, when that turned out to be her total for the day she felt very depressed. Only two soldiers out of the hundreds that must be aboard the ship—at that rate, she could go on for months without making an appreciable dent in the enemy's forces. And the enemy would not be standing idly by in the meantime, allowing her to get away with her actions. Sooner or later, they'd realize she was here and retaliate.

The next day was far more productive, though, as a squad of soldiers was killed in the pit she'd had some robots dig beneath a thin surface layer of street, and more of the enemy were electrocuted at another hidden trap. She was rapidly overcoming her initial qualms, throwing herself wholeheartedly into the effort to fight off her depressions at being alone. By keeping her mind busy and constantly planning new traps, she could keep her thoughts from the certain knowledge that sooner or later she would be captured and/or killed by these beings.

After the second day the aliens caught on to her sabotage, and it became harder to catch them alone. They traveled strictly in small groups, constantly alert for attack. No single group was large enough to make killing them worth exposing her position, and they were vigilant enough that, with four eyes apiece, it was impossible to sneak up on them. Fortunately, one group discovered an armory, and soldiers from all over the area were called in to investigate its contents. Michi watched from a vantage point on a rooftop several blocks away until she was sure no more soldiers would be entering the building, then set off the remote-control charge she had planted there several days ago.

The resulting blast was most satisfactory, leveling a number of square blocks around the arsenal. The explosion was so strong it even rocked the building Michi had been using as her vantage point. She hadn't expected quite that much power, but the result was worth it. She estimated she had killed at least fifty of the enemy in that one blow—a good day's work. But she did not fool herself; she knew the blast would also mark a turning point in her private war with the aliens. They could no longer afford to be charitable; she was not merely an irritant anymore. She was a full-blown threat and would be dealt with accordingly.

She couldn't count on having much more time before the enemy reacted in force; she would have to follow up the blast with a full offensive of her own, hoping to catch them far enough off balance to do some good. With Kagami following on her heels, she ran quickly to the secret cache of weapons she'd stored away.

The battle cruiser sat on a level stretch of ground just outside the perimeter of the city. The aliens hadn't yet discovered the underground tunnels that had held the motorized traffic, so they were a perfect way for Michi to travel undetected. She and Kagami reached a sheltered spot near the ship, hidden in the long afternoon shadow cast by an adjacent building. Using the shadow as cover, she crept over to the locked shed where she'd stored her weaponry behind some innocuous-looking garden tools. She strapped a native rifle over one shoulder, tucked some grenades in her pockets, and picked up a large, unwieldy device that Kagami had assured her was the native equivalent of a small mortar. Carrying the bulky weapon outside, she set it up on its little tripod in clear view of the invading ship.

Kagami could describe basically how the weapon was used, but the finer points of aiming it were beyond her specialized knowledge. Trusting to her luck, which had been excellent so far, Michi fiddled with the unusual controls until she thought she had them adjusted properly, then fired.

A ball of white-hot energy soared upward from the barrel, arching into the sky. Michi did not watch its full trajectory; she could see from the first few seconds of its flight that the ball would pass well over the alien ship to land beyond. Cursing her own inexperience—and Birk, for having deserted her—she quickly recalibrated and fired again.

The controls on the energy-mortar proved more complicated than she had anticipated. For a reason she was unable to fathom, they worked on some sort of geometric, rather than arithmetic, progression; the same adjustment did not produce the same effect twice in a row. She fired five blasts at the ship, and the nearest one hit a full fifty meters away from the target. Michi was furious with herself for being such a rotten shot, even though she'd had no opportunity for target practice beforehand.

After the first three mortar shots, the ship began firing back at her. Without bothering, at first, to ascertain her position, the ship laid down a barrage sweeping an area twenty meters in front of her, raising a cloud of dirt and debris that made further sighting difficult for both sides. Michi got off a couple more rounds of her own, but each attempt gave the enemy gunners that much more opportunity to pinpoint her own location. The mortar was not an easily movable weapon, even for her and Kagami together; when the alien fire came too close, Michi and the robot had to fall back, abandoning the weapon.

The air was now choked with dust raised by the enemy fire, which caused Michi to cough as she ran back to the tubeway she'd come through. She turned as she reached its mouth and could make out through the dust an army of enemy soldiers roiling out of the ship and down the ramps. She stopped, unslung the rifle from her shoulder, and turned the adjustment on the nozzle to wide-field fire. As the advance troops came nearer she squeezed the trigger and was rewarded with a thin line of blue energy that soared from the nozzle and raced toward its target. The beam hit five soldiers and each of them dropped, but that did not deter the others. Michi remembered only too well the suicidal ferocity of these aliens. Death meant little to them; they kept coming no matter how badly they were being decimated, and their sheer determination was enough to dismay even the staunchest foe.

Michi fired several more rounds into their midst, and still they kept coming. A few had weapons of their own and were returning her fire, but their dedication to forward motion worked to the detriment of their aim. Michi stood her ground and shot back at the enemy, each shot killing three or more of the troops—but all to no avail. At last she lobbed a grenade into their front ranks and dived once more into her tunnel, to the sound of a loud blast behind her.

She'd already ordered Kagami to black out the lights so that the tubeway would be absolutely dark except for those sections Kagami personally lit. Ahead of Michi, she could see the bobbing beam of intense light emanating from the robot, illuminating the path away from the scene of the attack. Michi raced forward, knowing the surface underfoot was level and free of obstructions. After she'd gone about thirty meters, she turned to look back at the entrance.

Silhouetted against the tunnel opening, she could see the enemy troops advancing, following her trail down into the underground labyrinth of Beta-Nu. She wondered about firing a shot back and discarded the idea instantly; it would do nothing to slow down the pursuit. Instead, she pulled another grenade from her pocket and heaved it with all her strength back at the aliens. The grenade landed twenty meters away and exploded on impact. The tunnel shook, and the roof cracked, raining dust and debris down upon the aliens. Encouraged by that result, Michi followed it with a second grenade in the same place. This time the ceiling there collapsed completely, burying the forward line of soldiers under a heap of rubble and sealing off the passageway from further pursuit.

She turned back to Kagami and started running. "Come on," she gasped as she reached the robot. "It won't take them long to start pouring in from the other entrances now that they know these tunnels exist, and I want to be as far from here as possible when they do."

Without even so much as a nod, Kagami accepted Michi's instructions and set out at a brisk pace. Michi followed the robot, running hard to catch up. No particular destination had been preset; in the back of Michi's mind had been the fear that she would never survive this raid at all, and she had not planned beyond this point. The robot, however, took it for granted that her mistress wanted to escape and planned the best route accordingly. They wove in and out of various tunnels, seemingly at random, until eventually they came out at an exit on the city's perimeter ninety degrees away from the ship.

It was night as they emerged from the tunnel—the dead black moonless night that characterized this world. Michi was gasping for breath as she tried to follow the robot, and her wounds were aching fiercely. She paused to catch her breath, holding one arm tightly against the scar line, and watched the robot moving away from the city. "Where are you going?" Michi called in a loud stage whisper.

Kagami halted and replied at the same volume. "There is a small forest in the hills just south of here. The invaders will be searching the city, but they probably won't think to look for you there. You will be safe."

Michi tried to take a step toward the robot, but collapsed on the ground instead as the pain from her wounds suddenly became more than she could bear. Kagami raced back to her side as Michi lay moaning in pain. "Can I help you?"

Through a fog of pain, Michi tried feebly to wave the robot aside and indicate she would be all right. "Just give me a few minutes," she gasped. "I'm doing too much too soon."

"I could carry you to a hiding place."

Michi shook her head. "No. I'm not leaving the city and all its weapons to them. I have to go back, keep trying. . . ."

"The forest is a safer course."

The pain was easing ever so slightly, enough to allow Michi to prop herself up on one arm. "If all I wanted was safety, I'd have gone with Birk. Running away will ruin everything. The aliens will get the weapons, and I won't be able to stop them. I've got a job to do here, and I intend to do it." *Or die trying* was the implied ending to her sentence.

Kagami did not argue further, but waited patiently at her mistress's side until Michi was ready to travel on. The robot helped the woman to her feet, and together the two figures slipped back into the city, working their way stealthily through the darkness of night to avoid detection.

Back in the direction of the alien ship, matters were not proceeding as silently. Every few minutes, Michi could hear a loud crash, and Kagami informed her that the invaders were systematically tearing down buildings in their hunt for the fugitives. They brought in banks of searchlights to illuminate the sector as bright as day. They would leave no sanctuary for Michi to hide in, and appeared ready to tear down all of Beta-Nu, if necessary, to apprehend the enemy saboteur.

I suppose I should feel flattered that they think I'm worth so much effort, Michi thought as she ran. But her body was in pain and her spirit was numb, and all she could feel was tired.

She tried to swim through the apathy that flooded her brain, tried to think of what to do next. Her body was being pressed to the limits of exhaustion, and she needed a spur to keep her going. She provided her own incentive by telling herself she could always quit the way Birk had. That thought so infuriated her that she kept moving despite all the pain and fatigue.

The arsenals were the key to this entire battle. Her principle aim was to prevent the aliens from capturing the Makers' weapons and taking them home for analysis. With those arms in addition to their own, they would certainly be unbeatable and Earth would stand no chance at all. If Michi could destroy all the armories, there would be little left in Beta-Nu that would do the invaders much good.

There were, of course, hundreds of other cities scattered about the face of this planet, each with its own armories. Michi refused to think about those. Her mind could handle only one problem at a time. She would deal with future battles when the need arose.

She had already booby-trapped the arsenals with remote-control detonators; it remained only for her to get within range and set them off. She informed Kagami of her plan, and the two fugitives turned back in the direction of the alien ship, hoping to avoid detection long enough to set the plan into action.

They did not make it. While running across an open plaza under the searchlights' glare, they were spotted by an enemy patrol, which immediately opened fire. A blast from an alien's gun hit Michi's left shoulder just as she dove for cover behind a building with Kagami right behind her. The woman cried out in pain and stumbled to her knees, trying to get up again to continue running. Her second try was successful, and she was on her feet and moving at a pace that was more a fast stagger than a run.

Destinations and plans were pushed from her mind. There was nothing now but pure survival: running to avoid capture and hiding to avoid detection. The patrol that had spotted her had sent up an alarm, and within minutes the aliens were concentrating their search in this vicinity, making escape all the more difficult. Michi and her robot ran a random course through the city for half an hour, finding only momentary respite before having to move on.

During one brief stop, Michi crouched on the ground and tucked her head down between her knees. "It's hopeless," she admitted. "I can't run forever, and they've got a whole army against just the two of us. Maybe Birk was right after all. It was stupid to think a person alone could make that much difference."

Kagami was silent for a moment. Then, quietly, she said, "Would you like to call for help?"

"Who could I call? There's nobody here but us."

"We can call Birk and Arthur. They may be able to help."

"We don't even know where they are."

"It's true we don't know their physical location. But Arthur thought we might someday need to contact them, and he informed me secretly of a way to do it."

"I won't go crawling back to Birk. I have some pride. And even if I did, he'd never listen—not after what happened before."

"Perhaps, not being alive, I misunderstand these things," Kagami said, "but I was under the impression that any alternative was preferable to death."

Michi hardly knew anymore what was preferable to what. She only knew she wanted to end this infernal chasing one way or another. "How do we contact them?" she asked resignedly.

"There is a room on the third floor of the tower where you

and Birk were living," Kagami said. "In that room is a communications screen tuned to a particular frequency Arthur specified. He said they could receive messages broadcast on that frequency if ever we needed to send them. I suspect this might be an opportune time to try."

Michi looked up dismally. "I don't know," she said softly. "I don't know anything anymore. My head's all turned around; nothing makes sense and everything is too much effort. What's the point of it all, anyway?"

"I am not capable of reasoning on quite that abstract a level. I was never designed for philosophical arguments."

"I wasn't either." Michi gave a little half-laugh, and that very act helped shake off the worst of the apathy. "All right, we'll give it a try and see if a samurai comes galloping to my rescue. Which way is the tower? I've gotten my directions so turned around. . . ."

Kagami pointed and Michi winced. In order to reach the desired building, they would have to pass through heavy concentrations of enemy soldiers, who seemed to shoot at anything that moved, even if it turned out to be their own people. This brief rest had given the pain time to catch up to her; not only were Michi's old wounds throbbing, but the burn across her left shoulder made moving that arm almost impossible.

"I don't think I can make it," she said. "Getting through their ranks in my condition . . ."

Kagami hesitated for just a second, then started off down the alleyway. "Where are you going?" Michi called after her.

"To create a diversion and draw the soldiers away from this area," the robot replied without stopping. "Without them here, you might have an easier time."

Michi couldn't think of anything to say until the robot was well out of earshot. She was startled that such heroism could be built into a machine—but, looked at from a robot's point of view, Kagami's action was a very practical one. What was heroism, after all, except doing the practical thing under adverse circumstances?

As she crouched in hiding, Michi could hear the soldiers' reactions to something, and the noise of pursuit gradually fading off into the distance. When she was sure the area was safe, Michi stood up once more and began her slow, painful trek back to Birk's home tower.

EIGHTEEN

Birk prowled the empty streets of Alpha-Xi like a lost poltergeist looking for a house to haunt. Alpha-Xi was a city that had never been truly alive before it died, and somehow—though Birk had never noticed it before—that made all the difference. The body of the town was intact, but its soul had been aborted centuries before Birk was even born.

When he first came into the city he was in no condition to measure such delicate feelings. He was still smarting from the sting of Michi's betrayal and still smoldering with the fires of his resentment. Sleep was difficult, coming in too-short intervals from which he fitfully awoke with his body dripping in sweat. He'd been most afraid of having nightmares, but he couldn't sleep long enough for any to come. He was reduced, instead, to restless tossing in his bed and nervous pacing along the floor. If Arthur observed any of this behavior, however, he was tactful enough not to comment upon it.

But if his nights were filled with restless energy, Birk's days dragged by with numbing fatigue. The loss of sleep was sapping his strength, robbing him of any pleasure he might have taken in this hidden fortress. Overhead, the illuminated cavern roof glowed its brilliant, ever-changing colors, and all he could do was yawn. The magnificent architecture, the majestic sweep of the skyscrapers left him drained and emotionless. When his anger at Michi died, there was nothing to replace it; Birk was a zombie haunting a city built for pleasure.

In an effort to cheer up his master, Arthur went to great lengths to provide diversions. He staged concerts of the strange electronic sound patterns the Makers had called music. He organized the maintenance robots into teams and presented sports spectacles of fierce and destructive competition. He ran the recordings of old plays and performances stored by the Makers for posterity, supplying Birk with subtitles where necessary. But his efforts were to no avail. Birk sat through all the presentations as though he did not care, as though his life had been stolen from him when he wasn't looking and his body was just going through the motions, afraid to admit the truth.

On the second day, Birk realized that this city was much colder than he'd previously thought, even though Arthur insisted that the air temperature was kept at the same standard as always. When Birk could not stop his shivering fits, Arthur turned the heat up higher until it was well past 30 celsius. Then Birk began complaining that it was too hot. From day to day the temperature seemed to fluctuate wildly, adding still more complaints to Birk's restless displeasure with what he'd thought was his paradise.

He wandered the streets, surrounded by beauty and yet apart from it. There were fewer maintenance robots here than in most other cities, a fact that only added to his feeling of emptiness. Spending the rest of his life here no longer seemed the ideal plan it once had been, and for that—as for everything else that was wrong with his life—he blamed Michi. The woman had ruined his perfect planet, despoiled it with the venom of her twisted soul. She had ruined him, too, shattering the tranquility of his mind and freeing the demon Hope from its dark imprisonment. She had brought a mirror of life, and he refused to peer into it for fear of seeing everything he'd sacrificed on his path to survival.

Then, on the fifth night as he prepared for another fruitless wrestling match with sleep, Arthur came quietly into the room and stood beside the bed. "Sir," he said, "I've received a message from Lieutenant Nakamura."

Birk tensed. "How did she find out where we were?"

"She doesn't know where we are," the robot explained carefully, knowing that this entire conversation was a potentially explosive one. "She merely transmitted a message along a specified frequency, without knowing our location."

"A *specified* frequency? Specified by whom?"

"By me, sir. I had informed Kagami that if ever communication was necessary . . ."

Birk banged a fist down hard against the side of his bed. "You did? And who in hell told you to do that?"

Despite his master's fury, Arthur retained his implacable calm. "No one, sir. It wasn't expressly forbidden, so I took it

197

on my own authority to establish the communications link. It did not seem wise to sever all possible ties permanently."

"Oh it didn't, did it? Well, you can break off your little tête-à-tête this instant. That woman is trouble incarnate, and I want nothing more to do with her. That's an order."

Arthur hesitated slightly. "She's in grave danger, sir."

"I don't care if she's fighting off the entire Mongol horde. She brought her trouble on herself. She could have been safely here with me. Anything she gets, she deserves."

"She could be killed," Arthur persisted.

"And I just told you, I don't care. Now I order you to forget about her and stop any communication."

"I can't do that, sir."

"What?" In all the time he'd known Arthur, Birk had never heard him deliberately refuse a direct order. There were times, Birk knew, when the robot could be stubborn and think of ways to circumvent his commands, but he had never before flatly said no. For him to do so now, when he knew how strongly Birk felt about this matter, was a major shock. "You'll do it if I tell you to."

"Not necessarily. I was endowed with certain discretionary circuits. . . ."

"You're a robot, goddamn it! You have to follow orders."

"I am several levels above the ordinary maintenance or factory robot, as you yourself know full well. I was created to be a servant, not a slave, with highly sophisticated, independent judgment." Arthur's voice was as emotionless as ever as he made his boasts; there was neither anger nor indignation in his tones.

"In other words, you suddenly think you have the right to do whatever you want."

"Not suddenly, sir. I've always had that option. I've served you because that was my function—but there are limits."

"And now?" Birk sneered.

"And now I must go to Lieutenant Nakamura's assistance. There is a chance that Kagami has been destroyed."

Birk's shoulders sagged, and he looked away from the robot. "Et tu, Arthur?"

"I beg your pardon, sir?"

"Are you going to betray me, too? I thought that, if nothing else, I could always count on you."

"It isn't betrayal, sir. In fact, I was about to ask if you wished to come with me. Your assistance and advice would be of enormous benefit."

"Never!" Birk shouted. "That little bitch dug her own grave. I'm not going to jump into it with her."

"As you wish, sir." Arthur started slowly out of the room.

"Just a damn minute," Birk called after him. "What about me?"

"You will be perfectly safe and comfortable, sir. There are plenty of robots to see to your needs. You can talk to them and order them about as you wish. They will obey your slightest command."

Birk was fighting to keep the tears out of his eyes. "Arthur, you've been with me for eleven years now. You've only known that woman for a few weeks. What did she ever do for you that would make you desert me after all this time? Don't eleven years count for anything?"

Arthur hesitated, longer than Birk could ever remember his doing before. Finally, the robot replied, "The difference, sir, is that Michi needs me now and you don't."

And with that, he was gone.

Birk tried to get out of bed and follow, but his feet got tangled in the bedcovers. In his struggle to free himself, he half fell to the floor in a welter of blankets. After a few moments he stopped his struggling and lay there awkwardly, feet on the bed and shoulders on the ground, trying to make sense out of the world that was falling to pieces around him.

Not need you? he thought. *How could you possibly think that? I've needed you from the first moment I came here. You kept me alive when I was dying, you told me what I needed to know to survive, you fed me and dressed me and talked to me when I was lonely. I've always needed that. I need it more than ever now that I'm stuck down here in Alpha-Xi.*

Birk was sobbing now, his body shaking as it lay in its awkward position amid the covers. *You were my friend, Arthur. My only friend. Someone I could count on to be there. And now you're gone.* He was crying so hard that he began to cough, wiping his running nose harshly against his bare forearm. The cold and the darkness of the night pressed in against him, reinforcing the loneliness that was now more total than anything he'd felt during the past eleven years. He twisted around within the blankets, wrapping them more tightly about his body and trying to hide himself within their folds. He wanted to die, to wipe himself out of the Universe without a trace, to become a nullity on the face of time. Gradually the sobs subsided, and he slipped into the first deep sleep he'd had since coming to Alpha-Xi.

When he awoke the next morning his eyes were dry. The tears and the mucous had dried on his upper lip, making his moustache stiff and crackly. The artificial light of the cavern ceiling flooded into the room, making harsh shadows and giving everything the hard edge of reality-made-brittle. The hurt had been replaced once more; he had adapted, as he always had. The emptiness within him was gone, and in its stead was a cold, calculating hatred that radiated from him like a frozen phosphorescence. He had transformed his loneliness into a tough, resilient rage that devoured everything in its path.

The mistake, he could see now, was in caring about anyone— even about a machine like Arthur. Once you let them in, once you let them past the defenses, then they could hurt you. And if they could, they would. That was a rule of nature as invariable as the laws of thermodynamics. That was a revelation of such crystalline purity, its shiny sharp edges so glittering with the light of truth, that he marveled at not having discovered it sooner.

But at least he knew it now. Now he could defend himself against the pain of rejection and betrayal. The ultimate rule of survival was to stay aloof and apart. If nothing mattered to him then nothing could hurt him. He could only be hurt if he cared. Now that he'd made himself independent of everything, he was free from pain forever.

He had cared for Reva, and she'd denounced him. He had cared for the people of Earth, and they'd turned their backs on him, leaving him to the mercy of Torres and his trained sadists. He had cared for Michi, and she'd tricked him to further her own purposes. Worst of all, he had cared for Arthur, and even the robot had betrayed him—deserting him at his time of crisis with a mechanical fickleness that Birk found impossible to explain.

One by one, everything he cared about had turned away and left him alone. He knew now the true meaning of that window he'd seen in the Beta-Nu art gallery. It was intended to point a lesson: Don't depend on the help of others, for they will invariably turn away. Reva, Michi, and now Arthur—he had lain on the ground in pain and agony, calling to them for help, and each of them had spurned him, pursuing their own selfish ends and sacrificing him to the wolves of necessity. If he was to live, he would have to get up off the ground by himself and not depend on someone else's hand to help him up.

He rose and dressed himself with great deliberation, then left the bedroom, ignoring the breakfast tray some well-intentioned robot had left on the table. It was his soul, not his body, that was hungry, and it needed nourishment of a totally different sort. The cold, cunning animal that now was Birk Aaland smiled. There were safe, harmless ways of feeding the anger that was consuming him. It was the only passion he dared allow himself, and he would treat it well.

No more would he be used. No more would he be a plaything for other people, manipulated like a mindless puppet. He stalked through the streets of Alpha-Xi toward the door to the surface, each step forceful and filled with his new purpose. He had been reborn, alive with renewed energy after Michi and Arthur had cast him into the abyss of despair. The new Birk Aaland would be free of the weaknesses that had caused the old Birk so much pain. He would see to that.

He made a brief stop to pick up a small handgun, then returned to the surface above the city's cavern. The crisp morning air of the forest glade did little to cool the heat of his spirit; he stood motionless at the entrance to the city with a slight breeze ruffling his hair. His eyes scanned the surrounding territory like those of a predator bird seeking its prey. Then, with sudden decision, he strode off in his chosen direction.

He stalked through the forest for half an hour, moving with an easy disdain that epitomized his new personna. After a time he spotted a motion to his right, and halted. There, perched on a tree branch, was a small fuzzy creature reminiscent of a terrestrial squirrel. The creature looked back at him with large black eyes and not a trace of fear; it thought it was safely out of his range and was confident of its ability to escape should there be any trouble.

Birk slowly lifted his gun and checked the setting to make sure it was on the lowest possible charge. He didn't want to kill the squirrel—that would take all the fun out of it. He merely wanted it helpless for a while.

Moving casually so as not to startle the creature, he took careful aim and fired. There was a small *bleep* and the squirrel tumbled from its perch to the ground. Birk ran to it, checking to see that it had not been killed by the fall. The animal lay on its back in the grass, panting in fear, but it was paralyzed and helpless in the face of the massive enemy that now bent and lifted it up in one enormous hand.

Holding tightly to the skin at the back of the animal's neck so that it couldn't turn and bite him if it shook off the paralysis, Birk took one of the squirrel's back legs between the thumb and forefinger of his other hand and began pulling and twisting it. His jaw was clenched as he thought, *From now on, I'm the one who'll do the hurting. I'll give back all the pain I suffered. I'll make them sorry they hurt me.*

The squirrel's eyes reflected the torment it was feeling, the fear and pain suffered at the hands of this hideous beast. It could not move, but tiny whimpers came from its throat in reaction to the torture.

The noises only fueled Birk's fire. He looked at the animal's face and imagined it was Michi lying helpless in his grasp, Michi pleading for mercy, Michi begging him not to hurt her any more. He grinned and twisted harder until he heard a tiny snap and the Michi-squirrel squealed in pain.

He took the squirrel's other leg, and the animal's face turned into Reva's. *You never wanted me, did you?* he thought as he twisted the tiny limb. *You were secretly laughing at me all the time I worshiped you. You ran out when I needed you, the worst betrayal of all.*

When that leg, too, broke, Birk grabbed the pathetic creature by its tail and began swinging it around over his head, finally beating its body against a tree. "This is for you, Arthur!" he shouted aloud. "The worst traitor of all. You made me care for you, you made me utterly dependent, and just when I couldn't cope without you, you turned and walked out. You're a goddamned calculating metal devil, and I hate every cog and gear in your fucking body!"

Blinded by his rage, his blows took on a savage ferocity almost sexual in intensity. He swung the squirrel against the tree trunk time and time again, until there was little left of it but a lifeless furry lump. Tossing it away, he went and cold-bloodedly stalked another, torturing it the same way, relieving more than a decade of pent-up hostility at his own incarceration and torture. The faces of his victims were constantly changing: Torres, Reva, Michi, Arthur, and the legion of nameless guards and soldiers who had beaten him for their own amusement during his imprisonment. He went through a total of six squirrels, feeding the dark and angry side of his nature with the bloodlust of his sickness. Only when it was late afternoon and he realized he should be getting back down into the city before dark did he call a reluctant halt to his activities and return home.

His body was glowing with life, the surface of his skin

tingling with the excitement of what he'd been doing. He was ravenous, wolfing down the large meal the robots prepared for him and demanding seconds, then thirds. He went to bed, lying in the darkness with his mind replaying the scenes of the day on the ceiling for his amusement. When he fell asleep, his rest was deep and dreamless, the sleep of a man whose soul finally knew peace.

Just as day was starting once again in the underground city, he was awakened by the gentle tapping of a robot at the door to his bedroom. Birk tried to ignore it and return to sleep, but the tapping persisted. He was tempted to yell "Go away," but knew that these robots with less imagination than Arthur tended to be extremely literal. If there was something important requiring his attention, he might never find it out.

Wide awake at last, he turned over onto his back and said, "What is it?"

"A message has come in on the communications screen." The robot's voice was a mechanical buzz, not nearly as smooth and mellifluent as Arthur's.

Birk gave a bitter snort. "It's probably that damn Michi again, begging for my help. Well, let her beg. The aliens can blow her apart for all I care."

"It is Arthur," the robot said.

"I don't want to talk to him either," Birk began. But it was too late—Arthur's voice was being piped into the bedroom through speakers Birk hadn't known existed.

"I called to say good-bye," Arthur said. His voice sounded strangely hollow, with a resonant burr to the words.

"Isn't this a bit late?"

Arthur continued slowly, despite the interruption. "Michi has been captured by the aliens. Kagami is still functioning, but greatly disabled. I was shot attempting to help Michi. I don't believe I can be fixed. My power is draining rapidly."

Birk felt a sudden chill up his spine. "Arthur?"

"I regret I could not serve you better."

"Arthur? ARTHUR!"

There was no answer, just a roomful of silence around him. Birk's body was covered with cold sweat. Arthur couldn't be destroyed. He had existed for better than two thousand years. He'd survived the Armageddon that killed his makers. He'd survived the centuries of boredom until Birk's crash landing here. He'd helped Birk through the most difficult times of his life, and Birk had more than once commented that Arthur would last until the Universe itself sank into its ultimate heat-death. Arthur was one of nature's constants— implacable as a mountain, eternal as the wind. Arthur would not—could not—die.

A fit of shivering wracked Birk's body. He remembered his earliest impression of this world, opening his eyes in the hospital and seeing Arthur standing before him. He remembered the long, often comical, language lessons while Arthur was learning Worldspeak. He remembered his first awed explorations of the Makers' cities with Arthur at his side, patiently explaining the planet's dim past. Every action Arthur took was done with the same uncomplaining acceptance of the world as it was—the gentle, unhurried pace of a being who had lasted more than two thousand years and had thousands more ahead of him.

The thought bubbled up from the depths of his soul that Arthur had gone voluntarily to help Michi, though somehow that concept no longer aroused the feelings of rage it had yesterday. *But why, Arthur, why?* he wondered, and back came the memory of the robot's parting words: *Because Michi needs me now, and you don't.* It was as simple as that. Arthur went where he was needed.

He wanted me to come with him. He asked for my help, and I turned him down. There was a sudden stinging in the corners of Birk's eyes, and he squeezed the lids tightly shut to stem the flow of tears. The robot he had thought of as his friend had asked a favor—the only favor in nearly a dozen years—and Birk had chased him off as though he were some malodorous street beggar.

I killed him, he thought, biting his lower lip to punish himself with pain. *If I'd gone, too, I could have helped him, warned him. We could have planned a reasonable approach. We could have won. The two of us could make that city do anything we wanted. It's all my fault he's dead.*

As he doubled up with guilt, the shame of it burning like a coal in his belly, he experienced a sudden snap as his mind divorced itself from his body. He found himself as a separate entity, standing in a corner of the room and looking down at the huddled, sobbing figure on the bed. From this strange perspective, he saw Birk Aaland as merely an animated skeleton on which some skin and hair had been decorously draped—a walking, breathing corpse that lived without life and experienced without feeling. It was a pathetic creature, that man who existed with neither reason nor goal, but it was not *him*. It had chosen survival as an end instead of a means, and that was the saddest testimonial he could conceive.

The destruction of Arthur had forced him outside himself, outside the narrow little sphere that encased his mind like concrete. Looking into his own soul, he could see himself for what he had become—an animal, a selfish, unreasoning beast who lived only for the next meal, the next night's sleep, the next morning's sunrise. He viewed himself without anger, but instead with pity, remembering the long chain of events that had brought him to this sorry state: his arrest, the betrayal by Reva, the imprisonment, the torture, the escape, the long years of solitude here on this dead planet, topped off by the frustrations with Michi. Here, in this unique way, he could view the events dispassionately as a rationale—but not an excuse—for the end result.

Memory of that artist's window in Beta-Nu came back to him with crystal clarity, but suddenly it had shifted into a meaning it had never held for him before. Now *he* was the standing figure, the one with his back turned to the person pleading for help. He, Birk Aaland, was the cold, heartless disdainer wrapped in a cloak of selfishness and ignoring the cries of the downtrodden. The figure in the background, lying propped on one arm with the other extended, was a protean being. First it was Michi, begging him to help her return to Earth. Her demands were not unreasonable; looked at from this new vantage point, he could see she was concerned with saving millions of lives that might otherwise be lost if the aliens managed sneak attacks on other Commonwealth planets. Even if he couldn't build a spaceship for their escape, the message rockets she'd suggested were not beyond the bounds of possibility. But, wrapped in his selfish need to spurn all things of Earth, he had turned his back on her pleas and left her alone to face the menace of the alien invaders.

Then the figure became Arthur, begging in his gentle, unemotional way to help him perform his duty to the living. Arthur was a servant of life; when Michi was threatened it was only logical that he should help her at the expense of Birk, who was in no danger whatsoever. But Birk, because of his wounded pride, had sent the poor robot off to his destruction without so much as a word of fond farewell. He had even cursed Arthur for deserting him when, in truth, the desertion was the other way around.

And then, much to his surprise, the figure on the ground changed once again and became Reva—pleading with him now, as she'd probably been too scared to do in real life, not to challenge the power of the government. She'd never been a strong woman; she had few resources of her own. When he was arrested and all his property seized, what was left for her? How had the government, in ways both subtle and obvious, bullied her into betraying him? If he'd thought as much about her as he'd thought about his precious principles, he might never have taken the foolhardy stand that ended so tragically for both of them.

The figure on the ground flickered, blurred, and divided into three—the three people he had, by his own callow selfishness, abandoned to their fate. He watched the scene in the imaginary window, watched the cold, dispassionate Birk Aaland scorn the pleading trio behind him. The pity he had felt a moment ago for this man who had undergone so many horrors vanished in a wave of self-hatred. Birk Aaland deserted his friends in their moments of crisis. Birk Aaland was not to be trusted. He was alone because, ultimately, he pushed away anyone who threatened to invade the inner circle of his soul. He would die alone and unloved because it was a goal he had worked hard for and richly deserved.

The visions were gone. Birk's mind rejoined that sorry piece of protoplasm sobbing on the bed—sobbing as much from self-pity as in mourning for a robot. But even through the shaking and the tears, insights were emerging in his brain—a belated sense of responsibility, a desire to stop the headlong rush away from reality, to return, however briefly, to the dimension of life once more. As Michi had said, there had to be an end to running sometime, even for him.

"Sir?"

That voice, seeming from thousands of kilometers away, brought his mind partially into focus. At first he thought it might be Arthur, miraculously returned; but then he realized it was much too mechanical and harsh. It was another robot outside the door, perhaps the same one who'd awakened him for Arthur's message. Birk realized with no little surprise that he couldn't tell how much time had elapsed between then and now.

"Yes?" he replied aloud, making no attempt to keep his voice steady. After all, what did it matter whether a robot knew he'd been crying?

"The robot Kagami is calling. Did you wish to speak to her?"

Taking a deep breath, Birk sat up in bed and opened his eyes. The room was quiet, the world waited.

"Just tell her to hold on," he said. "I'll be there as soon as I can."

NINETEEN

Things were settling back into place for Rafalyi and his crew. With the threat of enemy action now ended, he could concentrate on the real job of exploring the dead city.

The attack on his ship had been the turning point. When it failed in its first few volleys and he was able to regain the offensive, he could actually feel the tide of events moving his way. He ordered his soldiers out to capture rather than kill the enemy if at all possible, though giving them full permission to destroy as much of the city as necessary in the quest.

Klondanar-Nakonal gave him a funny look at that command. Any other commander would have ordered the resistance wiped out without a second thought—but Rafalyi was blessed/cursed with a probing imagination. He wanted to know the nature of the opposition, and why it chose so suicidal a plan as to attack his ship haphazardly. He knew his soldiers would have trouble remembering the capture-rather-than-kill order, but he hoped it could be carried out.

It took hours of searching and several false leads, but his troops searched diligently all through the night and the next day. One of the false leads turned out to be a robot; several soldiers got good shots at it and reported inflicting severe damage. For a while, the robot was all they could find, but Rafalyi stubbornly refused to believe that was all there was. The city was teeming with robots that were perfectly harmless and ignored his soldiers completely, so why should only one of them go on the warpath? If only a robot were involved, the attack on the ship would have been more thorough and better coordinated. He told his troops to search on and find a better culprit.

On the night after the attack, several hours past sunset, an alien being was spotted. It was in the custody of a robot much like the one seen earlier, except that it showed no signs of the reported damage. Whether it was the same machine or not quickly became immaterial; Rafalyi's troops incapacitated it with a rapid barrage of fire. It would have been easy to destroy the alien, too, except for Rafalyi's express orders to the contrary. Actually, once surrounded, the being put up surprisingly little fight. It had a wound across one shoulder, but seemed much sicker than that superficial injury would have made it. Rafalyi ordered that it be brought back to the ship for interrogation; meanwhile, the search for other aliens continued.

But it was now two days later, and no traces had been found. Judging by the guerrilla tactics used against him, Rafalyi was quite willing to believe there was only the one saboteur, aided by a robot or two—and, from the condition of the wrecked alien ship, it was scarcely surprising there weren't more survivors. Even this one was in bad shape. The miracle was that it had managed any kind of attack against him at all.

He was impatient to question it, but as yet had no opportunity. The creature was quite ill from its efforts, unconscious most of the time and delirious the rest. Not knowing the alien language, Rafalyi was uncertain how to proceed. Basic sign language would probably convey enough meaning for a start, provided the creature would cooperate. To ensure its cooperation, Rafalyi would probably have to torture it—but in order to torture it, he had to make certain the alien was healthy enough to survive its ordeal. In its present condition, it would not live beyond the first few minutes. So Rafalyi had it imprisoned under guard in a small room adjacent to his personal quarters, and waited.

In the meantime, the threat to his ship had been eliminated. He ordered his soldiers to cease their search and to return to their initial activity—searching what was left of the city to find anything of value. And, in particular, to find some more of those armories.

Kagami herself had barely survived her encounters with the alien soldiers, Birk learned from interrogating her over the communicators. Several shots had hit her dead center, partially paralyzing her motor circuits and slurring her speech pattern. She could barely move faster than a crawl, she said, and she had to speak slowly to make herself understood. She had, however, managed to lead the enemy soldiers away from Michi for a while and then lost them herself, giving Michi time to call Arthur.

Now, though, her heroics seemed to have been for naught. The aliens had persisted in their search, and Michi was in no condition to evade them for long. Arthur had found her just before the enemy did and was destroyed for his trouble. Kagami had eyewitness accounts from maintenance robots that Michi had been taken into the alien vessel, apparently alive, but that was some time ago. There was no way of telling whether the woman was still alive, or what might have happened to her in enemy hands. In the meantime, Kagami had had to use all her resources just to avoid the alien patrols that continued to scour the city for signs of more saboteurs.

Birk listened restlessly as Kagami gave him a detailed report of the aliens' activities. He listened with only half his mind, while the other half was working feverishly to develop some plan of attack against these creatures. He was no military expert; he hadn't had formal training in battle tactics as Michi presumably had. He knew there were giant military computers in other cities on this world, machines that delighted in solving complex tactical problems—but he didn't even know the right questions to ask. Without a sophisticated robot like Arthur or Kagami to act as an interface between himself and the computer, such a powerful tool would be useless to him. He would have to think of something on his own.

The only thing he really knew about the aliens was that they had an apparent disdain for their soldiers' lives. From Michi's descriptions of the battles on New Edo and from the way the aliens operated here, retreat was a shameful thing to them. When fired upon they fought back without consideration for personal safety. Michi had said the effect was overawing in battle, but it could also be a major weakness. In any event, it was the only clue he had to go by and he would have to use it.

"Try to stay hidden," he advised Kagami. "Make sure the maintenance robots do nothing out of the ordinary. Let's let the invaders think there was only the one human working against them. We'll try to lull them into a false sense of security for a while, and hope they won't take off immediately. I've got a couple of things to take care of before I join you there in a couple of days. We'll keep in touch by radio in the meantime, okay?"

Birk's primary concern was that the aliens might decide to leave at any moment. Once they were gone, the game was lost forever. They would return to their home world and come back here with armies of their soldiers, more than he could possibly cope with even using all the resources of this planet. Michi had realized that, too, which was obviously why she'd tried her abortive attack on the spaceship. Her methods were primitive and hurried and were doomed from the start. Birk had what he hoped was a more sophisticated method at his disposal, one that stood a better chance of success.

His main problem would be remembering where he'd left it. He'd always relied on Arthur to keep track of such things, knowing full well that the robot would always be there with a faultless memory. Now Arthur was not there, and Birk had to strain his recollection through years of petty details and repeated experiences. When he had narrowed the selection down to three possible places, he took a small car, camouflaged to avoid any chance of a stray alien patrol spotting him from the air, and left his hidden city of Alpha-Xi once more.

The car unfortunately moved at a much slower rate than a delta, and he had a long way to travel. The search was fruitless at his first stop, so he resolutely proceeded on to the next. He arrived two days after leaving Alpha-Xi, feeling hungry and exhausted; and there, in a makeshift laboratory he could barely remember setting up, he found what he'd been looking for: his hyperprop jammer.

He ordered the local robots to prepare some meals to take with him in the car, and waited restlessly while they did so. He was exhausted after two days' driving with little sleep, but he knew he could not rest yet. The aliens might decide to take off at any moment, and he had to get his jammer in place before they could leave. Otherwise, everything would be lost.

Birk drove day and night to reach Beta-Nu, pushing his car at top speed all the way. He used the car's radio to keep in frequent contact with Kagami. The robot reported that the invaders had stopped their search for guerrillas and had returned to their previous explorations of the city, apparently convinced there was no further danger. They had discovered two more of the arsenals and had begun greedily stripping them of their weapons. Michi had booby-trapped those buildings, too, before her capture, and it was a great temptation to blow them up while the aliens were inside—but, acting on Birk's orders, Kagami did nothing. The enemy must feel completely secure at last.

Birk timed his arrival at the city just after nightfall. Kagami arranged for a maintenance robot to rendezvous with him, since she was too damaged to do so herself; Birk and the robot carried his jammer and crept silently through the darkened streets to a building as close to the ship as he dared go. The aliens, no longer fearing mischief, had stationed no watch around their vessel, and the area was completely dark. It took Birk several hours to set up his equipment, but at last the job was done.

Unfortunately, there was no way to test whether his jammer would work or not. The machine generated a field that would cripple a hyperprop engine, but perhaps the aliens used a drive of a totally different design. Until the alien ship actually turned on its engines, Birk would not know how effective his invention really was. But at least it was in place, and Birk could rest a bit, confident he had done as much as he could to prevent a takeoff.

That accomplished, Birk retired to a safe niche in one of the underground tubeways and slept for five hours, instructing the robot with him to wake him shortly before dawn. Tomorrow would be the crucial battle, and Birk did not want to miss a second of it.

Birk used Kagami to help him in his scheme. Even though the robot had great difficulty moving, she could nonetheless plug herself into the city's radio link and coordinate individual units into a cohesive whole. Kagami would be an indispensable part of the coming battle, and Birk hated to think of how complicated the problem would have been without her.

By sunup all was in readiness. The maintenance robots went efficiently about their chores as always, ignored by the alien soldiers who came out of their ship for a new day's exploration. There was no sign that today would be any different from the days that went before. Peace and harmony reigned in Beta-Nu.

Birk waited until after noon and checked the situation with Kagami one final time. The robot, who could monitor various sectors, reported that the aliens were going about their explorations exactly as they had been doing in the past few days—walking openly through the streets with their

211

weapons holstered, searching through buildings for anything useful they might find.

Birk closed his eyes, took a deep breath, and ordered Kagami to signal the start of battle.

Throughout Beta-Nu, thousands of the little gray maintenance robots—whom the invaders had learned to ignore because they were completely harmless—suddenly lit their laser welding torches and began advancing on the aliens. The soldiers were taken totally by surprise. Nearly a hundred were cut down by the swarms of robots before they could even think to draw their own weapons. Those who weren't killed immediately made no attempt to hide; as Birk had assumed, that was not their philosophy of fighting. They stood their ground, firing valiantly into the mobs of machines that had surrounded them so abruptly. But they were vastly outnumbered. The machines carried the day, a credit to their creators. The battle barely lasted twenty minutes before all traces of the aliens were obliterated from the streets of Beta-Nu.

But before that, while the fighting still raged, Birk turned his attention to the area of most crucial concern—the alien spaceship. He did not know how the alien commander would respond to this new situation. If he simply sent the rest of his troops out to fight, they would be slaughtered along with the rest—but Birk could not count on the enemy to be that blatantly suicidal. A more reasonable commander, seeing that this battle was lost, might try to retreat by taking off in the ship, and the success of that maneuver would depend entirely on the effectiveness of an unproven invention.

Birk wiped his hands nervously on his clothes to dry the sweat. He knew the theory of his hyperprop jammer backward and forward. It *should* work—but then, every engineer was familiar with things that should have worked, but didn't. The jammer had never been field-tested, because there'd been nothing to test it on. Even if the theory was correct, the machine might have been assembled wrong by the robots working under Birk's direction, although Arthur had assured him that they were precision workers from an electronics plant.

The worst possibility of all, and the one that haunted his mind the most, was that the alien spaceship might work on a principle totally different from that of hyperprop—in which case, his projector would be about as effective as using mothballs to kill an elephant.

He could only watch the ship nervously, and hope.

Aboard the ship, the situation plunged quickly into chaos as reports came in about the robot uprising in the city. All the descriptions were the same—robots unexpectedly banding together and attacking soldiers with welding torches—and all ended with the same chilling abruptness. Something or someone had set off a time bomb out there, and Rafalyi's troops were paying the price for it.

When, after a few minutes, some sense could be made of the situation, Rafalyi's subordinates were unanimous that a counterattack must begin immediately. Rafalyi listened to their advice with surface politeness, then proceeded to issue orders of his own. The discovery of this world could not be jeopardized; it possessed secrets that would be of immense value to the race. Even so unthinkable a practice as retreat could be condoned when weighed against what the planet had to offer. Headquarters could send more ships here later to deal with the insurrection; right now, the intelligent move was to escape and live to tell Headquarters about it.

Rafalyi ordered the remainder of his crew to their takeoff stations and proceeded to the bridge himself. His subordinates—and particularly Ship's-second-leader Klondanar-Nakonal—were clearly dismayed by his cowardly behavior, but their thoughts could not have mattered less to Rafalyi. He was certain that once again he could salvage a victory from his seemingly iconoclastic actions; this planet was a treasure that would cap his career. He watched the instruments before him and, when all was in readiness, gave the order to lift off.

The engines roared to life, and the walls of the ship vibrated with the familiar feeling of strain against gravity. Rafalyi braced himself for the pressure of acceleration, but it never came. Instead, far below him, he could hear a series of engine whines and shouts and exclamations from his crew. The vibrations stopped abruptly, and his control panel was afire with danger lights.

Even cool, calculating Ship's-leader Rafalyi felt a surge of panic at this development. His control board indicated unheard-of troubles with engine overloads and malfunctions. Yet the ship had worked perfectly up until now. Coupled with the disastrous attack from the city, it suddenly seemed as though everything was going wrong at once. From being on top of the situation, he had suddenly plunged out of control. There was more danger here than he'd suspected.

He willed himself to remain calm, to think like a military officer. *If there* is *any Ideation in your blood,* he told himself fiercely, *it's time to use it.* Reaching out decisively, he pressed an intercom button. "Damage control, report," he demanded.

There were only confused noises at the other end. A Second Rank officer gibbered incoherently about the engines glowing white hot and fusing their parts. Rafalyi repeated his demand but still received no satisfactory answer.

He turned back to face the rest of his officers on the bridge. They all looked as confused as he felt, but he had to provide them with a symbol of strength. "It appears we shall get no intelligible damage reports for a while," he said evenly. "We must assume the ship is temporarily inoperable and plan our strategy accordingly."

"Now that we can't run, we must fight," said Ship's-second-leader Klondanar-Nakonal. "We must go out and achieve our noble deaths to earn our place in Paradise."

"Paradise can wait for me," Rafalyi snarled back. "I've got other plans."

"Do we wait for those robots to storm our ship, then? Do we sit like cowards and let death come to us?"

"We're not helpless. We've got a fortress here. Our ship's guns may still work—and if not, there are all the alien weapons we've loaded aboard. The enemy can't take us if we sit tight and wait."

But try though he might to project sweet reasonableness, Rafalyi could not calm his subordinate's temper. Klondanar-Nakonal drew his gun and aimed it at the ship's-leader. "I'm tired of your constant cowardice. Time after time you've denied us the honorable path to Paradise."

"Sometimes," Rafalyi said carefully, "it's braver to live than to die."

"I won't listen to your doubletalk anymore. Your heresies have brought disgrace to us all. From now on, I'll lead us to a proper fight. And as for you—" He leveled his weapon at Rafalyi's chest.

Rafalyi found himself overtaken by the greatest calm of his life. He knew he was right; if Klondanar-Nakonal killed him now, it would be the equivalent of death in battle—a hero's death, earning him his proper place in Paradise. He stared back at his subordinate unperturbed by the threat, willing to accept whatever fate might be in store for him.

His glacial calm unnerved the ship's-second-leader. His thoughts may have paralleled his commander's, for he lowered his weapon again and said, "You'll have to let someone else buy your passage to Paradise, mixed-caste. I won't do it for you."

Klondanar-Nakonal then turned to survey the other officers on the bridge. "Anyone else who prefers to spend eternity in the Pit of Cowards can stay with our ship's-leader. Those who prefer Paradise, follow me!"

Giving a fierce war cry, Londanar-Nakonal charged out the door. The rest of the officers followed behind him—some with equal enthusiasm, some with much greater hesitancy. The latter avoided looking at Rafalyi as they left, but leave they did. Within minutes, Rafalyi was alone on the bridge—and from what he could hear throughout the ship, the rest of the crew was deserting as well. Watching his monitors, he saw his troops pouring outside to face the equally fearless robot army.

Fools! he thought. *They'll go tripping over themselves on the path to Paradise. When I go, the road won't be as crowded.*

He turned back to his instrument panel. The situation could still be saved. If he could only find out what was wrong with the engines, he might still have his triumph. The ship could be run competently without much crew, if need be. He could still leave, pick up the soldiers he had left outside the cloud in the lifeboat, and return home with his information. There was still a chance for victory.

Rafalyi clung desperately to that thought as he studied his glowing board.

The time since her capture was all a blur to Michi. She was vaguely surprised the aliens had let her live—they hadn't shown a trace of mercy on New Edo—but she could hardly get up the energy to worry about it. She was in and out of consciousness at random moments, and little around her made sense. She felt feverish, and half the time she could not tell whether what she saw was reality or delirium.

She was kept in a small room with an improvised bed. An overhead light burned constantly. The door to the corridor was open, but on those few occasions when she could open her eyes, she saw two guards standing there, one on either side of the doorway. Not that it mattered much: She had little strength to try an escape.

A few attempts were made to feed her. Food was stuffed into her mouth, followed by water that tasted stale. She could only gag at the mixture and got little of it down—but it was enough to keep her alive for five days.

She was awakened from a sleep by loud noises in the corridor. Aliens were running past her doorway, their shoes clattering on the metal floors. They were shouting and screaming something unintelligible, making a terrible racket. Michi had an impression that, even had she understood their language, the yelling still would not have made sense. There was a taste of chaos in the air.

She turned her head to look at the doorway and was surprised to see there were no guards. She waited a few minutes, expecting them to be replaced at any second, but no one came. The ship grew deathly quiet around her. It felt totally deserted.

Old feelings stirred in her. She might be in pain, but she wasn't dead yet. She couldn't understand what had happened, but if the aliens had deserted their ship, they might have a good reason for doing so— in which case she should go, too. If she could get out of here and return to Beta-Nu, she might yet survive this ordeal. Even if she were killed trying to escape, that would probably be a better fate than being these aliens' prisoner.

She pulled herself slowly into a sitting position and groaned at the effort. The noise did not attract any attention, however, and after waiting a moment she rose painfully off the cot, leaning against the wall to steady herself. The world swam dizzily around her, and again she had to stop for breath until she could gather her resources. Then, ever so cautiously, she peeked out into the hallway.

She could see no one about, and the stillness was absolute. Staying in contact with the wall at all times, she staggered down the hallway trying to be as quiet as she could. The ship seemed deserted, but there was no point in taking foolish risks. She had no idea where she was going, but she might find some clue eventually. Anything was better than just staying in her cell.

She had just come to the conclusion that the ship was totally abandoned when she heard some faint noises farther down the corridor. She stopped, wondering whether to continue in that direction or head the opposite way. Her brain felt muzzy, and thinking was difficult. Her curiosity finally overcame her caution, however, and she started ahead once more.

She came, at last, to a large doorway, and could tell that

216

the sounds were coming from the room beyond. Peering in carefully, she saw that this was obviously the ship's main control room. Though it was big enough to hold a dozen or more beings, there was only one inside. He was seated with his back to the doorway. One of the control panels in front of him had been taken apart, and he was studying it intently. Beside him was an open tool kit.

Michi hesitated again and looked around the room some more until she caught sight of the monitors. The screens showed the area around the base of the ship, and they told a fascinating story. Hundreds of the aliens lay dead on the ground, amid shattered metal bodies of the little mainte-nance robots. There had been some sort of battle, then, though she couldn't imagine how it came about. Still, most of the aliens seemed to have left the ship to fight elsewhere. Perhaps the one here in the control room was the last one left on board.

That thought emboldened her. She slipped silently into the control room, and the alien was so deep in concentration that he did not hear her. She moved with painful slowness; she would have to cross an open area to reach him, and she didn't have the wall to support her anymore. Step by step she came up behind him and reached into his tool kit for an object to use as a weapon.

Her hand closed on something that looked vaguely like a small hammer just as the alien turned to face her. The face was ugly, but the startled expression in his eyes was plain to read. He tried to rise, but Michi found some unsuspected reserves of strength and moved too quickly for him. Swinging her hammer into the side of his head, she knocked him off his chair and onto the floor. As he lay there, stunned, she had time to regroup her resources for a second blow. She placed it more carefully this time, at the back of his neck, and the alien slumped, unconscious.

Michi was in only slightly better shape than her victim. She fell to her knees beside the body, panting from her exertions, and only after another couple of minutes was she able to pull herself up into the chair the alien had been using a short time before.

She was still sitting there, dazed, when Birk came in and found her. She wasn't surprised to see him; she hadn't the strength to be surprised. All she could think of to say was, "What took you so long?"

Then she passed out completely.

TWENTY

This time, Birk made certain he was in the room when Michi awoke. The young woman came slowly back to consciousness, blinked a bit, and tried to turn over. That act drew a stab of pain; she sucked in a quick breath and squirmed into a more comfortable position. Her eye-lids opened another little bit, and she caught sight of Birk. It took a moment for his presence to register in her mind, and then her memory returned.

She tried to speak, but her voice was hoarse and came out more as a croak. "You came back."

"Kagami did most of the work," Birk said. "I couldn't have done anything without her to coordinate."

There was an awkward silence, as both people wondered how to bridge the gulf between them. "I'm still awfully shaky," Michi said at last. She looked and found a cup of water on a tray beside her bed, and drank greedily from it to moisten her scratchy throat. "What exactly happened? What's the situation now?"

With a degree of modesty that surprised even himself, Birk related the story of his operation against the aliens, making sure to give Kagami most of the credit. He played down the success of his jammer and stressed how efficient the mainte-nance robots had been. He told Michi how the invaders had been cut down after they left the ship, and how he had waited to make sure they were all out before boarding with a party of robots.

Michi listened without interruption, apparently still in too much pain to do more than accept what happened. When Birk had finished, she asked another question: "Why?"

Birk could have pretended he didn't understand what she meant, but she would have known that for a lie. His coming back to fight the invaders was a dramatic turnabout in his life, and she was naturally curious. It was something Birk himself could not entirely explain.

It wouldn't be very flattering to her to tell the truth, he thought, *to say it was Arthur's death, not her own danger, that made the difference.* He sighed and said aloud, "As you said, there comes a time when you have to stop running. I've been running away for eleven years. There was no place else to go. I realized that sooner or later I'd have to stand up to the danger, or give up all claim to being human." He shrugged. "I suppose I got so mad at you because you were telling me the truth, and it was something I didn't want to face. It was easier to yell at you than to stop running. I hope you can accept my apologies."

"Under the circumstances, it's hard not to," Michi said. She lay back on the bed, accepting that explanation for the moment. "Are all the aliens dead?"

"All except the one you knocked out—I thought he might make a good prisoner. Since they have so little respect for their own lives, I've had the robots keep him under tight restraint. Unless he has a hollow tooth filled with poison, I don't think he'll be able to suicide."

Michi wrinkled her brow. "Why did you want a prisoner?"

Birk looked first to his feet, then to the window, avoiding eye contact with the woman. "Well, actually it's more for you than for me."

"The only reason I would need a prisoner is if—" She stopped and looked seriously into Birk's face. "Is if I were going back to the Commonwealth," she finished. "We have a ship now, don't we? That is, if your jammer didn't do too much damage."

Birk stood up and walked to the window, his back to Michi. As he gazed out over the city of Beta-Nu, he said, "I spent some time looking it over during the two days you were unconscious. The controls are all alien, but I suppose we could figure them out, given time. The engines melted down into a complete mess, but that's no problem at all. I could instruct the robots how to make new ones. They're very clever at things like that."

"Then that's one less excuse you have for not helping me." She said it as quietly and gently as she could, afraid to start their old arguments over again.

Birk clenched his fists tightly and beat his right hand against the wall. "Damn it, Michi!" he exploded, then almost instantly moderated his tone. "Sorry—old reflexes are hard to break sometimes. Yes, it is one less excuse."

He turned to face her. "Are you positive Torres is dead?"

"He's as dead as anyone can be. The coup happened the year I graduated the Academy. There were films of it and everything. By the time the assassins were finished, there wasn't enough of his body to use as dog meat. None of his people are in power anymore."

Birk wiped his hands nervously at his sides, trying to fight the decision. "You could still be lying."

Michi lay back on the bed once more. "I'm tired and I'm in pain. I don't want to go back to those games again."

"I'm sorry, but you didn't go through what I had to face—the torture, the beatings, the humiliation. I don't want to go back to those again."

"If anything, you'll end up the biggest hero we've got."

Her words took Birk by surprise. "Huh?"

"Just look at it. The Commonwealth is at war with these aliens. You captured one of their officers alive. You invented a machine that jams their ships. You discovered an entire planet filled with exotic weapons and new technology. I don't think any single person could make a bigger contribution to the war effort. Even if the government *wanted* to hold a grudge, they couldn't afford to. They need what you've got too badly."

Birk had never considered it from that angle before, but he had to admit Michi had a point. Even assuming the worst—that Torres and his gang of cutthroats were still in command—they would need his jammer and the weapons stored here in the Makers' cities if they were to beat the aliens. They would have to bargain with him.

"But what if the Commonwealth loses the war?" he asked. "I'm safe here whatever happens, but if I go back I have to take my chances along with everyone else. Even with what I can give them, our side might still lose. I could be killed."

"What do you want, a guarantee? No one can give you that. There aren't any guarantees, Birk. If you take a knife and slit your wrists, I guarantee that nothing in this life will ever bother you again, but that's the only assurance anyone ever has. Staying here is a slow form of suicide; even you admitted you can't keep running forever. If you go back, you'll have the same chance as everyone else—and maybe everyone's chances will be a little better because of what you can give. The choice is yours."

220

Birk was at a loss. He'd been over and over the arguments for the past two days and could still reach no conclusions. One thing, though, was certain—this was a decision he would have to reach on his own. Being around Michi only muddled his thoughts.

He started for the door. "I'll be back in a little while," he said to the woman. "I'll let you know then."

Birk left the hospital and went out onto the quiet streets of Beta-Nu. He tried to tell himself that if he strained hard, the events of the past month could be erased as though they'd never happened. But he'd never convince himself of that. The city wouldn't let him.

Beta-Nu was badly scarred from the battles that had raged through it. The aliens, in their search for Michi and other possible saboteurs, had destroyed nearly a quarter of the city. Once-proud buildings had been demolished, and the maintenance robots would be working for years to clear away the rubble. Now that the fighting was over they had returned to their regular duties, scurrying around busier than ever cleaning up the devastation. They paid him no attention as he walked randomly through the streets; they had other things to do.

What is there for me back on Earth? he wondered. *I've been away twelve years. That's a long time. Things change, people change. I'd be a stranger in my own world. My old friends may all be dead—and even if they're not, what would we have left to talk about? I don't even know if I could stand having lots of people around me all the time. Look how edgy I am now, with just one other person.*

And society would all be different. Events move so fast, and I've been left behind. I'd be a walking anachronism, laughed at behind my back.

And Reva. He pictured her as she'd been, then realized how foolish that was. She'd be a dozen years older than when last he'd seen her. She'd have given him up for dead long ago. She'd probably remarried and had kids by another man, maybe even emigrated to one of the colonies to hide the disgrace of having been Birk Aaland's wife. There was no hope there. He'd have to give up thoughts of her entirely. Reva and he could only be strangers now. That chain, once so strong, had been irrevocably broken.

He could be a hero, as Michi had said, but what good was that? He'd had fame once before, and knew it for the fleeting phenomenon it was. He could hardly put any stock in that. So

221

the question remained: What was there to gain from going back?

Nothing, his mind replied, *except the sensation of being alive again.*

He could always return to this world, he realized. The Commonwealth would be eager to exploit the Makers' riches. Teams of archeologists and military specialists would flock to learn all they could. But Birk was still *the* expert; if Earth ever became too oppressive, he would always be welcomed back here. That thought warmed him, somehow, more than he could have expressed.

He found, quite unexpectedly, that he had been walking in a specific direction with a particular goal in mind—the art gallery he had visited what seemed like ages ago, the day before Michi's ship crashed and sent his whole existence into a tailspin. He wanted to look once more into that window with the two figures, to see what new meaning it might have for him now.

As he came to that conscious realization, he found his pace quickening. That window had changed his life, several times. Now, when he faced the hardest decision of all, he needed to see it once more. Somehow, deep inside his mind, he harbored the superstition that everything would be all right once he reached that magnificent piece of art once more.

As he neared the site of the museum, though, his pace slowed again. Things did not look right, and he had a sinking feeling in the pit of his stomach. His fears were confirmed a moment later when he rounded a corner and gazed in horror at the sight before him.

That beautiful building, the inverted cone, lay in ruins, a victim of the aliens' heartless search for Michi. Tons of rubble littered the ground, and the maintenance robots hadn't even begun cleaning it up yet. He stood transfixed for a moment, and wanted to weep that something so beautiful and timeless could be destroyed so casually. It would have been but the work of a moment for the aliens to destroy the museum and all its art—art that had survived a holocaust and its aftermath, and centuries of neglect.

He fell to his knees and pawed frantically through the debris, looking for *his* window. He tossed aside chunks of rock and metal, stopping only when he cut his hand on a piece of glass. This was futile. Even if he could find that particular treasure, it would have been shattered in a million pieces by its fall. There would be no hope of reconstructing it.

You can't resurrect a dream, Birk thought idly. *You can only go on and dream new ones.* He took some consolation in the fact that, if ever any piece of art could be said to have a purpose, then that window had certainly justified its existence.

"Funny," he said aloud. "The only souvenir of an entire planet that I wanted to take with me, and now it's gone."

Then he turned and walked back the way he'd come. He couldn't afford to stand here gawking at a ruined building. For the first time in more than a dozen years, he had work to do.

From planet Earth you will be able to communicate with other worlds— Just read—

SCIENCE FICTION

☐ SPACE MAIL II Edited by Isaac Asimov, Martin Harry Greenberg, & Charles G. Waugh	24481	$2.50
☐ EARTH ABIDES by George R. Stewart	23252	$2.75
☐ ASSAULT ON THE GODS by Stephen Goldin	24455	$2.25
☐ GUARDIAN by Thomas F. Monteleone	04682	$2.25
☐ FIRE AT THE CENTER by Geo. W. Proctor	14417	$2.25
☐ THE SURVIVAL OF FREEDOM Edited by Jerry Pournelle and John F. Carr	24435	$2.50
☐ THE X FACTOR by Andre Norton	24395	$2.25